E2
B6m

D0835896

The Bridge

THE BRIDGE

by

Pamela Frankau

THE REPRINT SOCIETY
LONDON

FIRST PUBLISHED 1957
THIS EDITION PUBLISHED BY THE REPRINT SOCIETY LTD.
BY ARRANGEMENT WITH WILLIAM HEINEMANN LTD. 1958

MADE AND PRINTED IN GREAT BRITAIN BY
WILLIAM CLOWES AND SONS, LIMITED, LONDON AND BECCLES

TO M.W.

"with ease and affection"

*For the foolishness of God
is wiser than men,
and the weakness of God
is stronger than men.*

THE BRIDGE

I

NEILSON walked over the bridge. The coping on either side was too high to let him see the river. Ahead, he saw the backs of the slowly-moving crowd. It was a quiet crowd. There were no groups, each of them going on his way alone.

To right and left of him, they moved with the same intent and solitary purpose. They did not jostle one another; the bridge was very wide.

Neilson was aware of the man who walked with him, but when he tried to remember who the man was, he could not give him a name. Nor was there any necessity to turn to him and ask it. He was simply the companion of this journey; he had been here since the beginning.

'But when,' Neilson said to himself, 'was the beginning? What made it happen?' The answer, surely, was as simple as A.B.C. A moment ago, he had known. But now, and this was ludicrous, he could not even find the word for the thing that had happened. Only a violence, a suddenness, stayed on his mind, like the loud slamming of a door.

This ceased to puzzle him when he realised that his memory was gone altogether. He had felt it going, the landscape of the past breaking up, familiar names and things departing as he searched. That, he knew. But even as he knew it, the foggy, interim period itself went from recognition, stayed only in flavour and context, like the slamming of the door. All was gone. There was merely this moment of now. He existed only in the present, with a name but no other identity, crossing the bridge.

He seemed to be walking more slowly than the rest; the gentle traffic of people caught up with him, outstripped him, swept on. He was content to loiter along and let them hurry if they would.

There was a bay in the bridge; above the bay, the coping

rose into a small rounded turret, with the sun making a golden surface on the stone. At the foot of the turret a flight of steps ran down.

"We turn off here," said Neilson.

His companion hesitated before he said, "You know that . . ."

"I know we don't go on—to the gate."

A second afterwards, the words were beating hollow on the empty drum inside his head. They had echoed a meaning; now they had none. Baffled, he stood still, looking at his companion, and they moved aside into the bay. They leaned their backs against the turret. Neilson felt the sun-warmed stone on his shoulder-blades and reflected that, whatever came of this, he knew two kinds of peace. There was the peace of a mind without a memory; and there was the peace of a body without pain. (Pain was mixed with the violence, with the slamming of the door.)

The man smiled at him. He had, Neilson thought, most innocent eyes; clear-washed, blue and utterly serious eyes. The straight-featured face was so familiar that he might have been looking at it all his life. But the face was, in essence, foreign ('What do I mean, foreign?' Neilson interrupted himself. He had no basis for comparison. He, Neilson, was entirely disorientated, foreigner of foreigners, perhaps.) He looked at the man, puzzling it out.

"Why don't I know who you are?"

The smile widened. "Don't worry; you never did. I know who you are, which is more important. But I don't, at this stage, know what's in your mind. This stage is new to both of us." He did not seem disturbed by the thought; he spoke with placid authority. "When you talked of the gate—what were you expecting?"

"Nothing——" Neilson said. "I have no picture. I can't remember anything at all. Except that I must find them."

"You must find whom?"

Neilson frowned. "There are three people," he said. "That's all I know."

He saw the man looking at him compassionately.

"Don't be sorry for me. It doesn't hurt. They are somewhere at the back of my mind. Towering. Mountains that I can't see. But they will be there."

2

The crowd had passed; there was only himself and his guide, and the place where they must go; the way off the bridge.

"Where will they be?" asked the gentle voice.

Neilson shook his head. "It's no good asking me that."

"I didn't want you to hope too much."

"Hope?" Neilson said, "I hope for nothing. And now you look as though I'd made a joke."

"Well, I am entitled to think it funny. If you really hoped for nothing, we shouldn't be here." He added, "And I don't really talk in riddles, either. It's just that you're new to this."

As Neilson began to go down the steps, the guide said, "And you aren't much given to asking questions." He sounded relieved.

"I imagine," Neilson said, "I'll be told soon enough, without asking questions."

"Told . . ." the guide repeated. "Not told, exactly."

The steps widened as they reached the shore. It was a sandy shore and the span of the bridge was too great for Neilson to see to either bank. As they walked, the milky sunshine began to dazzle the bridge and take it away. Presently it looked far and gold, as though it were painted on the sky.

Now Neilson was content with the place, having a sense of rendezvous with the sky and the water, with the sand at his feet. He was not disturbed when the guide said to him, "You have a long way to go."

"I know I have."

"Do you really know—or are you guessing?"

"I'm guessing," Neilson said. "What sort of country is it?"

"Difficult. There's no map. There can't be; the times and places are charted, but not the distances between."

"*What* times and what places?"

The guide smiled at him. "The ones you appointed, Neilson."

"I don't understand."

"Go on—and you will."

"Straight ahead?"

"Straight ahead. It's a little misty yet, but you can just see the rock-point, can't you? At the foot of the cliff? Well,

3

that's where it begins to happen. Somewhere there. I don't need to tell you exactly."

"But you'll be with me?"

The innocent eyes looked at him and clouded. "I'll be with you, of course. As I have been all your life. But not in the same way. Because——" he hesitated, "well, my term of usefulness has come to an end. I can't help you any more. All I can do is keep you company. The steps that you take will be of your own choosing . . . like the survivors."

"Survivors?"

"Yes."

"Who are they?"

"Naturally you've forgotten. And at first you may think you don't recognise them. But since you chose them," he said, "you will—in due course. Remember, they're just images. Not real people."

Then he smiled again, looking past Neilson. Between them and the rock-point there was a belt of palm trees growing—bright green, wholly unexpected, giving the beach a sudden tropical look. The guide continued to smile at the stiff, glistening trees but he came no farther. He stayed on the edge of the palm-grove; the pointed shadows of the leaves masked his face.

"You're going in through his mind," the guide said. "It's the reverse of the usual procedure. But since you've lost your memory he can't very well come in through yours. Just go straight ahead and you'll find him."

2

Neilson went straight ahead. There was a sandy track running between the trees. He felt the air changing about him. Whereas the bridge, the gate and the steps to the shore had been understandable, this place was not. Its dimensions were odd. It had a flat brilliance, no true depth, just dazzle and colour.

There were crazy-looking flowers, half-orchid, half-poppy. One bloom as he stared at it became an enormous butterfly, purple and red-gold, that flapped away. In the branches above his head, green parrots flew and chattered. A white monkey leaned out at a level with his face and

4

offered him a coconut. Through the trees he could see other animals moving; two fat brown bears sitting up, holding their hind toes with their front paws, rocking to and fro on their rumps; a lion that prowled, tawny-gold and orthodox, twitching its tail; a baby elephant pulling down bananas; a surprised-looking giraffe. The animals had a pleasing, Noah's Ark quality. He said to himself, 'I feel as though I'm making this up.'

The palms divided in sudden perspective and showed him a coral beach, with a peacock-blue sea lapping against the coral. Looking west, wondering if he would still see the shore and the distant arch of the bridge, he saw only a tall square-rigged ship at anchor; the wind was in her white sails; across her bows a long low craft was pulling, and on a space in the foreground of the water he read the words 'Off Valparaiso' clearly printed. In smaller lettering, just below, there was the name of the artist: 'T. J. Somerscales.'

"*Off Valparaiso*," Neilson said, aloud and thoughtfully.

"My favourite picture," the boy explained. The boy was standing at his elbow; a skinny child of about eight years old, with a sunburnt skin and large spaniel eyes. There was a gap in his front teeth. His dark hair was wet and he carried a bathing-towel. There was, Neilson thought, something old-fashioned about the cut of his white shirt, the length of his shorts and the belt with the metal clasp in the shape of a snake. He waved his arm at the view.

"These are all my things," he said, "I can make them happen anywhere. Can you do that?"

"Well, presumably——" said Neilson, holding on to what the guide had told him, "I'm making you happen."

"Y-yes . . . And I suppose you must. But it seems a bit mean, doesn't it? To make me do it again?" He cracked the wet towel like a whip. "That's mean, surely. Of course you're in it too—I see that."

"Then you see more than I do," said Neilson.

"Don't you love me?" The question was flat, inquiring, spoken without wistfulness.

"How can I?" He put his hand on the child's shoulder. "Listen . . . You've heard of people losing their memories, haven't you?"

"Yes."

5

"Well, that's what has happened to me. My memory's gone. I don't remember a thing."

"Honestly?"

"Honestly."

"Not even your name?"

"Well, yes, I know I'm called Neilson. What are you called?"

"David," said the boy.

"So you see, David, it isn't a question of loving, or not loving you. I just don't know who you are."

"Oh, that's all right," the boy said indifferently. "Thanks for explaining, though. Come on. . . ."

He tugged at Neilson's hand.

The palm trees thinned away and there was no more coral beach. There was the shingle, and the rock-point curving around the pool. Between the foot of the cliff and the base of the rock-point there was a high, narrow crevice formed by one tall rock standing up and leaning over towards the cliff-side. The boy made for this gap; its rocky floor raised it a little higher than the shingle; Neilson could see the tidemarks and the slither of green seaweed on the floor. David scrambled up, then turned, spanning the crevice with his thin arms.

"Well, here we go," he said and Neilson saw that there was another boy standing just behind him, looking over his shoulder, a boy with grey eyes and pale fair hair.

DAVID

1913

I

As David walked up the beach towards his aunt's cottage, he flipped the wet bathing-towel and made it snap, a pleasing trick that he had learned from Bobby Lowther. All the Lowthers could do tricks; not only sleight-of-hand, but natural tricks. They could wriggle their eyebrows separately; they were equipped with mobile thumbs that bent backwards: two of them could move their ears. Even Tony, the youngest (his partner in this morning's disgrace and by general verdict soppy), had peculiar bones in his behind. Bobby said it was a double-jointed pelvis. When Tony was sitting on a hard surface he could make a sudden disconcerting bump with each side of him. Mrs. Lowther had forbidden him to do it.

David supposed that he should be sorry about this morning —at least sorry for having giggled just as Mr. Lowther reached his climax. He did not think that he could be. Mr. Lowther, bellowing like a seal, had—surely—made it clear that he gave up. "You, Tony, and you, David, are just a couple of rotten little water-funks, only fit to paddle." No more swimming, Mr. Lowther had said, and he would Tell Your Aunt Why, David, Do You Understand?

Mr. Lowther was no bully. When his children misbehaved, he was deeply, vocally hurt. He set up the same plaintive roaring every time. He wanted to know what he had done to deserve it. He would appeal to the heavens, and to Mrs. Lowther. He was a very big man with bright red hair (all the Lowthers except Mrs. had red hair) and when he got to the sad, roaring stage David always expected the round, bewildered face to crumple and a loud "Boo-hoo!" to emerge from Mr. Lowther. It was thinking of this that had made him giggle; and that had made Tony giggle too.

7

"So it's funny now, is it?" Mr. Lowther had asked in a weak, piping voice; his voice was at most times a little too small for him. "Funny, eh? Well, if you think cowardice is funny, I don't believe I want to talk to you any more." After which all the Lowthers had gone to lunch, by the path up the West Cliff to the hotel, Mr. Lowther leading and Tony last.

Though he pitied Tony, who was the only really likeable Lowther, David could not suppress a sigh of relief. He flipped the wet towel again, derisively, in the direction of the waves. They were enormous waves, no matter what Mr. Lowther said. The sea today was at its worst, ridged and grey-green, tearing at the sands, drawing back in dreadful arches, smashing in white disorder upon the point. It would be nice not to swim again.

There was little sting in Mr. Lowther's threat to tell his aunt. Since Aunt Rachel avoided the popular end of the beach, he would have to come to the cottage to do it; and Mr. Lowther was not happy at the cottage. Last time he had come, Aunt Rachel refused to speak because she was meditating and the time before she had pointed to a fly-button that was undone.

And even if he faced the embarrassments of the cottage, it was on the whole unlikely that Aunt Rachel would listen. Aunt Rachel seldom listened and never to the Lowthers. She regarded them as David's property and held him responsible for any outrage that they might commit, such as inviting her to a picnic. This wasn't fair; not that he much minded Aunt Rachel's type of unfairness; he had long ago decided that she was somehow separated from ordinary people, like the man-in-the-moon. But the Lowthers were his burden, not his pleasure; and it was odd that Aunt Rachel could not see this.

He had not asked for the Lowthers. They had begun it; last summer, when he was perfectly happy playing by himself. Aunt Rachel, who had watched their overtures through the telescope, said afterwards, "I saw you having fun with the red-headed family."

"It wasn't fun."

"Why wasn't it?"

He had brooded on the question, eating large mouthfuls

8

of what was said to be a curry. Presently he said, "They smell."

"What of?"

"Sort of foxy," said David. "They've all got the same smell. Except Mrs. Lowther; she doesn't smell of anything."

"Everybody smells of something—it's the skin," said Aunt Rachel vaguely. "What else do they do wrong besides smell?"

"They're all bumpy—and they barge—and I never want to see them again."

"You'll get used to them," said Aunt Rachel. Which had turned out to be true. He did not notice the smell any more. He accepted the Lowthers; they were part of the holiday, one of the minor flaws in its perfection, like Aunt Rachel's persistent prune-juice.

He thought about them warily, pausing with his back to the sea. Something was worrying him, but he couldn't hunt it down and give a name to it. He should, he thought, be happier than this. He was reprieved from the rough water. Everything was fine. Except that it was not. Why not?

He looked westward, up to the cliff, to the elaborate shape of the hotel perched there in its gardens. Its isolation from the town was complete. There was not much town; a scatter of grey stone houses in the crease between the cliffs, a short line of shops along the front, and a few cottages that straggled eastward, the last cottage being Aunt Rachel's.

The place, Aunt Rachel said, was being ruined; before they built the hotel, she added, you never saw a soul on this beach from one year's end to the other. Through the telescope, she kept a sharp look-out for trippers, the threatening race whom David had not yet identified. He thought of them as a line of black figures moving in a dance. With linked hands, they strung out across the curve of the little bay, from the breakwater below Aunt Rachel's cottage to the rock-point under West Cliff. One day she would see them there. Silent and black, they would trip, and all would be spoiled.

But what was spoiled today? Something was; and although a voice in his head told him otherwise, urging him to be happy with the reprieve, it wasn't, he thought, his own voice. It was the one that tried to make things easy; the one

9

that argued for doing as he liked. Sometimes it persuaded him with its arguments. Sometimes, as now, the result was a tug-of-war inside.

Aunt Rachel, too, heard a voice; but hers was outside her head and wholly benign. It was the voice of a Guru (not, to David's bitter disappointment, a large fuzzy animal, but a dead teacher who had lived in India many years ago). Before he came, Aunt Rachel used to get in touch with Uncle William when she needed advice. This was wrong. She did not explain why it was wrong, nor why the late Uncle William should be less reliable than a strange Guru. But there it was.

The last cottage stood fifty yards away from the last but one. It still looked like a fisherman's cottage; black and stubby, with a shingled roof and white-painted window-frames. There was a patch of weather-beaten garden in front, where the big brass telescope stood. David stopped for his ritual look through the telescope. As he swung it westward, the base of the rock-point slid into the glass circle. He saw the narrow gap where you could walk at low tide between the leaning rock and the cliff. Now the surf boiled and poured through it, tossing up white plumes higher than the leaning rock as though a whale were spouting.

It frightened him and he went on looking at it through the telescope. Behind him Aunt Rachel said, "Here is a banana because lunch isn't ready." There were four bananas; she began to peel and eat one herself.

David found Aunt Rachel's appearance pleasing. Big as she was, she still looked more like a toy than a person. She reminded him of Mrs. Noah in his abandoned Noah's Ark. She was dressed, as usual, in a smock that was wholly circular and shorter than you would have expected it to be, so that her downy bare legs appeared with great suddenness. Her square face was tanned brick-red. The Lowthers said that she had a jolly face, but David disagreed because of her eyes, which were large and brown and very sad. Perched on her head, she wore a raffia hat in the shape of an upturned flower-pot. She had made the hat herself. She liked to wear a hat even indoors. Her hay-coloured hair was bobbed, with a fringe across the forehead; the fringe showed under the hat.

"I ought never to make pastry," said Aunt Rachel. "But it's all right now—lunch is, I mean. It's a potato-pie instead. Be about twenty minutes."

"What happened to the pastry?" David asked with interest. Last time he had modelled it, grey and rubbery, into a family of mice.

"Most of it stayed on the rolling-pin," said Aunt Rachel, adding, "You can have a go later."

They sat on the grass beside the telescope, eating their bananas. Aunt Rachel did not say "Had a nice morning?" She looked him over and then asked, "Why are you miserable?" Sometimes her surprise-invasions annoyed him; this one made a short cut to the heart of the problem.

He said, "If something really frightens you, why do you feel that you ought to do it?"

"I don't know," said Aunt Rachel. "Are you going to do it?"

"Well, no, I don't think I'll have to. Because he said not, for a punishment. He got furious."

"Mr. Lowther?"

"Yes. Because we wouldn't swim; Tony and me. All the others swam. We stayed standing up. It was the only way not to get the waves breaking on top of us. And even then one did. We tried to jump it and we fell down and got scraped." He showed her his knee.

"Poor David."

"Mr. Lowther said it was all our fault for being rotten little water-funks. He kept yelling at us to come farther out where it was calm. Or he said it was calm. It wasn't—they were just those huge ones that don't quite break. And I don't like them either."

"You swim very well," said Aunt Rachel, wrapping the banana-skin round her finger and waggling it, "I've seen you go a long way out."

"Oh yes. When there aren't any waves. So does Tony. We just hate it when it's rough."

"How much does it frighten you?"

"More than anything in the world," said David without hesitation.

"Oh dear," said Aunt Rachel.

He was discouraged. "Why oh dear? Is it so very cowardly?"

"I said 'Oh dear' because I was thinking about Mr. Lowther. What did you say about a punishment?"

"No more swimming for Tony and me. That's what he said."

"But if the sea's rough that won't be much of a punishment, will it?"

"No. That's what's worrying me, I think."

"You *want* to be punished?"

"No," he said moodily, "I just don't want to be a coward."

"There's no such thing as sin," said Aunt Rachel, sounding cross, which was rather unfair because he had not mentioned sin. "Eh?" She looked at him suspiciously. "I've told you that before. There is only ignorance. I wish you didn't have to go to Sunday School." After which she embarked on her second banana and kept him waiting. Ignorance was beyond him. Sin he could understand.

"Is iggerance what God doesn't want you to do?"

"God isn't a person, David; He is everything."

"Well, *I* think he's a person," David said, "I can't help it." He bit a large piece of banana.

Aunt Rachel stared at the sea. "In ignorance," she said, "one makes mistakes. And the only bad mistake is to hurt other people. Will you remember that?"

"Am I hurting Mr. Lowther?"

"Please be quiet," she said, "I'm working something out."

She took so long to work it out that he had to remind her of the potato-pie. Fortunately only the top of the mashed potato was burned. They ate it all. There should, Aunt Rachel said, have been bananas and cream to follow; since they had finished the bananas they ate the cream with strawberry-jam. No worry, David thought, was so bad after lunch as before.

Aunt Rachel said, "Boys are *supposed* to be brave, that's the trouble. If you were a girl nobody would think it important."

"I should hate to be a girl."

"Yes, it's worse. But don't interrupt or I shall lose the

thread." She folded her hands on her round, smocked tummy. "Now, then, is it Mr. Lowther's business to teach you to be brave? No. Pooh to Mr. Lowther. And *I* don't mind in the least if you prefer not to swim in a rough sea. So there's no problem there. The only wrong thing that you can do—ever—is to hurt somebody, and who could possibly be hurt by your being frightened of waves?"

"I don't know——" said David—"Unless it's God. Or me."

"What *do* you mean by that?"

It was one of those infuriating thoughts that turned to jelly when he tried to put it into words. He could do no more with it, no matter how long Aunt Rachel sat there, looking at him hopefully, wearing the white moustache that the cream had left on the down of her upper lip.

When she repeated her question, he said, "I don't know," and when she asked fretfully if Mr. Lowther were going to write one of his little notes about all this, he made the same reply.

It was nearly four o'clock when Tony came to the cottage. Aunt Rachel was meditating. David, having scraped the rolling-pin, was using the proceeds to model a battleship on the window-sill. Deep in concentration, he had been only gradually aware of the return of the sun: a warmth on the back of his neck and on his calves; a sharpening of the shadows. Now as Tony whistled, he turned and saw a different day. The wind still blew strongly, but the sky was clear. The sea had turned from grey glass to peacock-blue; the ridges were still upon it and the waves still broke in white, thunderous foam. Inland, above the town, the colours had come back to the tilted fields.

Tony stood beside the telescope, his hair blown into spikes, his shorts billowing. From his expression David judged that this was a visit of importance. He left the battleship.

"They've all gone," said Tony.

"Where to?"

"It's a picnic at the Landslide; it's been planned for ages." He gulped. "I wasn't allowed to go."

"Because of this morning?" said David sympathetically. Tony nodded.

"I thought the punishment was going to be not swimming."

"Well, it is. But this is extra; for having giggled."

"I began it."

"I know," said Tony.

"Well, then it isn't fair."

"I suppose in a way it isn't."

"Did you tell him it wasn't?"

Tony shook his head. "Wouldn't have been any good."

"I'm damned sorry," said David; it seemed worth swearing about. He set his own fortune beside Tony's and could think of no amends to make.

"Want to have a look at the owl?" he suggested. It was a stuffed owl under a glass hood. Last time Tony had liked it; now he shook his head morosely. Then he gritted his teeth.

"I thought—well, let's show them," he muttered. He improved on it to David's pattern, "Let's *damn'* well show them."

"Show them what?"

"Show them we aren't . . . what he said."

"Water-funks?"

As Tony winced, he saw that he had been tactless. The words had hurt Tony more than they had hurt him. He frowned over this; it was so difficult to imagine taking Mr. Lowther seriously. Perhaps if he were Mr. Lowther's son— but that was even more difficult to imagine. His own parents were just two people in small silver picture-frames, not dead, but Passed On, according to Aunt Rachel.

He said, "How'd we show them, Tony?"

Tony jerked up his chin, saying to the air, "Go in. From the point. Off the rocks." He was breathless. "That'd do it."

"Mmm . . . Yes, I suppose it would," said David uncomfortably. He found the suggestion babyish. Mr. Lowther took them to the rocks for diving lessons in the pool. The two eldest Lowthers could dive. The rest of them jumped, holding their noses. He tried to follow Tony's line of reasoning. "D'you mean if we jumped first or something?"

"No——" said Tony. "Don't be stupid."

"Well, what?"

14

"I mean now. You and me."

For a moment there was panic in David's head. Then the look of Tony removed it; poor Tony, plump and pink-skinned, with his chin stuck out, his arms folded, in an attitude copied from the drawings in the *Boys' Own Paper*.

"Ha-ha," said David. "Jolly funny."

"What's funny? I'm not being funny."

"But don't be a cheese. We couldn't."

"Why not?"

"It's high tide."

"No, it isn't; tide's going out."

"It's just on the turn, that's all."

"You're a funk," Tony said.

"And you're a silly cheese. We aren't allowed to swim alone. *Or* go on the point."

"Well, of course we aren't," said Tony impatiently. "That's the whole idea."

"It's a cheesy, footling idea."

Tony reddened. "Mean you won't?"

"No, I won't."

"All right. You can boil your head."

"Here—stop." David caught him beyond the telescope.

"You needn't come. In fact I'd rather you didn't," said Tony distantly, "I'd rather do it by myself."

David said, "Go and drown, then; I don't care."

He stood watching Tony go across the beach. He bit his thumb-nail. He did not believe that Tony would do it, but he found it unbearable to see him tramping away alone on those fat legs, his head down and his arms swinging.

David bit off the last piece of thumb-nail. Then he said, "Oh, bugger." It was the worst word he knew and he waited for some sign of fury from the cosmos; when none came, he said it again.

Tony was past the breakwater now, heading west at the edge of the sea.

Tony was idiotic. And still he admired the idiot. Now he was more mixed up inside his head than ever, but he knew that he would have to stop Tony from doing this thing. He began to run.

Perhaps Tony was showing off. Perhaps when he got to the end of the beach he would not go to the rocks at all, but climb back up the path to the hotel. "Oh, *do* let him do that," David urged God, and deliberately slowed down to give God a chance.

No. Tony did not even look towards the path up the cliff; he went on his way to the point, growing smaller on the wet sand. David put on a spurt, running where the sand was firm, neither too wet nor too dry. He was catching up with the idiot now. He came under the shadow of the cliff, to the gap and the leaning rock.

The tide was lower; the waves no longer came through. Tony was climbing into the crevice; it was a high step up to the wet, weedy floor; he clutched and slithered. When he saw David he shouted, "Go to hell!" and jumped down on the other side.

The roar of the sea was loud. David stayed where he was, looking along the jumbled spine of rocks that formed the point. The waves were enormous. They came circling in like great crystalline bolsters until the rocks smashed them in uproarious foam. He could see them making the same horrid pattern beyond the point. But he could not see the pool from here; the height of the rocky spine was between.

He went through the gap after Tony. He jumped down. Tony was standing at the edge of the water, tearing off his shirt. Here the sand sloped down into the basin of the pool, that was protected from the open sea on this side by the rock-point itself; the rocks piled up in convenient ledges and slabs from which you could dive or jump. The far side of the pool was made only by a broken bar of low rocks, and the water was shallower there.

On calm days there was no ripple; when you stood on the ledges the water was clear enough for you to see far down. You saw the rock sloping on, different and whitened below the surface; huge dark clumps of weed grew there—blobs and flowers that were sea-anemones; sometimes there was a ribbon of small fish twisting by.

The pool was not like that today. It was in slow continual movement; the great swell pushed the surface up and up, then drew it down again, sucking at the seaweed; ominous, but not terrifying. The terror was just beyond; the crests rode high to the broken bar; there they were turned, and though the surface of the pool rocked with them, they drove

16

on, spending themselves in thunder high up the beach. If you swam too near the bar, David thought, a wave might catch you; otherwise there was no danger here. Tony's great gesture had turned to anti-climax.

He thought that Tony knew it. Tony kept his head turned away, desperately scrambling out of his clothes. David would have liked to rub in the humiliation with a biting phrase. Failing to find one, he straddled and made water into the sand. It was a satisfying gesture; but he feared that it was lost on Tony.

"Doesn't look so bad," he tried next.

Tony pulled on his suit in silence.

"Think I'll go in too," David said.

Tony began to climb up the ledges.

"Wait for me, you cheese."

Tony went on climbing.

The Lowthers had several methods for dealing with sulks, but these were more effectively contrived by six people than by one. David shouted a few half-hearted epithets, then stopped. For some unidentifiable reason he didn't like himself very much. The plump figure scrambling up the ledges had acquired stature, the Lord knew how. Savagely, David pulled off his clothes. Having brought no suit, he threw them down and went up, naked, after Tony.

He had no wish to jump. It was entirely horrible to have his head under water, even for a few minutes. (All right, you didn't sink, you didn't suffocate, you came up into the safe air; but if in your terror you forgot, as he frequently forgot, to hold your breath, you choked and it was like being dead. It was agony, with your nose blocked, your throat full, your eyes smarting and blinded. Mr. Lowther said that anybody could open his eyes under water, but that was obviously a lie.)

Since Tony ignored the lower ledges, there was nothing for it but to follow him up. The wind slapped David's bare body. His anger had gone; his censure of himself had gone. He was just cold and afraid to jump in. Tony, desperately aloof, now stood a yard away, looking as though he felt the same. They gazed down at the restless, tilting water.

"Ought to be warmer now the sun's out," David said through chattering teeth. This sociable attempt had an immediate effect on Tony. He took a step forward, held his nose and jumped. His foot slipped at the edge; it was less a jump than an awkward, slithering fall. He made a tremendous splash in the water. It seemed a long time before his head reappeared.

Determined on appeasement, David shouted, "Jolly good! damn good!" Even after Tony had finished spluttering, he made no sign. He swam his slow breast-stroke to the lowest ledge. The swell drew him down in its hollow, down and down, before it lifted him like a cork and he clutched and dragged himself out, dripping hugely. He squeezed the water out of his suit. Still with his head bent, not looking at David, he began to climb up again.

Presumably, he was going to do a second jump. Was it perhaps his intention to go on and on and on jumping until the rest of the Lowthers came back from the picnic? For the first time it occurred to David that this method of 'showing them' suffered because they weren't there to be shown. Still, he could hardly say so to this unfamiliar version of Tony. He gave a heavy sigh, shut his eyes and jumped. He sprang out as far as he could from the ledge; that way, Mr. Lowther explained, you didn't go down so deep.

It was every bit as nasty as it always was; the helpless fall through the cold air and then the great heavy sizzle as the waters shut over his head. Then he drew in his idiotic breath and choked. He flapped and rolled in the water; he was blind. He paddled in circles, blinded and spitting; striking out with his eyes shut. He threshed his arms, reaching for the rock; surely he must be under the ledge by now. . . . There was a blink of light coming back to his sore eyes, but he could not see clearly. His fingers touched rock, lost it; the water was pulling him; pulling him where? Rock again; now the drag of the current sucking him through.

He forced his eyes open. He couldn't believe it; he was on the wrong side of the pool, swirling in the eddies about the broken bar. High above his head there rose the monstrous wall of a solid wave sweeping in. He saw its green mottled slope towering up to a thin silver line on the crest. As he yelled, the silver line curled and the wall broke on top of him.

Now he would die. Down, down, down, down, bursting in the dark. Blind, strangling, below tons of water that roared and roared. Nothing had ever hurt so much nor been so dark; the dark was inside him, swelling him up; and the dark was outside, pressing him down. He was being squeezed into nothing at all.

He felt a bump that drove the last of the breath out of him; then he was rolling over and over in a pale green tunnel, with a stinging pain in his palms and his knees. The greenness fell away in a white smother and he was flung flat on the beach. But the stones and the sand were tearing back beneath him; there was another wave riding in. He remembered afterwards that trying to crawl up the pouring beach before the next monster came was really the worst of it. He couldn't crawl far; he crouched, hurting abominably inside; gulping and throwing up mouthfuls of sea-water that mixed with his lunch. He thought that he would go on making these noises for ever, that his chest would always have these knives in it and his stomach stay twisted in a knot.

When it stopped, he rolled over on his back and lay still. He rubbed his streaming eyes. He said "Thank you" limply because it was all over. Then he staggered to his feet.

He was only ten yards from the two heaps of clothes that were his and Tony's. He found this remarkable. He felt as though that thing must have happened on quite another beach. He went shakily towards the clothes. He picked up Tony's towel and began to dry himself carefully.

His hands and knees were raw. There were long scratches all down one leg from the hip to the ankle; his elbows smarted at the touch of the towel and left blobs of blood on it. 'I'm badly hurt,' he thought, with a weak sense of pride, looking at the stains; wishing that Tony were here to see.

Where was Tony, anyway? There was no sign of him on the ledges. But his clothes were still here. He must have climbed out along the other side of the rock-point, the side where the waves beat high. More fool Tony. Mr. Lowther had forbidden them to set as much as a foot on those rocks, even at low tide. They were steep and slippery, with no proper ledges.

'He *can't* be there,' David thought. He fastened his belt and yelled "Tony!" The echo bounced back at him.

"I'm going home!"

Again there was the echo, nothing else.

"I damn' near drowned!" David croaked. His throat was sore; he couldn't shout again. He headed for the gap, finding that his legs wobbled stupidly. When he got to the gap, he was afraid of slipping on the weedy floor; he poked his way through, pressing against the wall. He would not risk even the trivial eighteen-inch jump to the sand; he sat down and lowered himself carefully. Whatever else happened today, he wasn't going to be hurt any more. He trod like a cat as he went up the beach.

He looked back once more at the point. And then he saw Tony.

Tony had climbed out all the way. He was standing defiantly on the last high knob of rock, with the waves smashing just below his feet. He looked very small and not very well-balanced.

David clenched his wounded hands. He had been right, back there by the pool, before the terror came. Tony today was a person of stature, a better man than he. You couldn't just call him a silly cheese and be done with it; you couldn't say that he was showing-off; there was nobody there to see him. You couldn't dismiss it as the action of an idiot. Because it was brave; because you would not dare to do it yourself. And Tony dared.

Gloomily, David turned away. He tried to find consolation in his wounds, but they were not enough; they were only scratches. Even his elbows had stopped bleeding. There was nothing for it but to give Tony best and go home.

He set off along the beach, hurrying, forgetting to be careful of himself. The sun was fading; there were clouds piling up over the sea now and the gulls were flying inland. He heard a gull scream.

2

When he saw Aunt Rachel run out of the cottage, he thought that she was coming to meet him. Aunt Rachel did not often run. She was no longer Mrs. Noah but a big stuffed doll in jerky motion with striding legs and flapping skirts. She ran to the next cottage, waving and calling, and Mr. Burrell who lived in the cottage came tearing out carrying a rope and the two of them galloped down the beach together.

As they went past him Mr. Burrell yelled, "Stay where you are!"

Another cottage door flew open; old Miss Roxburgh with a teapot in her hand, screaming, "Help! Help! Come! Everybody come! Somebody's drowning!" A whistle shrilled. The blue policeman ran across the parade and leaped down, losing his helmet, staggering from the jump and racing on. David stood where he was, seeing people popping out of nowhere; out of the creamery, out of the baker's, out of the shop that sold spades and buckets. Two men who might have grown like mushrooms from the sand were shoving the black boat into the water. A line of little figures came racing down the path from the hotel. A yellow dog ran past him barking loudly.

The rock-point had changed in the blink of an eye; it was taken with a horrible meaning; like the corner where the car had knocked the cyclist into the ditch last year; a familiar place made hideously important, as though a finger pointed at it, drawing a plague of people towards it. After the people were gone and all was over, the corner never looked the same. Would the rock-point ever look the same?

They were scrambling over it, slipping into the water; he saw their heads and arms flung about by the waves. He did not want to look but he had to go on looking, at all of it; at the black boat hurled down by the breakers, rammed on the shore with one man falling under and rising drenched and the two still struggling to push it out; at a new boat coming round the point, a fishing-smack that danced and could not get near; at a chain of figures all holding hands, and the thin line of the rope. And at last he was looking at the end, the whole crowd coming away from the point, clustering, kneeling, stooping in a circle. Tony was in the middle of that.

As David began to walk towards it, Aunt Rachel broke out of the circle and came to meet him, turning him back. She had lost her flower-pot hat and her hair stood up like a golliwog's hair and her face was greenish and different, but she was saying, "It's all right, it's all right, it's always all right. Love eternal, light eternal, it's all right, David, he's just hurt his leg and cut himself a bit; he's sitting up and talking. O wisdom infinite you must have a hot bath. Mr.

Lowther's there now and it's all quite, quite all right." She pulled him along at top speed and talked to her Guru.

3

Mr. Lowther came to the cottage that evening, late and unexpectedly. They did not hear him coming because the wind had risen and there was every sort of noise going on outside. The storm noises made the room feel besieged and safe. The two oil-lamps had red shades; the oil-stove threw a star-pattern on the ceiling. These lights changed the treasures in the room, deepening the glow of the green glass bottle and the glass paper-weight with the coral inside. All the black wooden surfaces shone silkily and the stuffed owl wore a spark in its eye. Over the mantelpiece the outlines in the picture called 'Off Valparaiso' were dim, showing a paler ship on a darker sea.

The warmth was thick in the room. Aunt Rachel and David were eating bread-and-dripping, with the draughts-board between them.

"Now who is *that*?" Aunt Rachel said, as the knocking shook the door. David went to open it. Mr. Lowther was just a mackintosh bulk with a torch in his hand.

He gave his usual plaintive roar. "My goodness, aren't you in bed yet?"

Aunt Rachel rose, saying, "It doesn't suit David to go to bed too early." She was wearing the long blue djibbah with the bright green embroidered yoke, very fine indeed, David thought. She added, "He gets indigestion."

Mr. Lowther glanced meaningly at the bread-and-dripping. He looked squeezed in this room; he was too tall for the low ceiling and he bumped into the furniture, of which there was a great deal for so small a space.

"Well, I've come to thank you," he announced—"thank you properly, I mean. Wasn't a minute in all that scramble. If you hadn't been so nippy with the telescope—silly little ass—might have drowned. Oh *Lord*!"—his groans became less coherent—"What's one to do—I mean *what*? Bolt and bar? He knows perfectly well—can't imagine what possessed him—wife won't have any questions till tomorrow, quite

22

right too, but oh *Lord*!" He was blowing up for his Boo-hoo face.

"I make it a rule never to be angry," said Aunt Rachel.

Mr. Lowther said, "Eh?"

"But I must admit that I *am* angry with Tony."

"What? Well, so'm I," said Mr. Lowther. "Just saying so, wasn't I?" He sounded more injured than ever.

"Look at David's knees."

Mr. Lowther looked at them.

"And his hands." David automatically put them behind his back. "No," said Aunt Rachel, "show Mr. Lowther your hands. And your elbows." Mr. Lowther peered at the scratches.

"Now don't tell me boys always knock themselves about, a fact of which I am well aware," said Aunt Rachel. She offered Mr. Lowther the plate of bread-and-dripping but he shook his head affrightedly. She took another piece. "I don't mind how much David hurts himself, within reason, of course, as long as he enjoys the game, whatever it may be. But he didn't enjoy this at all. He only went into the water because Tony asked him to. Don't interrupt me, David, please. There's no reason why David should go banging himself about on the beach, just to amuse Tony; he happens to dislike swimming in rough water—*hush*, David—as who would not? My late husband," said Aunt Rachel, opening her eyes so that the whites showed all round, like those of a rocking-horse, "was drowned. At sea," she added, to make it quite clear. "So I should know."

"I'm sorry to hear that—very sorry," said Mr. Lowther peevishly.

"I don't know why you should be. It happened ten years ago and you are unlikely to have met him. Or do you mean you are sorry to hear that Tony *lured* David into the water—be quiet, David."

Mr. Lowther, bulging out of the arm-chair, began to look glassy-eyed. He said, "I don't understand any of this. I still don't know what Tony was doing out on the point." He looked at David. "I didn't know you were there—didn't see you. You tumbled in too, eh?"

"No," said David. "*Yes*," said Aunt Rachel. "*No*," said David. "You know I didn't; I told you; I jumped in and

23

then a wave got me. In the pool," he explained to Mr. Lowther, "and it wasn't Tony's fault."

"Certainly it was," said Aunt Rachel.

David sighed as heavily as Mr. Lowther. He remembered, too late, other times when Aunt Rachel had mixed everything up like this, stirring a simple story around and turning it into a kind of baleful porridge. He should have known better than to tell her anything at all. But she had not been angry about the scratches when she saw him in his bath; she had merely said Eternal Something-Or-Other and squeezed a sponge full of hot water down his spine. Why did she have to be like this now?

Mr. Lowther was saying that it would all have to be threshed out tomorrow.

4

The threshing-out was done at the hotel. David tried to think that Tony's sprained ankle was little to show for all the fuss. He changed his mind when he saw Tony established on the sofa in the billiard-room. There were several pieces of sticking-plaster on Tony's forehead; on his top half he wore a cherry-coloured golf-jersey belonging to Mrs. Lowther; a rug was spread across his lower half, with the bandaged foot left visible.

Mrs. Lowther sat in an arm-chair beside the head of the sofa. Mr. Lowther had pulled up a straight-backed chair to the billiard-table. He looked as though he were going to write down everything that they said, but he had no pencil or paper.

David wished that he could have come alone; if Aunt Rachel were going to behave as she had last evening it would be even more awful than was necessary. For the moment at least she seemed to have lost interest in the proceedings; she left him standing between the sofa and the billiard-table, and wandered to a further arm-chair, where she sat gazing dreamily out of the window. It was, of course, her time for meditation.

The billiard-room was large and light. Because the tops of the windows were open, the cords of the rolled-up blinds swung and tapped their wooden acorns against the glass; it was still windy outside.

David tried to smile at Tony, but Tony avoided his eye; he muttered "Hullo" and stared at his own bandaged foot. Mrs. Lowther smiled at them both. He approved of Mrs. Lowther, who was dark and neat and grey-eyed. She said, "Let's get it over as quickly as we can. I'm sure you're both sorry and that you realise all we want to know is just how it happened." Mr. Lowther gave a concurring groan and Aunt Rachel lit one of her long yellow cigarettes.

"Sit down, David." Mrs. Lowther pointed to the end of the sofa. He sat uncomfortably, on the edge, in the corner, giving Tony's foot as wide a clearance as he could.

"Well, now——" said Mrs. Lowther, "let's begin at the beginning. You thought you'd just go off and do something exciting—have an adventure, was that it?"

"No," said David, just as Tony said "Yes." Mr. Lowther groaned.

"Whose idea was it to go to the rocks?"

David looked at Tony.

"Mine," said Tony, with a smug note in his voice. Mr. Lowther barked, "When you knew it was forbidden, eh? When I've said it time and again, what? You both knew, didn't you?"

"Yes," said David.

"But you didn't think about that?"

"No," said Tony, "at least, David said something about it but I said, Oh pish, let's have some fun."

"What's the matter, David?"

"Nothing." He understood. Tony was still 'showing them'. Tony was keeping up his act. He was being the daredevil from the *Boys' Own Paper*.

"Well, what happened next?"

"We went to the rocks," said Tony, "and I jumped in."

"Wait a minute," said Mr. Lowther, sounding peevish and puzzled, "You didn't worry about its being rough?"

Tony chirruped, "No, not a bit," just before David said, "It wasn't rough."

Mr. Lowther said petulantly, "Now what *is* the point of saying a thing like that? It was beastly rough yesterday. Blooming great waves."

25

"But when we wouldn't swim in the morning you said you couldn't understand us being such cowards because it wasn't rough at all," David reminded him. Aunt Rachel puffed out her cheeks and made a snort in her nose. Mrs. Lowther raised her eyebrows and glanced at her husband, who gobbled some disconnected syllables that became, "Talking about the afternoon, aren't I? About the rocks, aren't I? Aren't I, David?"

"But it *wasn't* rough; not in the pool; there was just a swell."

"All right; there was just a swell. Whose idea was it to climb out to the point?"

"Mine," said Tony, "David didn't do it at all. After I jumped, I just thought, Well, I'll go and see what it's like out there." He flapped one hand, giving the words a swagger.

"You didn't try to stop him, David?"

"How could he?" Aunt Rachel interrupted. "When he was knocked down by a huge wave and badly hurt?"

"Were you, David?" Mrs. Lowther asked.

"Yes. But I don't know that I'd have tried to stop him. It wouldn't have been any good; we were quarrelling."

"No, we weren't," said Tony.

"Well, you were quarrelling with me."

"I just didn't feel like talking to you," said Tony in a high, lofty voice.

"Why not, I should like to know?" said Aunt Rachel.

"Oh lord, oh lord, oh lord!" said Mr. Lowther.

Aunt Rachel said, "If you ask *me*, Tony went off to the rocks as soon as he saw David was in trouble. *Not* a very nice thing to do."

Tony was scarlet. "Why, I didn't even *see* him."

"Didn't you?" said Aunt Rachel cooingly.

"No, I didn't! I damn' well didn't."

"Hush, Tony," said Mrs. Lowther, "don't get excited."

"Well," said Mr. Lowther, "we're getting somewhere near it. David stayed in the pool and Tony went out to the rocks by himself. And that's all you know, David, eh? You just dressed and went home, eh? Didn't wait for him? Because you were quarrelling?"

"No," said David, "that wasn't the reason. After the

26

wave had knocked me over I'd just had enough, sort of. I wanted to get home."

"And you couldn't see him anywhere about?"

David said, "Yes. Once I was through the gap I could see him; standing on the high rock. I just went on walking."

"You thought it was all right for him to be out there?"

David said, "Well, I hoped it was." He saw that they were all looking at him; except Tony. Tony went on looking at his own foot.

Mr. Lowther said, "I call that pretty stupid, for a start. You knew it was forbidden because it's dashed dangerous —— You——"

David interrupted him. "I knew he wanted to be there."

"A very sound attitude," said Aunt Rachel to the ceiling. Mr. Lowther said, "Wanted—*wanted?* What's that got to do with it? Well, all right, then; you didn't see him slip—didn't hear anything?"

"I heard a scream. I thought it was a seagull; there were lots of seagulls."

Mr. Lowther looked at him bulgily. "Are you telling the truth?"

"Of course he is," said Aunt Rachel in a far-away voice. "If he wasn't, he wouldn't admit to having seen Tony at all."

"Eh?" said Mr. Lowther. "Why not?"

"Because it would be so much easier. So much easier just to say he dressed and went home and that Tony wasn't anywhere in sight. That's what a real liar would say; that he'd seen nothing. David is telling the truth."

NEILSON

I

THE voices faded out of the room. The tapping of the blind-cords ceased at the windows. For Neilson all was quiet; this was a sheeted room in his own mind, where only the figure of the child remained clear; the child was alone and brooding, spaniel-eyed, with his chin upon his hands.

He felt a tenderness for the child. He was clear in judgment but not in condemnation. The child's truth was his own truth. There needed no excuses, no explaining between them.

'And you never did tell, David' . . . Neilson thought.

The child might have heard him think it. The child sighed and spoke.

"I never had to tell. Nobody asked me again. But I knew, I knew. I knew it wasn't a seagull screaming. I knew it must be Tony. But I couldn't look back. I was just too frightened. I couldn't think of him in that water, so I just went on, pretending not to hear."

Neilson watched him, silently, affectionately, until he was not there any more. Somebody moved up beside him; turning, he looked into the face with the straight brows and the innocent eyes.

"Who was the other boy?" Neilson asked abruptly.

"You saw him . . ."

"All the time. Who is he? The pale one, behind David's shoulder?"

The guide said, "He hasn't a name."

"Then what is he?"

"You will know. He is to be seen, and afterwards, not to be seen."

They were cold words.

Neilson passed his hand across his forehead. He was in pain. He felt as though he had been living for hours with a dentist's drill going through his body. Why it had affected him like this, he did not know.

"After all," he said uncertainly, "it was nothing to do with me."

"No?"

"No."

He was, he realised, deeply relieved that it was over. Yet, with the realisation, it was already forgotten. Nothing remained of it. There was the echo of an urgent and vivid experience, one that his memory should hold. Yet here he was, blinking at his companion, trying to recall just what had been happening.

"Like trying to carry water in a sieve," he said.

"It must be, a little."

"Where are we?" He could not see to the end of the room. It made a shadowy tunnel as they walked together.

"This," said his companion, "is one of the distances between."

"How far is it?"

"I am afraid there are no measurements by which I could tell you."

"I don't like it," Neilson said. "I don't like any of it."

"What is the worst of it, d'you find?"

"The worst of it? The loss of memory; that's the worst, by far. Having nothing to go on, as you might say. One feels——" he groped for the defining word, "naked."

"Oh, I'd make the most of your nakedness while it lasts, if I were you, Neilson." The voice, despite the laugh in it, was sorrowful.

"What do you mean by *that*?"

"I mean that remembering will be worse when it comes."

"I can't believe you . . . Why will it be?"

He peered at his companion, but it was impossible, in the shadow, to see the look on his face. "Why will it be?" Neilson repeated.

"I don't think I can prove it to you yet. But a few minutes ago, as you count time, you were feeling pain."

"Was I? What sort of pain?"

"You said—like a dentist's drill going through your body."

"Why did that happen?"

"You went in through his mind and lived there. You came out and brought the truth out with you."

"Don't understand a word of it," Neilson said. Light was

29

breaking upon them. There was no roof to the tunnel any more; it was an alley between stone walls with an evening sky above. He looked about him. "Which way do I go in this time?" he asked mockingly.

The guide said, "Well, you're still not consciously involved. And of course this one's mind isn't easy to follow, like a child's. That's the trouble with them as they grow older. Really the child is the only person you can see in the round; the only one with whom you can recapture contact completely. You can't have the same contact with this one. In order for you to understand him he'll have to set up the scene and let you watch it like an audience. You'll be more sensitive to it than most audiences would be. But if at the end you feel you haven't got the hang of the action, you must talk it out with him. His image will stay until you're quite clear. You've seen to that. Here you are," he added, coming to a halt.

There was a doorway in the wall. The guide stepped back, leaving Neilson to read the words 'Stage Door', to give them their meaning and to walk in.

2

He was reassured. Something was happening that had happened to him before. To be inside a theatre was familiar; though he knew it by instinct only, not by any association that he could recall. He recognised the stage-doorkeeper's office, the lighted cubbyhole with the letter-boxes behind it, the telephone on a ledge. There was nobody in the office. He went on down the short passage, took a right turn and found himself standing in the scene-dock, at the back of an undressed stage.

Between him and the proscenium arch he saw two stagehands. They were scrambling about on all fours, battening some flats together. Both were in their shirt-sleeves; although their heads, the pale fair head and the dark one, came close, not a word passed between them. This struck Neilson as odd; from what he remembered of stage-hands (and he was sure that he had known plenty) they talked all the time they were working. Though he passed close to them, almost stepping on them, they did not look up. Skirting the flats, he found the pass-door; he went down three steps into the auditorium. The house lights were up.

As he edged towards the middle of the empty stalls, the stage-hands raised the flats. They were exceptionally smooth and agile about it, Neilson thought, seeing that there were just two of them. The painted flats showed the back wall of a half-panelled room, with a window looking out into a London street.

The stage-hands braced the flats, tested them to see if they stood firm, then stepped back, warily and in unison. Their movements were precise, identical, the movements of dancers or drilled soldiers. (Which should, Neilson thought, be comical for stage-hands, but there was something worrying about it.)

They nodded to each other and walked into the wings, the dark stage-hand on the Prompt side, the one with fair hair on the O.P. side.

After a moment, as he had expected, the two side-walls slid in on trucks from the wings, hiding the last of the depth and the clutter, making the room complete. Still moving precisely and identically, the two men came back to dress the stage. They brought the unrelated furnishings of a bed-sitting-room in Bloomsbury; the original marble mantelpiece; a gas fire; a divan-bed with a piece of scarlet stuff thrown over it; a screen to hide the bed; a marble-topped wash-stand to do duty as a sideboard; gin, vermouth and whisky to put on the wash-stand. They steered a heavy desk to its place under the window and laid out foolscap on the desk. They put a vase of spring flowers there too. By the time that they had brought chairs, a modern gramophone and a bookcase, the stage was set. The house lights dimmed. This time the stage-hands bowed to each other more formally as they parted.

The lights rose on the scene.

Rain was falling behind the window. For a moment the room stayed empty; then the dark one entered by the door in the upstage wall. He was no longer in his shirt-sleeves. He wore a light overcoat, spattered with the rain, and a multi-coloured silk scarf. His longish hair was wet and untidy.

He was whistling as he shut the door behind him; he stooped to pick a letter off the mat.

31

DAVID

1929

I

DAVID was whistling the Skye Boat Song. By "the lad who was born to be King", he meant himself, though he would be slow to declare it. Hardly a supportable claim, for a copywriter whose days were spent at a desk in an advertising agency making puns about patent food. But this was Saturday afternoon and at his own desk there were true words to be written. Here, through the week-end, he could be alone with his daemon. The only threat to it was the possible interruption of Aunt Rachel at five o'clock.

Perhaps this letter, postmarked Putney, with the big, helpless handwriting yet bigger and yet more helpless, was to tell him that she couldn't come. In which case, he thought ashamedly, it would light up the afternoon. And would so compensate for being the wrong letter.

The right letter, the letter that he would, one day, pick up off the mat, came from a publisher. It began:

"DEAR DAVID NEILSON,
"We are very much impressed with your novel."

It could, alternatively, come from a theatrical management and begin:

"DEAR DAVID NEILSON,
"We are very much impressed with your play."

There were, as yet, two novels and two plays, but no letter.

Meanwhile Aunt Rachel's intention—of coming or not coming—remained obscure. She did not say which. These copious pages told him only that she had entered upon a legal phase. "It is a matter for a *good* lawyer; some really big man in the profession, you will know the right person," the letter said.

Her choice of rescuer was seasonal. Sometimes she wanted

a clergyman; sometimes a detective from Scotland Yard; sometimes a high-ranking officer in the Indian Army. This had been going on for years, ever since she turned against her Guru. He was no longer a chum, but a persecutor. He cut her pension by submitting false figures to the Inland Revenue; he stole her underclothes, employed hooligans to whistle at her in the streets and was, according to this latest report, going behind her back to Miss Brady.

David respected the long-suffering Miss Brady, under whose roof Aunt Rachel lived. Miss Brady's occupation—though her advertisement in *The Times* expressed it more subtly—was the care of borderline cases. He was miserably sorry for Aunt Rachel. Should she come today he would try, once again, to listen to it all.

Now the sunshine followed after the rain. April quickened the sense of wild adventure in his head. He opened the window; the last page of the poor letter flew down into the area, where it joined some dead flowers and sodden newspapers beside the dustbin.

He looked at the golden windows on the other side; up to the corner of the square, and the chestnut tree with the buds breaking. Nobody there. The silence of Saturday afternoon had come down. He stood watching, waiting, whistling his tune; in a moment he would turn away from the profound magic of the empty street. (Why do you wait? What do you hope to see? Get to your desk now, will you?) He longed to sit at the desk, to begin, and he longed to stay here.

A girl came walking out of the square. She stopped to look at the chestnut tree, carefully, as he did at this season. What was important about that? Reminiscent about that? She came on down the street. She took long steps; her fair hair was cropped and shining. He stared at the head, at the hermaphrodite body, and did not believe he saw them. This was the girl from Dijon.

He stepped back from the window. Of all the adventures that could come down the street this was the one that he would have asked for (had it occurred to him to ask). So the impulse to hide and let her pass by was absurd. Still, it was strong. Quite possibly she had forgotten his name; certainly she had forgotten where he lived. She did not know that he was here.

But she had looked, as he looked, at the chestnut tree. There was the echo. When he had found her in Dijon she was doing the thing that he was doing; on a hot summer afternoon; tramping straight through all the galleries of the museum, looking neither to right nor left until she came to the last room that held the tombs of the kings. Their footsteps had sounded together; their search had been the same.

They had paced, in silence and separately, feasting at the gold angels and the couching lions. She had moved slowly along the sides, as he moved, recapturing, one by one, the small stone shapes of the weeping followers. David resented her; he had come to think of the tombs as his own discovery, his own private treasure. The similarity of their methods irritated him. He wished that she would go. Turning suddenly, he collided with her; their bottoms bumped; he looked at her sourly. "I'm sorry."

She smiled at him. All the beauty here was carved and painted and still. By this her animal beauty was exaggerated. She had a wide forehead, a short-nosed leonine face, a skin that glowed brown. Staring at her, he forgave her.

He did not forgive her for quoting Huxley's views on the size of the sternum that would be necessary to support an angel's wing. She laughed at his anger, saying that she liked facts, she liked to know.

"I prefer truth to facts."

"What sort of truth can there be without them?"

"What sort of truth can there be *in* them? . . . How I hate scientists anyway. You aren't a scientist, are you?"

No, she said; history was her passion. It was, he decided, a legitimate passion and he forgave her for calling things that had happened by the dreary name of facts. He forgave her for having a car; she was American and all Americans had cars. He had made his own pilgrimage here in hours of sweaty third-class travel; there would be hours more of it before he reached La Colle.

"La Colle? Where is La Colle?" They were sitting by then at a café table in the shade. He explained where it was, but he could not explain why it meant so much; nor could he describe the valley where small vineyards and coloured squares of cultivated earth sloped up to the Roman wall. Above the wall there was the town. One day he was going to build a house on the side of the valley that faced the town. He did not tell her so.

She had wished that she could drive him part of the way; she was going back to Paris. The word 'Sorbonne' reduced him to uncomfortable admiration and she did more and worse to him as they talked. She was dangerously easy to talk to. He had not before met a mind that he liked in a body that he wanted. When she rose from the table he looked at the body, in the linen shirt and trousers; its magnetism was unexplained; if it were not for the line of the breasts just showing, one might think that this was a boy. She said without coyness, "I hope I see you again." They wrote their names and addresses on the postcards of the angels that they had bought in the museum, exchanging the postcards. He still kept her postcard on the mantelpiece. In a way he had been relieved that he could not afford Paris on his way home. Anyone who could leave him as sensually and spiritually disturbed as she had left him would be perilous company. She should remain LINDA PLATT, 27 Rue du Cherche-Midi, on the back of the postcard. But she stayed on his mind; she had stayed for ten months. Sometimes he wrote to her and always he tore up the letters.

Now she must pass the window. Standing behind the curtain, he watched her pass, neat in line, vivid in colour, co-ordinated in movement, with a catlike solitude. She went, a bright foreign shape, down his street. And now he must run to catch her; he had not known that he would. Leaping across the room he heard the bell ring at the front door. It was as he had often remarked, the loudest and rudest of bells, like a fire-alarm.

"Hello," she said, standing on the step. "Does it always make that noise?"

"Yes. I am very glad to see you."

"Well," she said, "since you didn't come to look for me in Paris as agreed, I thought I'd better come to look for you when I got to London. There was always the British Museum if you weren't here." She gave him an unexpectedly vulgar wink. She strolled about his room, refusing chairs. "I like to move around until I get comfortable in a place, the way a dog moves around." She had lit her own cigarette before he reached it with his lighter. He faced her cool stare;

35

her eyes were grey, with very large eye-sockets and heavy lids.

"How is work, David?" she asked formally, almost primly.

"Work is fun, Linda. But so far unrewarded." He added, "I'm on the last act of a play now."

"I wouldn't want to get in the way of the last act."

"Have no fear."

"I mean it; if you want to work, tell me."

"I will . . . when I want to work. Have a drink?"

"Too early for me. And I should hope it's too early for you."

"Why are you in London?"

She said, "Parents pending."

"Parents . . . I shouldn't have thought you had any."

"Why not? People do."

He said, "They aren't taking you back to California, I do trust."

"Oh no."

"You'll never go back there and teach history," said David. "Mark my words."

She raised her eyebrows.

"Because I can't believe you want to."

"Go on——" she said coolly.

"Be a *teacher* . . . so odd. Not a bit like you."

"On the contrary, exactly like me."

"Why is it?"

She hesitated. "You could say it's because I'm a show-off as well as a scholar." He waited for the truer explanation that she implied; it did not come. She was looking at him, thinking about him. He wondered what she saw. Something more than the reflection that he knew from the shaving-mirror, the slanted brows, the spaniel eyes and the straight nose. He was moderately satisfied with the reflection.

Linda turned away, picking up the Dijon postcard from the mantelpiece, turning it over, reading her name and then looking at the angel again.

He said, "Now don't say that thing about the sternum arch and the span of the wings, there's a good girl."

"Why does it make you so mad?"

"Because it's a typical snigger-boy-scientist's observation."

36

"You believe in angels."

"I believe in God."

"Do you, though?" She sat down in the arm-chair.

"How can anybody not?"

"You fascinate me."

He began to hate her. "When we talked about Chartres and Vézelay, I thought you did too."

"No. I only believe in man. And man's endeavours. Among which, at the risk of offending you, I number Chartres and Vézelay. Don't look so miserable." She waited and when he sulkily refused to speak she said, "God may well be; I don't know. And unless I know, I can't believe. My quarrel is with God's middle-men down the ages."

"Why?"

"Because they sell fear. Life anyway is all of terror and must be faced with courage; why drag God in to make it worse? Oh, as an historian, I know why; as a psychologist I know why."

"Psychologist too, eh? Good show," he said bitterly.

She looked puzzled. "What are you? Denominationally? Episcopalian? Catholic?"

"Neither."

"Well, what?"

"Hybrid, really. My mother mistrusted churches. She says she only had me baptised because she was nagged by some nuns. She is slightly crazy. I'm inclined to think it was an R.C. baptism. School was straight C. of E., of course; and at Bristol I was vaguely Anglo-Catholic; and now I don't go to church any more."

"Well, what d'you *do* about your God?" she asked severely. He resented this from an agnostic. He snapped, "I know he's there."

"Do you pray to him?"

"Of course."

"And that's okay—just to believe in him and talk to him?"

"Why shouldn't it be?"

Linda rose and paced with her hands in the pockets of her suit.

"I don't get it. I guess I never will get it." She went to the window and back. "You think he knows all about you?"

37

David said, "You sound nauseatingly like Christopher Robin:

> 'D'you think the king knows all about me?'
> 'Sure to, dear, but it's time for tea.'"

She disarmed him by laughing. "Anyway," she said, "we're quits. I can't say, as I'd like to, 'There is no God'; any more than you can say, as you'd like to, 'There is a God.'"

"Oh yes, I can," said David obstinately.

"You can . . . What's he look like?"

"Shut up."

She said, "Were you always so umbrageous about the gentleman?"

"I'm not really umbrageous, darling." He was aware that the word darling stuck up at the end of the phase like a sign-post; so, he thought, was Linda aware. "If one's entirely convinced that there is a personal God, one gets impatient with hecklers. To be fair, Aunt Rachel used to get equally impatient with me. In her view he has no personality; he's just a sort of enormous electric current."

"Aunt Rachel . . . ?"

"Well, that's how she used to think. Now, poor darling, I don't think she pays him much attention. As I said, she's slightly crazy."

Linda frowned. "You said your mother——"

"Aunt Rachel is my mother."

"Come again?" said Linda.

"I'm illegitimate. She brought me up to call her Aunt Rachel."

"You sound very placid about it."

"Why shouldn't I? It's no trouble."

Linda said that it usually made for a sense of insecurity, for a chip on the shoulder. "Goodness me," said David in derision, "I didn't know till I was twenty-one and it's never really registered. I always thought of her as my mother anyway. There never was anybody else. In her fubsy way she couldn't have been sweeter or more sensible about it."

He watched Linda's face; which at first expressed mutinous doubt, as if determined to be at odds with the situation. Then the corners of her eyes crinkled; her smile was loving.

"Compassionate fellow——" she said. "Aren't you?"

"Am I?"

"I made a note of it in Dijon." She stared at him again. "Are you still a pacifist?"

"Heavens, yes. Aren't you?" said David.

"Certainly." She went on staring at him. "If you weren't British, I'd assume you were homosexual."

"You would, eh?"

"Yes, I would, *eh*."

"Saved by my passport? You must explain."

Linda said that young Englishmen gave this impression to Americans. She added, "You aren't, in the least, are you." It was a diagnosis, not a question.

"No," said David, "I can cross that off my list of worries."

"Were you never?"

"Oh, at school, I suppose . . . in so far as I was anything. All one's first loves are for one's own sex."

"And all intelligent people," Linda said, "are bi-sexual."

"Oh pooh——"

She looked forbidding. He was not, however, in the humbler mood of Dijon, where once or twice she had managed to rob him of his own resources; making him feel that his intellect was less than hers, that he was a woolly and second-rate romantic. American fluency could do that. Linda's forbidding look changed to wariness as he said "Oh pooh" again.

"It is a fact."

"You'll remember my aversion to facts."

Again he had the impression that she was holding back; she wanted to say more of this, but she did not.

A comfortable silence came between them; he felt no need to talk while she moved to his desk and began to rearrange the flowers that he had bunched so clumsily in the vase. After a moment he saw the flowers looking as they should look; she loped back to her chair.

"Like some tea?" As he heard his own voice, the casual ordinariness of it suggested that they had been married for years.

"Yes, let's have some tea," said Linda lazily.

"Then we might go to a movie or something."

She nodded and picked up his newspaper to look for

39

movies. He stood staring down on the bent head; the back of the neck where the silky hair grew into a point, looked defenceless; he stared at the thin hand with the signet ring, that turned the pages of the newspaper. "There's a French one here that's good. I'd like to see it again, and I'd like you to see it."

He saw the miracle that she made for him. It was the simultaneous knowledge of safety and of danger. This was homecoming. Yet this was the moment of setting out upon adventure. This was the end of search and this was the beginning of everything.

2

"That toucan," said Aunt Rachel, as she paid for her coffee, "ought to be let out of its cage. So large a bird must have liberty. Disgraceful."

The waitress said, "Pardon?"

"I shall let it out myself, I warn you."

The waitress seemed mystified.

"I'm talking about the toucan." Aunt Rachel pointed with her small red umbrella. The waitress looked where she pointed. "Oh, the *parrot* . . . I didn't catch."

"Parrot or toucan," said Aunt Rachel, "its beak is unusually large and the light in here very poor—I must ask you to release it at once. Perhaps you would prefer me to summon the R.S.P.C.A.?"

Naturally the waitress, being a boot-faced girl with no initiative, had to call in a second authority. "Mrs. Gowan, this lady thinks Cocky ought to come out."

"I beg your pardon? Was it something about the bird, madam?"

Aunt Rachel repeated her order. Mrs. Gowan, a foolish-looking woman, though not necessarily in league with the Enemy, disagreed. The parrot was old and preferred its cage. It used to like to sit on the backs of chairs, but that was when Mr. Gowan was alive. Meanwhile she didn't advise going too near; that bird could give madam ever such a nip.

"You would appear to be kind-hearted," said Aunt Rachel after due reflection, "I shall send you a Christmas card. At Christmas, of course, not before." She made a note

40

of Mrs. Gowan's name and the address of the tea-shop in her Film-Goer's Diary. As she went to the door, she was not sure that she had been wise. The little waitress was snickering in the shrill unpleasant way that Aunt Rachel associated with the younger employees of the Enemy. One could not be too careful.

Turning left into Tottenham Court Road, she walked slowly; the rain had stopped, the sun shone and she was tolerably certain that she had given him the slip. This being Saturday afternoon, the street crowd was thin enough for her to recognise and challenge one of his people, should such appear. She always challenged them. That was the way to deal with them; they never stood up to it. Sometimes they blustered, sometimes they simply backed away with a frightened look in their eyes. It was a mystery to her why he should employ such dolts. He was clever enough himself; he never showed his face.

That was his trick; and that, before anything else, must be impressed upon her defending counsel, who might expect the Enemy to be an ordinary man. Aunt Rachel paused, nodding agreement with her reflection in the window of a furniture shop. She wore her best clothes. The Enemy had, of course, rigged the weather forecast, but she had fooled him by bringing her umbrella. Not a drop of the downpour had fallen on her orange velvet beret; her heavy blue cloak was just a little splashed; no harm had come to the white, beaded flannel tunic. She looked very nice. She rather wished that she had remembered to put on her shoes, but these rosy slippers were comfortable for walking. (What a horrible piano! No need to make even an upright in that cheap yellow wood, and she wouldn't, she decided, have the bedroom suite as a gift.) "Pooh to mass-production," said Aunt Rachel aloud and moved on to the next window, an ironmonger's. She wanted to take David a present; if Miss Brady and the Enemy together weren't forever robbing her, she could buy something worthy of him. As it was she chose a small pearl-handled knife from a card and complained about the quality of the wrapping-paper.

She hoped so much that David would really *listen* today. He was always sympathetic but he had a way of cutting through her more important explanations. And he must have all the evidence for this barrister; otherwise they would just be wasting the great man's time. David, like most young people, was inclined to be slapdash and happy-go-lucky. She repeated, "Slapdash and happy-go-lucky"; then she tried it the other way, "Hapdash and Slappy-Go-Lucky." Always she had derived pleasure from words.

That was how David got his writer's gift. She did hope that this new play of his would be a little more human and down-to-earth than the last one, which had been set in Eire and whose characters were all, in her view, crazy. If he would only write about *real* people, she was sure that he could get a public. It was high time. Genius he might have, but he was, after all, twenty-four—and take Keats and Mozart . . . now what were those two cheeky girls doing loitering outside the shut doors of Maple's on a Saturday afternoon, she would like to know? She sailed across the road.

Yes, of course. They were both giggling as they waited for her. What possessed him to employ stupid children of the housemaid class? "That will be quite enough from you," Aunt Rachel said. "And don't imagine," she added as she passed them by, "that I am in ignorance of your mission." Their giggles became screams behind her. She turned, shook her umbrella majestically and went on.

It was a pity that Miss Brady had not seen the incident. Miss Brady stubbornly protested that these hooligans were all imagination. "Imagination, my foot," said Aunt Rachel. She looked back, from the corner. She had, she thought, frightened the two horrid girls out of following her to the square. Of course she would have to expect more of this sort now that the case was coming on. He would do his best to break her nerve before the trial. And he would be bound to get at her witnesses, who must be placed under police protection. Another point for the barrister.

Oh, there were so many points; so many things to be decided. How, for instance, to defend the fact of David's birth? (That old scandal was where all this began. Once the Enemy had got hold of it, he was in the strongest position possible. She would never know exactly who had given her away; she thought the little Eurasian woman in the hotel at Folkestone, but it was difficult to be sure.) How to defend it? She would never deny it. Besides, no good barrister was likely to advise perjury. It was fortunate for David and for herself that such cases were always heard in camera. Ah, fortunate indeed. And sucks to the Enemy, when one thought about it. She came to the Square.

There was David's chestnut tree, most magically alight with green. It had made spectacular progress since last week. Aunt Rachel throve upon spring. "Spring," she said, "is the time for birth—and action." Birth, she repeated more doubtfully, and action. David's birth . . . action for slander. Words could be maddening as well as delightful. (The words embroidered in pink cross-stitch on the sampler that hung above her bed when she was a little girl: BE SURE YOUR SIN WILL FIND YOU OUT.)

What a thing to put in a little girl's bedroom . . . It had set her against sin for life. Not that the Enemy's counsel would admit this. Oh, dear no. He would use the word Sin for William and the big sofa after the dance; he would argue that David was the proof of the finding-out. "This woman who sinned," he would say, pointing his finger at her across the court.

Lots of people had taken that line, including her poor misguided mother, who saw William's drowning as a punishment for sin and nothing to do with the Merchant Service.

"Pooh to sin," said Aunt Rachel, peering happily at the chestnut tree. She forgot about it the next moment because a cat came through the railings and greeted her most politely, with a halt and a chirrup. She persuaded it to pounce at the ferrule of her umbrella. It was soon obliged to go; cats always had an appointment somewhere else. Aunt Rachel began to walk down David's street, looking carefully for spies.

None in sight.

Yes, though. Just one. Standing under the portico next door to David's house. The insolent fellow wasn't taking the trouble to hide. He stood out on the step, with his back to the door, staring at her. A seedy man in a mackintosh, he carried a bulging leather bag, anyone could tell that it was full of forged evidence. She confronted him on the pavement; she waited for him to declare himself. He didn't.

'I'll stare him out,' Aunt Rachel decided. After a moment the strategy succeeded; he came down the steps. He said, "Looks as though everybody's out. I've rung three times."

"That for a story," said Aunt Rachel, leaning on her umbrella.

"Pardon?" said the man.

"I'm surprised you don't tell me you're waiting for a friend. Or a bus. Either statement would be equally convincing."

He looked alarmed. Behind him the front door opened suddenly and a woman with a sheepish face screamed, "I'm *so* sorry; I was at the top of the house. You've come about the cistern?"

"That's right," said the man and he went up the steps, vanishing into the hall at a cowardly speed. The sheepish woman blinked nervously at Aunt Rachel and shut the door. Really the clumsiness of their devices was pitiful. She would have to say a word to David about these neighbours of his. Crossing his doorstep, she rang the bell.

He was a long time answering.

3

"You see . . . you disturb my peace. You've been doing that ever since Dijon."

"Well—fair enough. It's what you do to mine," said Linda.

"I do, *eh*?"

"Yes, you do—*eh*."

They were laughing still, but, he thought, it is out; it is said; the beginning of this beginning is over.

"But don't you——" she asked, "like to have your peace disturbed? Now and again?" There was no art in the question; it was serious and exploratory.

"Well, yes . . . except—this wouldn't be the same."

"Same as what?"

"Same as the others." Then he kept silence lest he should say, "You see, I could love you for ever."

She said, "I can't be cagey. Any more than you can. That's the only way we're alike."

"The only way?"

"Oh, sure." She spoke with careless authority as though she had been analysing their two characters for years. Now he mistrusted further talk. But she would still do no more than hold his hand tightly and go on talking.

"I'll hurt you," she said, "more than you'll ever hurt me."

44

"I won't hurt you, ever; I don't believe in hurting people. I think it's the worst thing anybody can do."

"I'll do it to you, just the same. That's the way it'll be."

"Cassandra," said David, drowsy with lust, "how d'you know?"

"You have the most vulnerable face of any man I ever saw; men oughtn't to have vulnerable faces," she said. "I could love you the way I once loved a woman. And I hurt her plenty."

"A woman . . ."

"You can guess that thing about me, can't you? Most people can."

He was interested, not repelled. "That's why you said all intelligent people were bi-sexual."

"They are."

He thought about it. "Is being in love with a woman like being in love with a man?"

"Only worse . . . It's too close. There's no privacy, d'you see? Your minds are too much alike; there are no thoughts you can hide. The wave-length's too strong. And a man can't be in love twenty-four hours out of the twenty-four. But a woman can. It's a kind of steady, remorseless pressure; no let-up. She doesn't go off by herself in her own head; and forget your existence over a golf-game or the Wall Street prices. I couldn't take it. I loved her very much, that one," said Linda, "but it ended by giving me claustrophobia. And I quit."

"Are you warning me that I might give you claustrophobia? I never study stock prices—or play golf."

She said, "You don't have to draw a moral; I was just talking."

"Suppose we stop talking?"

"If we stop talking, we'll never get to the movie."

"No, will we?" said David.

He took the fragile boy's skull between his hands and looked down into the eyes that looked up at him solemnly, thoughtfully, as though the person behind the eyes knew what he knew, that this could not change anything because all was already changed.

The front door-bell rang its abominable peal. Though he had trained himself to go on writing and let it ring its head

45

off, just as he could ignore the telephone, this was different. It came as an urgent scream from the world outside.

Nor did it wait a decent time before it screamed again. This was Aunt Rachel's manner of ringing, he reminded himself, with a sensation of tumbling cold inside him.

"Will somebody do something?" Linda asked.

"Not on a Saturday afternoon. I'm alone in the house."

The third peal sounded.

"Want to see who it is?"

"Not in the least."

"Well, you'd better; it makes me nervous."

"They'll go away," he said.

"You know who?"

"No." And that was true. If he didn't go to the door, he couldn't know; not for certain, anyway.

The thought made a shadowy reckoning in his mind; a piece of unwelcome arithmetic that equated this moment with another moment, when a boy walked up on the beach, hearing the cry of the gull, looking resolutely ahead lest he should know the truth. It would be like that, not to go to the door. The moment was spoiled.

It was spoiled in any case, with the fourth peal screaming on and on.

"I'll answer, David. If it's somebody for you I can just say you're not home."

"No, you mustn't do that; stay here, darling; I'll have to go."

As he crossed the hall, he did not know what he was going to do or say. He could see the highly-coloured bulk of Aunt Rachel shimmering through the glass panels in the door. Here came familiar impatience and pity, the reflex of boredom beginning. He was without his armour against it. Unprepared, cross, plucked painfully from all adventure, he opened the door.

She was looking even sillier than usual. Or had a new detachment come to him so that he saw her as Linda would see her? An absurdly-dressed, billowing old creature, with thick white patches of powder put on at random and a crazy eye. . . . He looked all down her, from the orange beret to the embroidered bedroom slippers.

"Oh, darling," he said wearily, "I can't see you now."

46

She looked startled; her mouth sagged.

"I'm awfully sorry. But I've got somebody with me."

"Oh, David——"

"Sorry. It really isn't possible."

"But . . . this is my time."

"No, it isn't—not always," he said as stubbornly as he might have argued at eight years old. "You didn't let me know."

"Oh I *did* . . . I wrote . . . About the lawyer. It's so important." Her eyes began to fill with tears.

He went on holding the door. She did not try to come in. She repeated, "The lawyer . . . I asked you . . . Haven't you done anything about him?"

"Oh lord . . . I only got your letter this afternoon."

"But you *will* do something, won't you? You will help me."

He had never before felt this finality of impatience. All he wanted was for her not to be here at all, not to be anywhere in the world.

"A really good barrister, David—not just some little man."

He said, "Darling, we've had all this before. Try to remember. Try to understand. A barrister won't be any good."

"Won't be any good? Won't help me?"

"How can he?"

"For the case."

"Darling, there *isn't* a case. You know that. When you think about it, you do know it; don't you?"

The tearful eyes wavered.

"It's just that you let yourself imagine it all. And then you get worried. Everything's all right."

"*No*," she said desolately. "I must talk to you. I do want to talk to you."

"Not now. Please, darling. I really am busy."

"But I was looking forward to it."

"We can do it tomorrow. Why not go to a movie? There's a good one at the Dominion. You do that—and then tomorrow——" He wished that she wouldn't stand there, looking away from him, with her lip quivering. Her voice was a tiny croak, "Oh please, David, do let me in."

"I *can't*—I've told you."

47

She mumbled something and began to search in her enormous Florentine bag; all sorts of things came out and went back and still she searched.

"What *is* it? What are you looking for?"

She didn't answer.

"Want some money? For the movie? I can give you some—— Look," he said. "Here's five shillings."

She did not take it. She muttered, "The present. I bought you a present . . . Can't find it—doesn't matter now," and shut the bag again. She turned and went heavily down the steps. He called after her back, "Have a nice time. . . ."

He shut the door.

He came into the room again. He saw Linda waiting for him.

"All right?" she asked.

"Yes."

Because, of course, it was all right. Aunt Rachel would go to the movie. She would enjoy it; she always did. And to-morrow she would tell him the whole plot of it and he would listen to every word. She wouldn't go on being sad; she forgot things so quickly.

He did not want to think about it. Above all, he would not remember her searching in that chaos of a bag for his present. Perhaps she had forgotten to put it in the bag. Or perhaps she had imagined it. There was the time when she was convinced that she had sent the Mayor of Putney a silver épergne.

'Damn——' he thought. 'It isn't so bad, is it? I've never sent her away before. I never will again. This is the only time . . . And I did try to give her the money for the movie. It's all right, it's a little thing.'

It was a little thing, surely. What could it matter when he set it beside the magic in this room?

But the magic was out of the room. It would come back, perhaps; now it was gone; there was only David, hating David.

48

NEILSON

I

As the curtain fell, the house lights came up and Neilson was still alone in the theatre. The dark stage-hand who had played the part of David came through the tabs. He wore no make-up; his face was pale and sweaty.

Through the pain that made him weak, Neilson thought that he saw a similar weakness in David; who clung to the curtain for support and looked at him beseechingly. Dizzy with pain, Neilson tried to rise.

"Is it clear to you?" David asked.

"No . . . none of it. But let me go."

"I can't. It is you who must let me go, don't you see? You brought me here—kept me here. It was for you I had to do it again. Now set me free." He let go of the curtain, swaying on his feet. "Question me. I'll answer."

"You must question him." The voice of the guide came from somewhere above Neilson's head. It hurt still more to turn and seek for him. He was standing at the front of the dress-circle, with his hands on the rail; he looked down at Neilson.

"Any question you like," he said gently. Neilson followed the direction of his eyes. The fair stage-hand was standing before the curtain on the O.P. side. He leaned against the wall of the proscenium arch, with his arms folded and his ankles crossed. He took no notice of David; nor did David now seem aware of his presence; he stood, limply, his eyes fixed on Neilson, waiting for Neilson to speak.

With an effort, Neilson began.

"Why are there two of you?"

He looked from one to the other. The cold fair figure did not move, might not have heard him. It was David who replied, hoarsely, with the beads of sweat dropping off his chin, "Because—well, because there are always two of me. Surely that's so of everyone."

49

"Are you responsible for his actions?" Neilson asked, addressing the question again to David. The fair one smiled, not agreeably. David said, "God, no!"

"Then where's your cause for self-reproach? It wasn't you who shut the door in your mother's face, turned her away. It was the other one. I saw him."

The fair stage-hand appeared gratified by this; his smile broadened.

"You—saw him," David said through clenched teeth, "that's interesting." Agony, courtesy and courage were in the words; so might a man have replied to his doctor's diagnosis, "Cancer? That's interesting."

"I can still see him. Can't you?"

David shook his head. "Doesn't matter. I know he's there."

"And it was his doing, not yours."

David said, "No. I may not be responsible for his actions, but if I let him be responsible for mine—well, then, I take the rap."

"I don't understand," said Neilson.

"Don't you really?"

"No."

"It's true, though. I did that thing. Shut that door."

He looked as though spikes were piercing him; or was that, Neilson wondered, a trick of the spiky pain that pierced his own body?

"Why does it hurt you so—to have done it?"

"Because it was cruel."

"But very understandable, surely. Any young man might do it. Any young man falling in love, selfish and excited. Naturally you didn't want her there at that moment."

David shook his head. "Not good enough, I'm afraid."

"Not good enough, maybe. But human. Look—she wasn't easy company at the best of times, was she? Not the mother you'd have chosen to meet the young woman you loved?"

The fair stage-hand nodded agreement. David said, "All the more reason to bring her in."

"You are harsh with yourself, aren't you?"

David said quietly, "So are you."

"Meaning?"

David smiled and was silent.

50

"Anyway," said Neilson, "surely you can't go on suffering for it. That's not reasonable."

David's eyebrows twitched. "Can't I? Can't I though? You tell me."

"How can *I* tell you? I don't know." He saw David lift inquiring eyes to the dress-circle. The guide's voice said, "No; he doesn't know. Tell him if you can."

David nodded briefly, wiped his face and moved a step forward. He dropped on one knee, leaning towards Neilson across the orchestra-pit. The fair stage-hand stepped away from the proscenium arch. He was tense and rigid now, staring at David.

"It's like this," David said: "one talks about 'putting things right', about 'making it up to' the person one has wronged or hurt." He snapped his fingers impatiently. "As though one could cancel out an action by an opposite action; wash out a moment of cruelty with a moment of kindness. And it isn't true. The thing has been done. It can never be undone. That moment is still there; it still happened. I can never make it not have happened. Whatever kindness and thoughtfulness I may show to my mother for the rest of her life, I am still guilty of that."

He looked into Neilson's eyes. "You knew it," he said. "You couldn't condone it or write it off. You're only trying to excuse it now because you've forgotten. It looks a little thing, doesn't it, when you watch it? But not when you live it. That's why you kept it here; and that's why you kept me."

He rose. Fighting to understand, Neilson gazed at him and saw that he stood alone. The fair stage-hand was gone.

Then David smiled at him and he remembered.

"Yes," Neilson said, "I kept you; you and your failure in compassion. All these years."

"And I can go now . . ."

"Yes, you can go now." His voice was as quiet as David's and his pain was over. "Just one more question," he said as David turned away. "What happens to *him*?"

David halted on one foot; he looked puzzled.

Neilson said, "The fair one . . . the one who is to be seen . . ."

"Oh, he goes on, I make no doubt . . . Here's the man who

tells you the answers," he added, with a gesture towards the guide, who came strolling down between the rows of empty stalls.

"Not that answer," the guide said, "or not yet. Think it over, Neilson."

"He goes on, you make no doubt," Neilson repeated, thinking it over. "*He goes on.*" The words brought fear.

"Oh, but you——" he called after the vanishing, lovable figure of David, "at least, now, *you'll* be able to live without him."

"Live?" said David, laughing. "What d'you mean, live? I've been dead for years; much longer than you have. Goodbye, Neilson."

2

When they came out of the theatre by the stage door, they found themselves again in the alley. The light was grey and sad; a false twilight, Neilson thought; no dark would follow; there would be just this continuing greyness. He stood uncertainly, trying to recall the immediate past. But it would not come. All he knew was that something had recently hurt him and that he dreaded being hurt again.

The face of the guide, watching his doubt, was sharpened and anxious.

"You will go on?" he asked.

"Have I the choice?"

"Of course."

This astonished him. "I have free will?"

"Yes. Here, as there. You can take, or refuse."

Neilson thought about it.

"I wish," the guide said, "I could tell you that it will get easier. But it will get harder."

"And if I refuse? But why should I refuse?" he interrupted himself. "I don't know what's ahead, any more than I know what is behind me. You say harder. Harder than what? I've no comparison to make."

"Nothing stays—of what happened in there?"

Neilson shook his head. "I don't even know what you mean by 'in there' now," he said, looking at the wall; the

52

last of the curtain had fallen in his mind. "So let us go on."

"Good." They began to walk down the alley. "This," said the guide, "is another of the distances between."

For a while, nothing changed. The grey light remained itself, ominous but not unkind. In the hush their feet sounded loudly on the flagstones. Then, far away, Neilson heard the sound of hammering. It grew; it swelled into the racket of buzz-saw and mixer, drills and steel.

"What the devil's happening now?" he asked.

"They're building," said the guide. "You'll hear the builders again, more than once."

"Would you mind telling me why, to add to every other abomination, there have to be builders?" For the first time in this acquaintance, he had made his companion laugh. "You're beginning to sound more like yourself, Neilson."

"Well—why the builders?" The noise was growing less and the light in the alley was changing; this was the beginning of sunshine.

"I can tell you why. But since the immediate happenings aren't staying on your mind yet, you may find it difficult to understand. Do you remember the theatre?"

"Wait; I remember *a* theatre, yes; hazily."

"And a scene you saw played there?"

"No."

"Nor the stage-hands who built the set?"

"That rings a bell," said Neilson. "Two stage-hands putting up some flats. Yes. That I do remember." He felt a sense of achievement.

"Nothing else?" his companion asked.

"No; I just have that isolated picture, as though I'd dreamed it."

"Well, let me put it this way. As you become more deeply involved, the scenery will become more solid, more real. And for this process you need builders."

"I don't get it," said Neilson. "*Am* I becoming more deeply involved?"

"You must. It's inevitable."

The sky above the alley was now brightly blue, with a white cloud passing; their two shadows became sharp on the flagstones. "This survivor," said the guide, "the one that's coming now, won't leave you in any doubt about the issue. You won't need to ask *him* questions afterwards. And you won't—except at the very beginning—be perplexed by the Two."

"The Two——" Neilson murmured, memory stirring again.

"I told you that he was to be seen, and afterwards not to be seen; the pale one, remember?"

"He is evil." The words came automatically; he did not know how he knew.

"And you will lose sight of him, at the end of this happening; just as the survivor does."

"But why——" Neilson asked, "does it make you sad? Surely, it is good if he goes."

The guide shook his head gently. "It is only the power of vision that goes."

"What do you mean?"

"You'll find out." Just ahead on his right there was a gap in the wall.

"You take that turning," his companion said, "and you'll be there."

3

Neilson took the turning and found himself standing on the edge of a cobbled pavement. A low wall with an iron gate in it faced him across the pavement. Over the wall he saw green grass and gravestones. A gravel path ran from the gate to the door of a country church with a square Norman tower. Around the top of the tower the rooks were flying. The battered blue face of a clock looked out from the golden-grey stone. The chestnut trees that grew beside the church were heavy with their thick, tired leaves and spiked fruit. In the lazy autumn sunlight, all looked familiar, peaceful and threatened.

'Why threatened?' Neilson said to himself and as he asked the question a man brushed past him and put his hand on the gate. He too was familiar, a dark-haired, sun-tanned fellow in his thirties; good-looking because of his straight nose and the slanted eyebrows above the large, sad eyes. He was frowning to himself; when he opened the gate it was a hunted gesture, as though he were seeking sanctuary.

Perhaps he was. For a second man came after him, walking lightly and easily, a man of much the same build, with pale fair hair and grey eyes. He followed through the gate and went on in pursuit, up to the church door.

DAVID

1939

I

THE church door was locked. 'Might have known it,' David
said to himself as he turned away. So lately returned from
France, he had forgotten the habits of English churches.

He came down the path again, loitering, looking at the
peaceable graves and finding it in his heart to envy William
Cox, Departed This Life, Aged Ninety-two Years. The
church clock chimed the half-hour. He could, of course, go
up the hill to the other church, to Madeleine's ugly little
church that was always open. But the half-hour chime was
beguiling. In this shifting mood it was easier to drink than to
pray. Perhaps a couple of drinks would make him certain.
He badly needed to be certain before he went home.

In the small Devonshire town of Harloe the leading pub
was the Golden Dragon. David got back into the car and
drove to it; down the wide street that should be sleepy with
its Saturday afternoon. It was not. There were more people
about than usual and the physical town seemed to him to be
standing on tiptoe, every house on tiptoe, the shops and the
flat-faced Georgian houses, the whole familiar street, silently,
attentively waiting for war.

As he parked the car in the yard of the Golden Dragon, he
could hear the sound of the radio coming through the windows. Among the collection in the back of the car, the farm-
tools for Ricky and the garden stuff for Madeleine, Linda's
notebooks and the toy rabbit for his daughter Anne, there
was a new portable radio. For the last few days he had found
the old, feeble set at the farm an exasperation; and the
others were always turning it off when he wanted to listen.
A new radio, the man in the shop had told him, was an
investment now. They were going to be short, like everything
else.

56

David crossed the yard. He preferred the public bar to the saloon; he had a weakness for public bars and there was always a risk of meeting the local squirearchy in the saloon. The squirearchy bored him. But in this mood it would be easier to hear the squires' talk than the talk of poorer men. He went into the saloon. It was a low-ceilinged room with dark beams and dark, polished tables. Horse-brasses and shining tankards hung in rows. Over the open fireplace there was a framed print, frail and speckled, an ancient drawing of Plymouth Harbour when the Armada came. David glanced automatically in its direction.

Phil, the owner of the Dragon, a pink man with small blue eyes and a plummy, gentlemanly voice, was serving the squirearchy in the person of Duchesne. Duchesne was in his sixties; a J.P.; narrow and brown and military, with crows-feet at the corners of his eyes. He made a cliché of an Englishman, standing by the bar. Both men said "Good evening" a little stiffly to David.

According to Linda, they had reason to be stiff. He himself did not belong. Neither did Linda belong; nor Ricky Powers; nor Ricky's wife Madeleine. They were strangers; it was less than a year since they had bought the farm; and they were, by local standards, suspect. Ricky and David were writers. Ricky and Linda were Americans; Madeleine had French blood. And their hint of community life was locally indigestible. Or so Linda assured him. Being, as she told him, wholly abnormal in his lack of self-consciousness, he would not notice. "We make them feel uncomfortable," Linda said.

He did not mind the thought. He had no use for neighbours, except at La Colle, where *les voisins*, the peasants, lived in stately independence, minding their own business and taking it for granted that everybody wanted to do the same.

'If only we could have stayed at La Colle,' he said to himself. Already it seemed lost and long ago. ("*The gates are barred on the summer side.*") But it was just nine days back in time, the day with the news of the Russian Pact, the sudden frenzy that turned all the tanned, half-naked English to a worried mob in travelling clothes, jamming the trains and the roads. They had joined the mob. He had said his good-bye standing under the mimosa tree on the terrace, staring

57

across his beloved valley; turning with Linda's hand in his to look at the stone cottage with the cypress topping the crinkled tiles; going out through the wooden door in the wall, hearing the clapper-tongued bell over the door jingle for the last time. It was only their second summer at the cottage. As he shut the door, cutting off the sight of the terrace and the valley, he shut the door on France. Home to England with the rest, and home to war.

'If we could have stayed——' But that was impossible. Thanks to Linda, they were organised to the hilt here in Devonshire. They had made their plan, with Ricky and Madeleine, immediately after Munich, pooling the money for the farm. And he had been party to the plan; he had agreed to all of it. As Linda said, it made sense. Linda wasn't crying inside for La Colle. The place meant less to her than it did to him. He was the sentimentalist of their team; she often told him so.

Still he had the feeling that in France he would be less sentimental, untroubled by personal scruples. At La Colle he could see war as *les voisins* saw it, impersonally, with a rueful calm.

And here? Here in the saloon bar he felt on his guard, defensive. He ordered a double whisky instead of a pint of bitter. Drink, he agreed with Linda, had been sneaking up on him this year.

"All the same," Duchesne was saying, "I'd give my eye-teeth to be in it—not out of it. A war's no time to be old."

Some of the conscripts, David reflected, might be thinking that a war was no time to be young. Phil the landlord sucked his teeth and said he couldn't say he was looking forward to the evacuees. Slum families by the hundred, according to the Reception Committee; and the billeting orders were, to say the least, high-handed. "How many have they managed to dump on you, Mr. Neilson?"

"A mother and baby. We haven't much space. It's not a big house and there are seven of us already, four adults and three children. And the farm-bailiff's cottage couldn't take another cat. I wish," he said levelly, "that we could manage more."

Duchesne was silent. Phil said plummily, "Well, you'll
58

change your tune when you see them. It's going to be hell in every reception-area. Though personally I'm willing to bet they'll all be back in their slums before you can say knife. You can't change 'em. That doesn't," he added to Duchesne, "go for my Four-by-Twos upstairs. Judging by the stuff they've brought with them, they're here for the duration. Another Munich, and they'll look pretty silly."

"There won't," said Duchesne, "be another Munich."

"Sure?"

"Sure. I was telling my conchies that, in court last week."

Phil said, "Only one thing to do with *those*, if you ask me. Shoot the lot." He laughed uproariously. "I would, honestly. Save their keep."

Duchesne filled his slim, elegant pipe. "Oh come," he murmured, "no need to emulate Hitler yet, is there?"

"Ain't there though? Haven't I been saying for the last five years—what this country needs is a dictator?"

Duchesne chuckled, "Well, you'd better cease and desist, Phil, my lad. From now on, that kind of talk's going to commend you to M.I. Five."

"If my son was a conchie," Phil said, "I'd shoot him."

"Why?" David asked. The limpid question brought the two heads round to face him where he sat in his corner; Duchesne's narrow, greyhound head and quizzical eyes; Phil's fat round head with the mouth spluttering, "*Why? Why?* That's a dam' funny thing to say, isn't it?"

"It isn't meant to be. I truly want to know why you'd shoot him."

"Fair question," said Duchesne, with a benevolent snap of his jaws.

"Well, but, Lord——" said Phil. "I'd have thought it was obvious. Because he's a louse. Because he's no good. What's the good of a man who won't fight for his country?"

"He might do infinite good; if you take the long-term view."

"I'm afraid I'm too old to have time left for a long-term view," laughed Duchesne, wrinkling up his eyes. Phil continued to look po-faced and outraged. "Well," he said, drawing himself another tankard of bitter, "if that's all the good he can do, he knows where he can put it."

"He might"—David brought his glass to the counter—"have a moral objection."

"To what, for Christ's sake?"

"For Christ's sake; exactly; to war."

There was a moment's silence; then Phil said, "He knows where he can put that, too," and refilled David's glass.

Duchesne said, "And I could do with another dry sherry. You respect the conchie, do you, Neilson?"

"Too much to call him by that name."

"M'm," said Duchesne thoughtfully, "calling names doesn't help. All the same——" he raised the thistle-shaped glass and appeared to study the sherry—"what d'you do with a pacifist in a country at war? That's what I've been stirring round in my head all through these damn tribunals —ever since conscription came in. He's just a passenger in the boat, isn't he? Question is—can we afford passengers? Mind you——" as he took a sip of sherry, the thin cords of his neck extended—"if they were all Quakers it would be easy. I saw what those fellows did in the last little shemozzle. Up in the front line getting blown to bits on ambulance-work. And don't believe Jerry doesn't shell ambulances. He does."

Phil was roaring. "*Look!* We're all of us going to be in this thing, aren't we? Whether we like it or not. Chaps with no choice—conscripts—civil-defence workers—poor bloody little clerks going for soldiers—everybody mucking in because they've got to. That's it, isn't it? Who's got the right to sit on a bloody fence and say, 'Soh sorreh, ai don't care to pahticipate'?"

"Everybody's got the right," said David placidly.

"Oh, *have* they? That's lovely. That's gorgeous," said Phil, his voice less plummy and less gentlemanly. "Everybody, what? Including you?"

"Certainly. And you."

Duchesne flickered his eyes. Phil flounced towards the shelves and made an unnecessary business of straightening bottles. When he turned back his voice was quiet and injured. "I'm sorry—I know I'm not brainy like some people. I just don't think this is the moment to discuss it."

David saw Duchesne's warning, half-sympathetic signal to him, and chose to ignore the signal. "I can't imagine a more obvious moment to discuss it," he said. "There was never a better one in your lifetime and mine. We're on the edge. It'll be here—tonight or tomorrow. It's the eleventh hour. We're about to shed our theories and start on practice. All right. What I want to know is how a Christian reconciles his faith with killing his brother. Eh?" He grinned at them. Duchesne looked politely embarrassed; Phil reddened and puffed. "No answer? Well, can you convince me that the man who says 'No' to all of it *isn't* doing humanity a greater service than your poor bloody little clerks who muck in? For the sake of other poor bloody little clerks fifty years from now? I don't think you can. Because if he has the courage—yes, I said courage, then someone else who cares for the brotherhood of man may find the courage too. And that—unless of course you like wholesale murder and waste and ruin—would be a step in the right direction. War solves nothing—means nothing. You may give me another whisky."

Phil, now purple, said furiously, "Oh, may I? Well, I don't know that I want to."

"Phil, don't be an ass," said Duchesne. "Free country, isn't it? So far? Neilson's just expounding a theory. Perfectly tenable theory. I don't happen to subscribe to it, any more than you do, but what's the point of losing one's temper?"

"Who's losing their temper?"

Duchesne's eyes flickered again. "He's a writer, remember. He uses his loaf where you and I just muddle along." He turned to David. "Must say I enjoyed that play of yours no end. Took my missus last month when we were in Town. 'Got to support a local talent—what?'—that's what I said. And we both had a thoroughly good evening."

"Thank you; I'm glad you liked it." Oil on the troubled waters a speciality, David thought. It was the first time that Duchesne had ever referred to his work. Phil was still glaring at him. "Is that the way they're talking on the Riviera?" He pronounced it Reeveeyaira. "The frogs, I mean? Jolly lookout if it is . . ."

"Never talk to frogs," said David; "can't understand their language." Just as Phil was beginning to show a truce flag, he added, "They croak in the garden all night under my window." Duchesne said quickly, "What d'you do about

61

your place in France—time like this? Just shut it up and leave it?"

("*The gates are barred. . . .*")

"All one can do. Here's to it." Grudgingly, Phil had poured the third whisky.

"When did you get back?"

"Last week."

"Everyone pretty panicky, I suppose?"

"Only people like me," said David—"the English—hurrying to get home."

"Don't blame 'em, do you?" Phil barked.

David said purringly, "Have I blamed anyone for anything, so far?"

The door of the saloon bar opened to let in a runnel of regulars, local blood who said "Hullo" to Duchesne. There was one self-conscious figure in officer's uniform; a middle-aged man with greying hair who said, "Excuse the fancy dress." The group formed around Duchesne, with David out of the group, listening. The middle-aged man had what he described as a War Office billet; he was driving back to London tonight. "Not my form, really, staff and all that. A ruddy desk-wallah, that's the drill. Thanks, Phil, I looks towards you." A dark boy in battle-dress was saying solemnly to a blonde girl who held a bull-terrier in leash, "What in the name of God are they going to *call* this war? Got to have a name, hasn't it? And the last one was The Great; so what's this? Greater? Greatest? Don't just giggle; it's terribly important."

"You mustn't worry, Gerald. I'm sure the best brains in the B.B.C. are working it out. By the time you're back on your gun-site they'll have the answer."

"Well, cheers."

"Cheers."

"Cheers!"

"God bless . . . And if that silly little Birmingham umbrella-merchant calls it off again, I swear I'll go to Downing Street and clock him a fourpenny one. In person."

"Darling, he *can't* call it off; it's all laid on. My brother in the Board of Trade says——"

"What do I owe you?" David asked of Phil. He was aware of the group now, suspended and watching him, of

62

Duchesne watching him, bird-like and non-committal. Phil's large hand took the money. Phil's small eyes were studiously lowered. He could guess what Phil would say about him after he went. He would, he thought, be more interested in hearing Duchesne.

The sitting-room of the Golden Dragon was opposite the saloon bar; a small room and little used; there were few resident guests. The door of this room was always open.

Here now sat the family whom Phil had described as "my Four-by-Twos", an elderly Jewish couple and a young woman, presumably a daughter. Their attitudes somehow suggested that they were waiting for a visa from an over-worked Consulate. The young woman was hunched, reading a Left Book Club volume in a yellow jacket. The mother, in velvet and pearls, leaned strenuously towards the radio; it was a prettily-fashioned white radio, placed on a stool between her chair and the sofa. On the sofa the father, with a parchment face, a stiff collar and a little paunch, was listening also, nodding patriarchally.

All three stared at David as he came out of the saloon bar. He said "Good evening" and was surprised by the lively chorus of their reply. Their eyes looked grateful.

"Are you staying in the hotel?" the mother asked eagerly.

"No—I live a few miles away; just beyond Axminster." He wondered what in the world had made them choose Harloe.

"Will you have a drink, sir?" said the father. "It's quite the moment for a drink, isn't it?"

"You're very kind, but I've had three. May I—as we say in America—take a rain-check?"

"You're an *American*?" It seemed to delight them.

"Only an honorary American." David explained, "I married one."

"How *very* nice," the mother said. The father's eyes, bright and tired and immemorially old, rested upon him. "What will America do?" he asked.

"Stay out," said David.

"Not for long." The verdict was Olympian. "This is a world war. This is everybody's war."

"Thank God it is coming," said the mother. The girl said, "And about time, too."

David left them. As he crossed the yard to the car, he reminded himself that the object of the drinking had been to give him certainty. All that he had achieved was detachment; the drinks had raised a comfortable wall against the pain of the truth. When you drank, the truth could be there without the pain. He looked at the truth. It was this. All his adult life he had vowed himself to pacifism; he had sworn that he would never kill, that he would go to prison as a conscientious objector rather than fight. And now, on September the Second, 1939, he was not sure.

He drove up Axminster Hill, sunny and detached, seeing it not as his problem alone but as the problem of any man who, in Duchesne's carefully democratic slang, "used his loaf".

War was abomination. So was Nazism. Phil was a Fascist bully; Duchesne was a master of compromise. And the Jewish father had said "Everybody's war" and the mother had thanked God for it. 'Confusion worse confounded,' David said to himself.

Linda would say that he must expect confusion if he admitted emotional evidence; emotional evidence weighed nothing against pure logic and pure logic condemned war. Her sweeping lucidity sometimes reminded him of Aunt Rachel saying, "There's no such thing as sin, I've told you that before." He blew Aunt Rachel a kiss in his mind and said a prayer for her soul, one of his usual childish prayers, "Look after her, please, and let her be happy." He missed her, in spite of all. And there was one memory of her that still tortured him, one thought that he would not think. Not all the kindnesses after could wipe it out. It was easier to think of her death. She had died quickly of pneumonia, caught by getting out of her bath to chase the Enemy down the garden, dressed only in water-drips on a day of sharp frost. Her last word had been "Pooh".

Had she been living today she would no doubt have said "Pooh" to Hitler. Linda would approve. The only emotional evidence Aunt Rachel ever admitted was her own.

And his own emotional evidence—what to do about that? He couldn't cut it out. There was Linda and there was Anne. Not to fight would be not to fight for them. Ricky, with a wife and two sons, thought differently. Ricky said that writing should be classified as a Reserved Occupation and cited a medieval Irish law by which bards were immune. David could counter with the poets who had died fighting and Ricky could retort that they had owed it to poetry to stay alive. "A man of genius," Ricky said, "is more of a miracle than Chartres. Chartres can't protect itself from destruction. He can, and he should."

'Not that I have genius, oh dear no,' David thought; this truth gave him no pain, though the boyhood certainty that he would be the greatest writer in the world was sometimes a troubling whisper. Ten years' industry had made him a popular demand. Today he was a good, successful middlebrow, with a light comedy running in the West End and the Book Society Choice of last January. In America, he got more respectful reviews and smaller sales. And nothing that he put on paper ever measured up to the magic in his head. But he was a lucky fellow; one of the minority who could earn his living by doing what he liked to do.

What happened to that living, in a war? Linda prophesied a boom in book sales; the shut theatres, the bombing and the black-out would force people to stay at home and read. Linda could study and prophesy any number of practical developments; as an historian, she was trained to the long view. And there had been moments during this week wherein he had wished that she would exhibit some signs of a nervous system. She did not feel, as he felt, that a huge black cloud was piling to put out the sun. She did not read as he read, hungrily, the bravest words in poetry, nor call on them for courage. The pacifist who gorged himself on the fighting poets was surely a mixed-up creature. Linda was never mixed-up. How did it feel, he wondered, to be free from the crossed wires, the side-tracks and the gratuitous bruisings?

'And now,' he thought, as he drove through Axminster and out along the ridge, 'you're just where you were at three o'clock this afternoon. When you elected to take the car and do the errands, shake off the others because you had to be alone and make up your mind. You wouldn't even take Anne.' (She had cried, and said, "*I* couldn't leave me; I'd be too sorry for me.")

65

"Oh hell . . . I should have gone to church and not to the Dragon."

He came to the gate. He got out, opened the gate and drove on up the grassy track to the farm.

2

He stared at them, sitting around the dinner-table in the candle-light; he saw Ricky's good-humoured jowls and red tie; the harlequin elegance of Madeleine; Linda looking like a beautiful and sensuous choir-boy. Sundered from their mood, he heard them talk.

"Roosevelt will bring them in," Ricky was saying, "first moment he can." (Like Linda, Ricky now spoke of Americans as though he were European by birth.) "And, however unattractive life's going to be over here, we're lucky; the United States at war will be a lot worse."

"I wonder," said Linda, "if we'll any of us live to see mankind begin to make a little sense . . ."

"Don't see why we should; nobody else has," said Ricky.

"It would be reasonable," Madeleine observed, "if God lost patience with humanity this time and allowed him to destroy himself completely."

Hold on to Madeleine, David said to himself, she believes what you believe, or something like it. The other two were needling Madeleine about the powerlessness of the Pope in this. Ricky was composing a clerihew:

"The trouble about the Pope,
in war-time, is his inability to cope."

"Mind if I leave you?" David said to them.

"You aren't going to glue yourself to that blasted radio again?" said Ricky. "Nothing's happening."

"I am going to say good night to Anne. With your permission," he added scrupulously to Linda.

As he shut the door he heard Ricky say, "Drenched in Byronic gloom tonight," and Linda replying, "Drenched in whisky too, bless him."

He went up the crooked staircase and along the passage to the nursery rooms. He could smell lavender. The leaded window on the landing was open and he could hear a dove gurgling to itself on the roof. Below the window the apple trees were solid with their fruit; he looked over the tops of the apple trees to the twilit hills. It seemed to him that these richly-wooded hills, like the houses in the town, stood on tiptoe, waiting.

Quietly he opened Anne's door. This small white attic belonged to her; two steps led down from it to the larger room where Ricky's and Madeleine's children slept. They were already asleep, two motionless mounds in the two beds. Anne also; Anne was doubled up on her face like a frog, with no bedclothes over her and her night-gown hitched up round her middle; on the pillow beside her there was the new rabbit. David began to adjust the night-gown and the sheet. She threshed and wallowed and did not wake.

He loved her more selflessly than he had ever loved anything or anybody. This was love as it should be, he thought; love at its simplest. This was the way that one ought to love God, without demand. He put his finger into the small curled hand; she clasped the finger without waking. He dared not draw it away.

How could he leave her? This was more of his own emotional evidence, but on the other side, on the non-combatant side. It was impossible to think of leaving her, of sitting in a trench somewhere, pretending to be a soldier, letting Anne grow and change, and he not there. He would settle for all else that war might seize from him, comfort and fun and chosen companions, the magic in his head, time and money and France. All could go, if only he might stay with Anne.

Now he caressed the palm of the curled hand with his finger and she opened her eyes; large grey eyes, like Linda's; her hair was as dark as his.

"Hullo," she said sleepily.

"Hullo, Anne."

"Have the Germans come yet?"

"No, not yet. In fact, it's extremely unlikely that they'll come at all."

"What a shame, what a *shame*," she moaned and burrowed into the pillow, clasping the rabbit. In a moment she was fast asleep again. He stood there giggling and cherishing the words. He could be as boring as any father he knew, repeating his child's remarks.

67

He laid his hand on the dark curls. How, he wondered, could he be so sure that Anne was his kindred spirit, having his own cast of mind? Absurd to think that a five-year-old child had a cast of mind at all. Yet sometimes he could feel as close to her as though she were already adult, already a friend from whom he could have no secrets. When their eyes met, and they laughed together.

He sat down by the cot. He sighed and put his head in his hands. "Oh, Anne," he said softly, "I wish I knew."

How many fathers were saying good-bye to their children, here, in France, in Germany? How many had said good-bye already? Phil's truculent words came back to reproach him— "Chaps with no choice, poor bloody little clerks going for soldiers—everybody mucking in."

Was that a part, perhaps, also of the brotherhood of man, to take your share in the common martyrdom? There were other words than Phil's.

> *"Their shoulders held the skies suspended;*
> *They stood, and earth's foundations stay.*
> *What God abandoned, these defended . . ."*

Oh, emotionally, yes. On short-term, yes. He could feel it. But he could not make himself accept it. The plain truth, as he believed, was to stand firm and say No; in the faith that one day all mankind would say No. 'That is your belief, before God,' he said to himself. 'Have you the strength to live up to it?'

Linda came softly into the room. Nobody could have looked less like a mother than Linda, in the white silk shirt, the narrow black trousers and scarlet slippers. But Linda, perversely, made the best of mothers. Her tenderness for Anne matched his own. Along with her animal love, she had the endless patience, the expert touch, the kindly discipline, of a trained Nanny. And the balance that she held between him and Anne was faithful. Never, since the baby's birth, had Linda let him feel that he was diminished in importance for her. (The fact that they never quarrelled over Anne was doubly remarkable. One of the proofs of their love seemed to be in the violence of their quarrels, which ended leaving them weak and desolate.)

He watched Linda's luminously fair head bent over the

pillow, and rose and put his arm about her. He kissed the top of her head. They went from the room hand in hand, at peace.

Peace might have endured a little longer had Ricky not embarked on the subject of conscription. David was standing by the window, peering through the clumsily-rigged black-out curtains at a searchlight-beam wheeling over the hills. Glancing surreptitiously at his watch, he saw that there was another twenty minutes to wait for the midnight news.

"Six months from now——" Ricky was saying, "we'll be up for trial."

David turned back into the room; the long farm-house room with the 'civilised' furnishings. Ricky and Madeleine had just finished a bagatelle game. Linda, curled on the Knole settee, was making notes. War or no war, the London University term began this month; Linda gave three lectures in the term. She had a devotion to the University. Before they decided to move to the country, she had talked of working there full-time.

"Six months from now," Ricky repeated, "it'll be conscription for everybody up to forty-five. The tribunal will be hearing David and me. This is the reasoned opinion of Richard Jay Powers, adopted Britisher, corny best-seller, phony farmer and minor prophet."

"Make a note of it, Linda," Madeleine said, and added, "I wonder . . . Are we allowed to accompany our husbands? Pity to miss the pearls. No tribunal's going to have a chance against you two articulate types."

David came slowly back from the window. Ricky said, "What'll they do with us? Can't be sure, can we?"

"Of course you can; they'll direct you into non-combatant jobs. Use your head. What's the farm for? Why are we here?"

On Ricky's domed forehead the lines deepened, corrugated. With his frown and his laughing, pagan mouth, he looked wicked. "I hate to tell you, but there's still one piece of grit in my spiritual works," he said.

The words came to David like a lifeline; Ricky spoke and the lifeline vanished.

"It's this way. Can one's conscience honestly accept the ruling of a Government that's at war? If we're directed into agriculture, then that's because the war-effort needs our services, surely? We're helping the war-effort again."

"Yes," said Linda without looking up.

"Helping to kill people."

"Feed people too," said Madeleine.

"Feed killers," said Ricky. "That worry you, David?"

He was silent. Madeleine said, "Do we hold, then, that the only honourable course of action is to go to prison?" She looked coolly from one to the other. David studied her face, the ivory skin, the blue eyes, the upright forehead below the gleaming cap of black hair. He knew why he was studying their faces tonight; he was trying idiotically to see through their foreheads to their true thoughts. Surely, there were doubts behind those foreheads too. Surely, all three could not be so glib and certain. He moved to the sideboard and the whisky decanter.

"Oh well," said Ricky—grinning, "it's the counsel of perfection; and who's perfect? Fix me one, David—one for the jail."

David brought his glass to him. "I see a flaw in your argument, chum," he said. "Long before you get near the jail." His voice sounded harsh and truculent, as though, he thought, some note of Phil's voice had got in.

"All right . . . And for heaven's sake stop looking like Hamlet," said Ricky. "We wait upon your words."

"You do—*eh*?"

"Yes, we do—*eh*——" Madeleine mocked him.

"Well, here's the pretty flaw. If it's against your conscience to accept the rulings of a Government at war, why did you and I spend two soul-searing days putting up the black-out? And what's that respirator doing out in the hall, with 'R. J. Powers' inked so legibly on its cardboard box? And do I take it that you'd rather starve than use your ration book?"

"Why, bless you," Linda said, "the boy's majoring in logic at last."

Madeleine said, "*Touché*, Ricky; give him *touché*. He's entirely right. As long as we live on this island we're subject to a Government that's at war."

"We're all compromising, of course," Linda said. "There's no alternative."

"I guess not," said Ricky, "but Hamlet here looks as though it didn't suit him."

"It doesn't," David said, "none of it does. I can't help seeing us as a bunch of woolly theorists looking for a way to be comfortable. And I begin to doubt that war's the time to be comfortable."

"Blinding-Glimpses-of-the-Obvious Department," said Linda. She was looking at him steadily. 'She knows,' he thought, 'she knows.'

He snapped, "For all the good we're going to do our beliefs we might as well be in the trenches."

"Are you serious?" Ricky's mouth still laughed. Madeleine said, "Dearest David—that's a little exaggerated, no?"

He gave her moody attention. "You're a Catholic," he said. "It doesn't matter to you that plenty of your fellow-Catholics will die, believing in the rightness of their cause?"

"And kill, too. I'll pray for them," she said, smiling and assured.

"You don't feel any comradeship with them?"

"Where *are* we going?" Ricky asked the ceiling, as Madeleine replied, "Not with them as fighters, no. But I don't condemn them, either. This is a matter for the individual conscience."

Ricky prodded David. "How's your individual conscience right now? Judging from your face, it feels like a stomach-ache." He slapped David on the back. "Cheer up. Different grades of lice, that's all we are, all of us. Hiya, brother louse."

"Oh, be damned to you!" David shouted. Linda rose as he did. He said, "I'm going for a walk."

"I'll come with you," said Linda. In the hall he said, "Please don't. I want to think."

"Do it aloud. Better."

She picked up an electric torch from its place beside the pyramid of gas-masks in their cardboard holders. She put her arm through his, determinedly, and they walked out under the apple trees.

He could not make himself talk; she spoke first, when they leaned on the gate of the cornfield.

"You're having hell, aren't you, suddenly?"

"Yes."

"Just why, d'you know?"

"If I knew, I wouldn't be having hell."

She hugged his waist gently, kindly, and waited. He listened to the stiff patter of a rabbit's feet running through the corn-stubble; he looked at the stars. He said, "I find myself hating Madeleine and Ricky."

"And me?"

"Oh God no, not you; just them . . . On the other hand," he said, "I didn't much care for the types in the Golden Dragon, sold on war." He repeated, " 'Jerry'; 'conchies'; 'four-by-twos. . . . How desperately important words are. One can love—or hate—people for their words alone."

"Darling," Linda said, "I've told you—and you've told me—ever since this thing began to break, that there's only one standard: one's own standard, one's own credo, what you'd call one's own soul. What's it matter if Ricky is slap-happy and gets under your skin? What's it matter how Madeleine figures—or fails to figure—about the Pope? And, on the other side of the ledger, what's important about British slang? Stop your ears to *all* the words. You're alone in this, with your God; just as I'm alone in this with my own ethic. Don't let yourself be side-tracked by inessentials."

When he was silent, she said, "That's what you're going to find hardest to take, though. All along the line. The things people say. It's always hard to take. Poor darling, you didn't know that before, did you? You've always been unnaturally immune from public opinion . . . and now you'll meet it head-on."

It was true. He wished that she were not so remorselessly knowing and accurate.

"It would be worse, darling, if we'd stayed in London. You'd have every one of your chums to face. We're insulated here. Imagine . . . All the theatre boys dressed up as Air Raid Wardens, people dropping in for drinks wearing every kind of corny uniform . . . And another thing you'll feel badly about—if they start bombing London. You'll feel you ought to be bombed too. I'll have difficulty in keeping you off the first train you can get." She pressed close to him. "Oh, it's easy for me. I wasn't born sentimental-compassionate. All I care about is you and Anne—and, one rung lower, the part of myself that's laughingly known as my integrity."

72

('Won't you please——' he said to her in his mind—'stop talking?') She went on.

"I know that if we'd stayed in the States as of last year, you'd be having all these same feelings. With a double guilt-complex for being three thousand miles away. There's *no* place a pacifist can be at ease in war, David darling. Not even——" she hesitated—"not even the front line."

She spoke the words with a challenge. When he did not answer, she said, "It's in your mind; I know it is."

Still he was silent.

"I warn you, if you do it, you'll be quite horribly wrong. In your terms of reference, it will be a sin."

His voice asked coldly, "Are you a judge of sin?" He felt her body shiver. "You hate me for saying that, don't you, David?"

('It is true at this instant. I hate you. You are the love of my life and the mother of my child and I hate you with all my heart. For being right.')

3

Having spent the third morning of the war cutting wood, David came into the kitchen to get a glass of beer. A large, vivid woman in khaki was being fed by Linda with bacon and eggs. The clumsy uniform disguised her for a moment. She was Valentine Brooks, one of the faithful of the theatre, who could turn her hand to any work connected with the stage and make it fail to pay. Valentine loved Linda hopelessly. Merry-eyed and foul-mouthed as usual, she greeted David:

"Pardon my clothes; I came straight from the f—ing Buckingham Palace Garden Party."

"She's an At," said Linda, "A.T.S. You address her as Volunteer Valentine Brooks. Overloaded, I call it."

"And underpaid," said Valentine. "Still, it's the biggest laugh I've had since Mother dropped her pearls down placey. Bliss, these eggs. Cooking for two hundred, I never seem to have time to eat meself, like."

"Why are you cooking for two hundred?"

"Because I'm a cook."

"An Army cook . . ." he said.

73

"Best sort of cook I'm fitted to be," said Valentine, "seeing I can't really cook. But my heart's in my work."

"Who are the happy two hundred?"

"Training camp at Colyton."

"Why on earth did you choose that?"

"It chose me. Ta awfully, Linda," she added as Linda put two more eggs in front of her, "I do have what's known as a Big Frame," she added excusingly.

"But explain, for my sanity, why they make you cook when you can't?"

"Well, but that's the Army for you," said Linda. "Square pegs in round holes."

Valentine made a vulgar comment on the round holes. Then she abandoned the eggs, looking at Linda, suddenly serious and authoritative. "No, my love."

"No?"

"No. The plain bloody fact is that the A.T.S. are only needed for a limited number of jobs."

"There must be plenty of women who *want* to cook."

"Not on Army pay, darling. I'll get by," Valentine said, "cooking's mainly common sense. And I've the strength of an ox, which helps. Ox roasting ox, as you might say."

David watched Linda as she came to the table and began to lay the places for the children's lunch. Beside the bulk of Valentine, she looked small-boned and elegant, in a pale grey sweater and slacks. She murmured, "But, darling, why do it at all? Joining the Army's pure waste of you. Someone of your talents and intelligence——"

Valentine roared with laughter; she looked like Charles the Second when she laughed; black curls, grape-bloom eyes and white teeth. "It's just too bad about my talents. Plenty of talented, intelligent little boys are going to get themselves killed—and soon. Aren't they? Christ, Linda, what have you *got* to give to a war except you?" She finished her eggs.

Linda was silent, smoothly aligning knives and forks. David knew that she was waiting for him to answer on their side. Valentine did not appear to need an answer. She pushed back her chair and spread her legs, which were encased in baggy stockings of greenish khaki; at the ends of them the brown shoes looked like boxes. "Sweetly pretty, aren't they,

74

David? Want to see my knickers? Bockers, rather. Khaki bockers at my age—look. Where's your tot?"

"Anne . . . She'll be along," David repeated. " '*What have you got to give to a war except you . . .*' "

"Eh?" said Valentine.

"That's what you said."

"Oh . . . yes. Well, that's it," said Valentine. "No two ways about it."

He saw Linda's heavy-lidded, watchful look; he said, "If you happen to approve of war."

"Oh, f—— that for a start, if you'll excuse me. Who approves of war? Who the hell could? Might as well try to approve of a motor accident. Only thing to be said for war is that one doesn't have to do anything about one's debts."

When the children came, she taught them a macabre trick with their thumbs that reminded him of the Lowthers' tricks in his childhood. When she said that she must get back, David said, "I'll drive you."

"But I can hitch a lift with the next man. That's what I did coming here." When he persisted, she said, "Petrol—petrol." "We're all right," said David. "Agricultural necessity; coupons by the yard." He watched her take Linda into her arms with a man's embrace; he thought that Linda rather liked it.

Valentine loped beside him to the car. She was, he supposed, a figure of fun in her ill-cut jacket and clumsy skirt; they exaggerated her breadth. The flat peaked cap like a muffin was disastrous. But the clamour of envy and admiration went on inside him. She scrambled into the car, saying, "Nice to have you chaps around; I was lucky, getting posted here. Linda says I can come for a bath any time."

"No baths?"

"Well, no hot water. What's the matter, David? Hangover?"

"That too," he said. "It's the fourth in a row, which doesn't help. At this rate I'll have cirrhosis before the war's been going six weeks. Which should solve all problems." They bumped down the grassy track to the ridge. "Valentine, I think I'm going mad. I'm a pacifist. I've never been anything else; and now all I want to do is fight."

Valentine said, "That's easy. A hell of a lot of people stopped being pacifists at eleven a.m. on Sunday."

"I haven't stopped. It's still against my conscience to kill."

"Cheer up, chum, you may not get the chance. You could find yourself with the Pay Corps in Nottingham."

"Dear Valentine."

She cocked her head, looking at him narrowly. "Linda making it tough for you? I wouldn't be surprised. I'll always be in love with Linda, you know that, but our heads don't work the same way. I haven't the patience to analyse it all and make little measured judgments and hold to them. I'm a gambler; and a sloppy type; and what's good enough for my buddies is good enough for me. You're the same sort. You'll never get anywhere if you try to steer by your head."

"I don't. It's not the same for me as it is for Linda; my heart's involved. And my faith. One minute I can hear the monk saying, '*And waste the folk who cost our Lord so dear.*' The next, it's 'I have a rendezvous with Death, at some disputed barricade.' And I go on feeling cut in half."

"Well, poor old boy. But you could feel like that in uniform, too," she said consolingly—"people do. And think how pretty you'd look—unlike me."

"How do you square war with Christianity, Valentine? With God?"

"Cor stone the crows, is it my business to square war with God? If He couldn't square it with Himself, I presume He'd stop it."

They came to the gate with the sentries. Valentine said, "And another thing. The Army may be tough on the feet, but it's a beautiful rest for the ego." She saluted him and loped off down the asphalt path; he saw the sentries exchanging grins. She did look funny.

"The ego . . . Is that what I need to take a rest from?" He asked the question to the air. "Is that all that plagues me?" Perhaps it was. Still wondering, he drove back through Harloe. He found the church door locked again (might have known it) so he wandered round to the back of the churchyard and sat down on a tombstone under the chestnut tree.

His hands, one each side of him, pressed hard against the rough, lichen-blotted stone.

"*Let's talk of graves. . . .*"

Tombs of the Kings of Dijon, with the gold angels watching over, and the lions couched. Tombs of the knights with their stone feet crossed from the crusades.

"What have you got to give to a war except you?"

("*And waste the folk....*")

It was all very well for Linda to say, "Stop your ears to the words." He couldn't. The words besieged him.

"Go hang yourself, brave Crillon!

We fought at Arques and you were not there." "*Debout les morts!*"; "Mithras, also a soldier——"; "I shall go back to Imbros, at morning, over the sea——"; "Davy Gam, Esquire.'

"*Thou Shalt Not Kill.*"

But, "Valour and Innocence
Have latterly gone hence
To Certain Death by certain shame attended.
Envy—ah! even to tears!—
The fortune of their years
Which, though so few, yet so divinely ended."

He clasped his hands across his eyes.

"Forgive me, God," he said. "This is against all that I believe, but I cannot help it. I've got to be with them."

NEILSON

I

NEILSON knew these things. The country churchyard faded from his vision and still he knew them, remembered them. Now he saw nothing but the face of the man, gazing into the dark.

The face of the man endured. Only for the blink of a second did it seem to Neilson that the face had a colder, fairer look, that the eyes were pale. Perhaps the waning light had done this to it. For afterwards it was again the dark and vulnerable face of David.

"Of the man I was," Neilson said aloud. He held on to the words. They rocked in the hollow of his head; they danced and jangled, but he knew that he must not forget them.

The man who once he was went from sight.

Now all was dark, but this was darkness with a difference; this blacked-out street was familiar. He could feel the pressure of memory stirring, unburying itself, quickening to come alive.

A car was crawling along the black street beside him; the pale beam of its single, masked headlamp skimmed the surface of the road. Overhead the gunfire bumbled and barked. High to the west the searchlights lanced into a cone, catching the tiny shape with wings and keeping it caught. Now the sky was thunder and the ground shook.

Below his feet the ground grew rough, uneven; familiar, too, this stumbling forward in a foreign place. There was the pounding of heavy artillery, the crash of a trench-mortar, a shell that screamed. Light coming through and a landing-craft sinking in rough water; a white road breaking up under shell-fire, a tank on its side, ablaze. He saw the Italian hills and the blown bridges; Anzio; Rome; Florence; Forli; he saw and remembered as they poured past him, each intolerably real and vivid, too real to shred away so fast.

Each put a barb into his flesh, hooked and hurting, but to be welcomed with joy because he knew it, because he had been there before. This was memory returned, the film unwinding where there had been no film. But the speed was impossible; if only, he thought, he could find the trick of controlling it; he was dizzy with the cascade of the past.

Whole sequences went by, uncaught. That was the Grand Canal, surely, and the Lion of St. Mark; that was the skyline of the Alps, seen from the air; Mont Blanc shouldering by, under the wing of a bomber. That was a train sliding home through green fields, and this was a city where flags flew above the noise of bells.

The pealing of the bells changed, hardened, to become the ringing of steel on stone. Neilson stood, hearing it, with his guide watching him.

2

"I remember," Neilson said.

"You know who you are?"

"Yes. I am David. Those things happened to me; all of them, from the beginning."

He looked into the straight-featured face with the innocent eyes. "But why does *that* make you sad?" he asked. "I'm not sad any more."

"Nor in pain?"

"No, nor in pain."

"Nor troubled—by the Two?" the guide asked wistfully.

"The Two—wait." It was hard to think, against the racket of the builders. "That was different—as you said it would be. I saw him at first—the pale one. He was following David—I mean me—up to the door of the church. But I never saw him again after that. Except, just at the end, when it was fading out, I thought——" He hesitated, feeling cold.

"What did you think, Neilson?"

"I thought, for a second while I was looking at David, that it wasn't David at all, but the other one. His eyes looked pale, and his hair . . . It must have been the light, the light was going fast. In another second I knew it was David."

The guide said nothing. Neilson felt colder still.

"It—it doesn't mean they've merged into one person, does it? That the other one's moved in?" He pleaded with the silent face. "Please don't tell me it is that."

"Not quite that. Remember what I said of him."

" 'He is to be seen; and afterwards not to be seen,' " Neilson repeated.

"Yes. It happens, as one grows older. One learns to accept him."

"I wish one didn't."

The guide looked at him sympathetically.

"It began there, did it? But——" Neilson pleaded—— "David was mixed-up in his mind; I mean *I* was. You understand, don't you? One minute war looked right; to refuse looked wrong. And then I was back at the truth of Christ. And then the word 'Pacifist' shamed me and I wanted to fight. Either one could look like the brave thing— or the coward's way. Till at last I didn't know what was good and what was evil; there seemed to be both in each." He sighed suddenly. "And that's why I couldn't see the Two this time?"

The guide nodded.

"Shall I ever see them again?"

"Differently," the guide said.

"Now?"

"No, not yet."

"But now? What happens now?" The guide took him by the arm and turned him about. He saw the builders.

3

'The singing masons,' was the phrase that came first to Neilson's mind. But the words echoed with beauty. He did not find these beautiful. The men were all dressed alike, in white powdery rags; all were barefoot; all the faces and arms and hands were deep brown. And they were all much of a size, dwarfish and broad-shouldered. Their song had no audible words; it was a low, strong chant, a chorus as of bees. Remorselessly they worked and chanted, laying stone on stone. He did not like the builders. But he had to watch them, because they were doing the thing that he had never done. They were building his house, at La Colle, above the valley.

There was no mistaking the valley; he knew every coloured patch that chequered the further slope of it, up to the Roman wall. He knew the bell-tower of the church, the clustering façades above the rampart. Beyond the end of the southern wall there was a cemetery, with its tall white monuments and black cypresses silhouetted. The long town made a crest on the hill; above it there shone the Mediterranean sky. He looked at the orange trees growing beside the north wall; he saw the hotel of tangerine-coloured stucco; all was as it had been when he first came to the valley, in his far youth.

The builders confused him. Because the house too had been here always; old when he bought it; the stone cottage with the cypress making its tiled roof more squat, the purple bougainvillæa flaming round the windows; the well-head, and the mimosa tree, on the flagged terrace, where every evening as the sun sank he stood to watch the shadow walk up the hill towards the town.

The guide was saying, "Know where this is?"

"Yes, of course. It is the house at La Colle. But I don't understand. It's always been there. We were so frightened that it wouldn't be—when we came back after the war. But it was untouched. Did something happen to it since? Why must they build it again?"

"Oh, they aren't building it at La Colle," the guide said. "You've reached the confusing stage where you can see the two worlds—the world you lived in and the world where you are now. The builders are of now; they're building it here. Always a little disturbing, seeing the wheels go round."

"Why don't I like them? Why do they seem hostile?"

"Hostile . . . They're not, you know. Except in the sense that all the mechanics must now seem like the devices of an enemy; mere obstacles. Your impatience is natural." He paused, looking sad again. "Of course, you may have a hint that they will, sometime, build something that you'd rather not see. But, for the moment, they're merely in your way. You don't need them. You can remember the place."

"Perfectly."

"And the time . . . ?" said the gentle voice. "Do you know the time that you've appointed?"

Neilson frowned. The mountains behind the valley were playing a trick that he knew. A carven-looking edge of cloud, that had been the merest small, bright hem beyond the ranges, had towered up suddenly to hide the sun. All the colours of the valley went out, and the rising wind rattled the dry leaves drifting on the terrace.

"The time," he repeated. "No, I don't know which year. We got back in the summer of '47. Is it then?"

"No. It is the year 1950."

He shivered; there was some horrible echo sounding. "Why that year?" he asked sharply.

"You chose it, Neilson. That is where you are."

He looked about him.

The builders were gone. He could no longer see the terrace because he was standing in the narrow dusty road outside the wall. The cottage and the terrace were on the other side of the wall. The sun was high. Along the top of the wall the geraniums looked as though they were splashed there in red and green paint.

Now he heard somebody whistling the Skye Boat Song and David came walking up the road from St. Etienne. He had silver-grey patches in his hair. He was tanned to the colour of Indian tea and he wore his Riviera clothes: a yellow singlet and trousers of faded pinkish sail-cloth, rope-soled shoes on his bare feet. He gave the stolid wooden door in the wall a nudge with his shoulder; the clapper-tongued bell inside jingled loudly as the door fell open.

DAVID

1950

I

As David came through the door, the bell jingled above his head. He heard the pause in the click of typewriter keys beside the open window on the first floor; Linda called, "*C'est qui?*" "Only me," David called up to the blue, fluttering curtain. Reassured, she looked out above the bougainvillæa.

"Where did you go?"

"Just walking around, brooding."

He was at the brooding stage that was the best. If only this were all that there was to the writing of a novel, he thought wistfully, as he had thought before; this stage wherein you walked accompanied, with the characters coming into focus; beginning to be real people who made their own lives. All you had to do was to watch the dream grow solid. It was magic; the first magic, and the last, he reminded himself, the only magic there was. It must die cold when he put pen to paper; and he must put pen to paper soon or it would die by its own hand—the sadly simple suicide committed by all stories if you let them cook too long.

'Tomorrow,' he thought, 'I must begin.'

Anne, who had not appeared for breakfast, had now vanished from the terrace, leaving her traces; the mattress spread for sunbathing, a pair of dark glasses, a volume of Proust and an American thriller. David sat down in a deck-chair under the mimosa tree and gazed across the valley.

The church-bell from the town rang the Angelus. He said a shapeless prayer; he had been aware of twinges of piety all the morning; he felt well and one could, he had noticed, mistake feeling well for what the Catholics called a state of grace. One's health, in one's forties, became noticeable. He was a healthy man. Certainly there were more hangovers than there used to be. There was a morning cough that went as soon as he stopped smoking, but it was some time since he had tried to stop. There was regular influenza brought by the English winter and the variety of minor troubles, known as 'bugs', that he caught in America.

'Middle-aged, that's me,' thought David, without rancour and without believing it. He did not feel middle-aged. In this perspective, the war years, the years that should have increased him in mental stature, did not look like a part of his own life. He had hung up his own life on a peg and turned himself into somebody else, into a soldier. Looking back on the long nightmare of boredom tempered with terror and incredulity, he could make little of it. Good things had come of it, and evil things. It was a period without shape or pattern; nor could he know whether he had been right to choose that way. The ethics had faded. He could, when he willed, remember the torture of decision, but it was a flat, far memory. It was out-of-date. The thunderous, improbable years intervened.

Sometimes he knew that the decision, like the years, had separated him from Linda; that for all their enduring love they saw each other now in a different perspective. More often, he could fool himself that all was as it used to be.

He had come back to real life feeling, if anything, younger than before. Perhaps, he thought, one should be allowed to leave out the war years when calculating one's age. It was not, surely, to them that he owed his greater tolerance, the hints of a sense of proportion, a tendency to skip moral judgments and take life easy? These were the desirable results of being happy and successful.

When he got to there in his mind, he felt the smallest sting of reproach—that came from whom? From a boy who looked as he had looked once, a boy with honour in his eyes? In a blink of his imagination he saw that young man for an instant; quite clearly, standing on the terrace, laughing in the sun. His hair was black; his forehead was smooth; his face looked out upon adventure. The innocence, the untried quality, of him was a little pathetic. Then the man who had known war and peace forgot him. He began leafing back through the summers that had passed since their return to La Colle. This was the fourth summer. Three years, then, since he had stood on the terrace, thanking God.

He had said, "We're here again. We're back. France is back; the sun's come back. The Germans have gone; the bogey-men lie dead, the ogres, the pantomime-villains of our day. It is all over, the thing that could never be over. Oh please, let me be grateful always. Let me not forget to be grateful."

But one forgot. It was, perhaps, the shortness of human memory that made all wars possible. Only five years since it ended, and now, he thought, the self of these five years dominated the scene, obscuring the grateful man. Nearer and more beguiling, there was the upward curve of his fortunes. But he did, he argued, say 'Thank you' for hitting the jackpot.

Linda said that what he had developed overnight (if the war years could be counted as the night) was the common touch. She thought even less highly of it than he did. She was a little too ready to agree with him when he classified himself as a skilled craftsman with just the requisite lack of taste.

This, he believed, made the novels and the plays popular, shareable; he still wrote himself down as a middle-brow, but the hairline, he knew, had advanced a little instead of receding. He could still say with truth that he was doing what he liked to do. It was cause for gratitude that this should bring movie sales and Book Club choices.

"And the play, they tell me, will run for ever. So it had bloody better," David said to the valley, "seeing I never mean to write another." This was a regular vow; made when he was still convalescent from the long slaughter of casting and rehearsals. The theatre was the most maddening of loves. He was through with the theatre. Back to a novel and peace and solitude with only himself to call the tune; he wanted nothing more. He was done with producers, directors, actors, rows and rewrites. Till next time.

Drowsily, he contemplated the girl in his novel, who was already beginning to have a fatal look of Anne; just as the older woman began to look too much like Linda. One of his limitations was to have to write of the things and the people he knew. Hurriedly he allotted the girl red hair and a Domestic Science Degree. She seemed to resent both allocations. Then she turned opaque, as they all did at this stage

85

when he stared at them too hard. So it was time for a drink.

The inside of the house was, as ever, violent in its coolness after the sun on the terrace; there were three rooms, linked by arches cut in the thick stone walls, and a short, rounded stone stairway leading to the upper floor. Blind with sunshine, he groped his way through the third arch into the kitchen. He found a glass and came back to the well-head outside the kitchen door. Here, by a system of rope and pulley, two wire-baskets hung in the cool depth of the empty well. Next week, *MM: les Fabriquants* permitting, they would have their refrigerator. But he was sentimentally attached to the well. There was little here that did not pull on his heartstrings. This house, to him, was home. To him, not to Linda. Linda had sunk roots in Devonshire, on the farm, in his years of absence. She had sorrowed for it when Ricky and Madeleine broke up the partnership and went back to America. But she had, somehow, as he had not, managed to sink palpable roots in London; in the maisonnette on the wrong side of Eccleston Bridge, the only post-war lodging that they could find. It was nice now; she had worked on it. And the façade, like its neighbours, was at last repainted; the street revived. There was a new house going up where the bomb had fallen three doors away. Linda liked the London flat and the London life; she never longed, as he longed, to live in France. She had not his fool-proof love of it; even on holiday, she could become impatient alike with French politics and the French post office.

Besides, her work was in London. His, after all, was a portable profession; Linda couldn't carry classes and students across the Channel. No, he thought, we'll never live in France the year round.

He stood by the well, hauling up the basket with the bottles, restoring in his mind the only other place that he had loved as much as this, Aunt Rachel's seaside cottage long ago. He could see the black, tarry shape of it, the brass telescope standing in the ragged garden above the shingle; the crowded, cosy room with the stuffed owl in its glass case, the coral paper-weight, the picture 'Off Valparaiso' hanging above the mantelpiece.

"What I have today is total recall," he said to Anne as she came out by the living-room door.

"Would it be something you ate?" said Anne. She looked, as was to be expected, fragile with tiredness; there were dark smudges under her eyes.

"Want a glass of *rosé*?" he asked her.

"It would help, I think. Short of sleep," she explained unnecessarily.

"H'm," said David, "just what time *did* you get in?"

"Oh . . . around three, not too bad . . ." She went on quickly, "But the local cocks have such a conscience about cockcrow, do they not? And when they're through it's time for the dogs, and after the dogs it's the milk-van—and the bread—and the vegetable-truck; and all those hobnailed boots. I see them quite alone, without feet, the boots, always; just unoccupied boots going by under the window, talking in *patois*; don't you?"

"No," said David, "and if I did I should be seriously worried." He stood the bottle of *vin rosé*, cold and splendidly coloured, on the parapet of the well. When Anne brought her glass from the kitchen, he said, as he had not meant to say, "What went on last night? Something special?"

She looked wounded. Linda said that Anne's face was, in defiance of likelihood, more vulnerable than his own. "But it was René's birthday——" she said, "his birthday-party; I told you."

"I'm sorry, I forgot." She was waiting for him to give her what in the Army he had called a rocket. He stalled, saying, "Did you have fun?"

"Oh, *wild* fun, yes." She doubled up like a jack-knife in the canvas chair until she appeared to consist only of a face whose chin rested on two brown legs that were very long from knee to ankle. "We dined at Felix au Port."

"You did, *eh*?"

"Yes, we did, *eh*?"

"Who paid?"

"I don't know; René, I suppose; or Joe van Merren. Then we drove. We stopped at two places to dance; one new one, in Villefranche, but we had to leave because of the sailors."

"What did the sailors do?"

87

"You know what sailors do."

"And then?"

"Then we just drove home rather slowly and had a swim on the way. There was a moon."

"There was a moon. As I should know. I prowled around by the light of it in my dressing-gown till two-thirty. Your mother insisted on taking over after that."

Anne looked him straight in the eyes, unsmiling now and ready for trouble. The click of the typewriter was still sounding steadily from the window above.

"Before we go further——" David said. "If Linda's given you hell this morning, I'll pend mine till the afternoon. No need to look grateful; my object is to be effective. I'll be less so, coming immediately after Linda. You've had it from her?"

"Well, I have and I haven't, as you might say. She's what's known as put her foot down. But she didn't take long about it."

"Ah," said David, drinking his wine.

"Is 'ah' all you're going to say?"

"About last night, yes. For the moment."

She uncurled and walked across the flagstones to the edge of the flower-bed, where she stood looking across the valley. In the droop of her shoulders he saw dejection. Linda was right, of course. And Linda had got her salvo in first, while he walked between the gardens of the Quartier St. Etienne, letting the novel simmer. He would rather that she had not. He wondered how she had tackled the situation; he was tempted to ask Anne where the putting-down-of-the-foot left René and the others. Nothing disloyal to Linda in asking, but better to let it ride. He had to guard always against sounding as sympathetic as he felt; the wave-length between him and Anne was powerful. Not, he told himself, that he was on her side now. He was on Linda's side. But the damnable truth remained: temperamentally Anne was exactly like him, not in the least like Linda.

She drained her glass, with a gesture that seemed to be a dispirited toast drunk to the valley, and turned back to him. In looks, she was neither his nor Linda's, and the only beauty in her face was the *beauté de diable* of her youth. She had brown curly hair, a bumpy forehead, eyes now more green than grey; Puck's nose and a wide mouth whose white teeth were crooked. (A hockey-ball at school had done that; Linda talked of getting the teeth fixed on their next trip to America.) She was really all legs and the wide grin, David thought, looking at her. Anne's magic was the charm that made slaves. A dangerous thing to be born with. And the foot must be put down on René and the other rich playboys who came under the spell. She wasn't eighteen yet.

Her grin faded. Now she looked quite ugly with misery, a sad sprite tiptoeing painfully across the hot flagstones. She flung herself down on the mattress, her chin pointing at the sky.

" 'With rue my heart is laden'?" David suggested. A sigh was his only answer. Still the typewriter clicked away upstairs.

"You aren't in love with any of them, are you?"

"*Gosh*, no." Her voice could be all-American as easily as it could be Oxford English. There had been Americans in the party last night.

"Well—that makes it easier."

"Makes what easier?" She rolled over on her stomach, propping her chin on her hands, looking up at him. The grin had come back.

He said, "Makes the veto easier . . . the put-down-foot."

"I suppose it does. It doesn't feel as though it does. But I can't know, can I, until——"

"Until?"

"Until love and the veto run concurrently," said Anne.

"This is not inevitable," David reminded her.

"Mean, if he's the right young man I can stay out with him till all hours?"

"Depends what you mean by the right young man. In terms of your own choice the right young man, as I recall, is the one who keeps you indoors."

"Does he, though?"

"Yes, he does. All day. Sitting by the telephone which fails to ring."

Anne giggled. "Why do you fancy I'm doomed to love unrequited?"

"It isn't a serious fancy."

"Oh yes, it is. I can see. Just as I'm confident that you and Linda will both hate him, however perfect he is."

89

"He won't be perfect."

"There you are," said Anne. "Anyway, he's doomed too. I propose to be as cold as ice, as chaste as snow *and* escape calumny, except at the hands of the critics . . . I shall care for nothing but my career."

"The theatre—as I've told you—is not a career. It's a particularly besotted form of martyrdom."

"Then why did you agree to let me go to R.A.D.A.?"

"Because I have no spine."

Anne said, "Oh what bliss," and appeared to go into a stupor.

"What is bliss?"

"Your having no spine and Linda having so much psychology. Other parents might have thwarted me. You know," she said, sitting up, cross-legged, "it's frightening to look forward to anything so; you think God will stop it, the way, as a child, you used to think he'd stop picnics; so mistrustful and silly. And really so unfair to him."

"One's nearly always unfair to him," David said moodily. God was shared ground between them. As though the subject had cued it, the typewriter stopped clicking upstairs. Anne's eyes met his as the two of them heard Linda coming down. He was disturbed by the conspiracy of the look; they might have been children signalling to each other. 'Here comes Teacher.'

Nobody could have looked the part less, he thought, as Linda came on to the terrace; she was still, in these clothes, the girl from Dijon; the girl with the fair, well-shaped head and the boy's body. Middle age made her a little thinner, a little more tense. The lines on the forehead were thinking lines; the heavy lids were heavier. Her tan showed up the whitish wings in the hair just above her temples. In London she kept them skilfully blonde.

"Thirteen pages since nine o'clock," said Linda. "I defy the best-seller to improve on it." It was an article on the Code Napoléon for an American historical magazine. He was still a little awed by the things that she knew; when she said, "You don't have to read it, you'll be bored," she meant, "You won't understand more than half." Her lucidity could still fool him into believing that he would remember facts and dates as she expounded them, but he never did. The old cloud of unknowing persisted. Just a woolly-minded trader in fiction, David said to himself, thinking humbly about the Code Napoléon.

He put Linda's glass into her hand. She moved her chair back under the shade of the vines; their shadow-pattern made her face non-committal. Then she smiled at Anne, as lovingly as though there had been no veto. She cocked one ankle up on her knee with her usual boyish gesture. She waved her cigarette at David, for a light. Seeing Anne's look, he thought, 'Now we're both afraid of Linda. . . .'

"Well, darling——" Linda said to Anne.

"Well?" said Anne.

"Now David's here, shall we talk about it?"

"As you wish," Anne said, courteously and gloomily.

"I don't think I'm unreasonable," said Linda. "In fact I think I'm a touch more reasonable than some mothers would be. Anne——" she added to David, "doesn't agree."

"Well, but I've said it won't happen again. That was the first thing I said to you; I said I was sorry and it wouldn't happen again."

"This has been said before," David reminded her.

"Last night just got out of hand."

"So did Thursday night; and Monday," said Linda.

"I'm on your mother's side, Anne."

"You subscribe to the veto?"

"I don't know what the veto is, but I'm pretty sure I shall."

"I've told her—that there's not to be another evening with René, or the van Merrens, or any of them. She can go and swim—and lunch—and spend the afternoon, but she's got to be back here for dinner. . . . Fair enough, don't you think?"

He said, "What do you think, Anne?"

"I think it's perfectly bloody," Anne said in her Oxford voice.

"Well, so do I," said Linda, "but you've bought it."

"You have, in a sense, bought it," David agreed.

"Look, sweetheart——" said Linda. "Don't for the love of heaven think we don't understand, because we do. We know you find these chums highly desirable and there's every reason why you should. They're a bunch of amusing, cosmopolitan kids, all older than you, which is flattering and fun for you. They're a little too rich for sense. And they drive too fast and they stay out too late and that's what I can't allow. I'm sorry. I don't ask you to try to see it my way. You'll go on thinking I'm a martinet and I'll go on knowing it's the only thing I can do. You forced my hand, you see. You could have steered it all much better. You could have been more intelligent from the beginning, and made a point of getting home at the time you said you'd get home. You didn't. And this is the result. And you have my full permission to hate me for it, see?"

As ever, David thought, she was overplaying her hand, thrusting her assessment of the situation too far, making too much of her understanding; in brief, subjecting Anne to the same ordeal-by-verbiage that he himself had often suffered. He saw it take effect on Anne precisely as it reacted on him; he saw her squirm and retreat into silence.

"And I don't want you to feel I'm trying to make a fool of you to your friends. So you needn't tell them; David will tell them," Linda was saying limpidly, "then they'll just hate us and sympathise with you."

2

The ordinary days at La Colle were good enough. Linda, David knew, would have liked them all to be ordinary. She despised the cheap glitter that had come back to the coast-line in August; the yachts and the Casinos; the playboys and the playgirls, the flashing cars that clogged the sea road. On the ordinary days they remained aloft in their small fortress on the edge of the valley; working and cooking, gardening and sleeping in the sun; driving down to Cagnes to swim with the commoners from the pebble beach that was most simply and uncomfortably different from the rock-terraces at the villas of their rich friends. They liked the pebble beach too.

At evening they sat under the mimosa tree and watched the shadow walk up the far side of the valley, the last light shuttle along the Roman wall, leaving the town bleached and bare with evening. After dinner they lit the lamps. They would play gramophone-music, or David would go on working while Anne and Linda played chess. Before they went to bed, they would go out on the terrace to watch for shooting-stars.

But all the days could not be like this. They knew too many people. Sometimes David was appalled by the number of people they knew. There was a telephone in the cottage and voices came over it; English voices, American voices; the voice of Valentine Brooks bellowing Anglo-Saxon greetings and a request for a loan from St. Tropez; publishers; actors; professors; strays from Linda's California; there seemed to be more voices than ever this summer. David's new play had, as usual, expanded the always widening circle. Linda received the invaders as though they were his fault. Fair enough. She could say No and he could not.

"Darling—it's Bob and Gloria. They have just got here. They want us to meet them for drinks and dinner, and then . . ."

"And then go on to the Casino, *if* we feel like it. I know. Well, having the gift of prophecy," Linda said, "you'll feel like it; Anne and I'll go home. Transportation arrangements over to you."

That was how it had happened this morning; and now he stood beside the bar in the Casino, drinking a brandy. One for the wheel. Anne and Linda were gone, driven back up the hill by Americans staying at St. Paul. Bob, who wrote thrillers, and Gloria, who turned them into radio-scripts, had taken their places for *chemin de fer*. David was—as usual—the only one of the party who played roulette.

Childish, he thought; reprehensible, superstitious; the game that could become too important; and nobody who hadn't the virus in his blood could understand what you meant when you said 'the game'. To the non-addict, roulette was simply a wheel that spun and sent a ball by chance into a socket with a number. The chances against your chosen number were thirty-five to one; and that was all; and it was idiocy.

To David and his kind, roulette was not only the most beguiling of all battles between oneself and the gods, it was a mystical experience.

Like other mystical experiences, it was largely unshareable; not to be communicated. Any attempt to communicate with those who did not know turned you into something one degree sillier than the golf bore. Your talk was gibberish, "I had a *mille* on the *quatre premier*; two came up and I doubled, and, damn it, three came up twice running. After that, of course, I had to cover the twenty-six, but I *didn't* forget my darling twenty-one, which, in simple arithmetic, was pretty obvious, coming after the three." Only a fellow-mystic would see the beauty of it. (Only a fellow-mystic knew that you could fall in love with a certain number and remain faithful; or find suddenly that your ardour had cooled and that this year you loved the seventeen instead.) Linda, like other sane persons, would ask, "How much did you win?" Or, should she know what had happened next, "You ought to have stopped there."

David drank his brandy at leisure. He was in a mood of luminous tranquillity. The novel, for better or worse, was inching its way forward on paper. He had given eight hours to it every day, for a week. He had drunk nothing stronger than *rosé* and he had kept out of the Casino for what seemed a lifetime and was in fact eleven days.

Last time, Linda had been with him, staying away from his table, never asking how it went, ready to drink with him when he took time out from the enjoyable warfare, demonstrably content to wander and watch the play; the gambler's wife wearing her psychological approach on her sleeve. Nor had she asked him about his losses. "Because," she had said before this, "you'd only lie. You're pedantically honest. Outside a Casino, you're the most truthful person I know. The moment you connect with this imbecile game, you become the biggest liar in five continents."

He set down his glass. The hot room, with the windows open to the Mediterranean night, shimmered for him with the magic of Tom Tiddler's ground. He lingered, lighting a cigarette. This was his last chance of detachment from the crowd before he went down and in and was one of them; the murmurous devotees, solemn and savage with concentration, held at each table by the invisible threads of their faith. Really, he thought, they were extremely funny. And the tables themselves were funny too; each one a point of heavy significance in the room, as though surgical operations were taking place on them. They looked a little like operating-tables, with the lamps above them hanging low.

94

Supposing, after all, he decided not to play tonight? That was an idea: to drink and stroll around the tables, in glorious freedom from the drug, pitying the addicts. . . . Think, he said to himself, of the nervous energy that you will save; think of the agonies you will be spared; think of the utter peace that comes from not caring what the wheel is doing; and think (since you're thinking) of how it will feel to leave this place with the same amount of money you had when you came in. To say nothing of leaving it without a sense of guilt. How would *that* be for fun? Magnificent . . .

He went down the three shallow steps from the bar.

As he joined the thinnest of the crowds at the five-hundred-franc table, he saw that Anne's forbidden friends were sitting beside the window; René in his white dinner-jacket and cummerbund, van Merren with his crew-cut and red satin tie, Mrs. van Merren, aged twenty-two; the little Austrian girl with the gentian-coloured eyes and her beau, the Spaniard who drove the racing-car. Enamelled children, chattering round a bottle of champagne, not playing, though René had a pile of chips in front of him. Just as well, David reflected, that Linda wasn't here.

And now the insane magic began. The wheel was still; they were paying out on the last spin. The ball lay in the socket below the number twenty; the pink woman with the mysteriously rectangular bosom had covered the twenty with eight separate *mille* plaques. She was a fellow-mystic and she acknowledged David's congratulatory grin with the only sort of smile that the mystics allowed themselves when in full play; a fleeting, precarious signal; no more, lest the gods should see and reverse the luck.

After the twenty, David said to himself, the twenty-one; simple arithmetic; and, to juggle with higher mathematics, the three and the twelve; naturally, the *quatre premier* because of one's old friend Zero, and the *dix-douze* because it was a habit.

The first three spins, in David's superstition, foreshadowed the evening's play. If none of his numbers came up in the first three spins, he could look out for trouble; any sort of win on the first three augured a painless evening; and a *plein* on the first spin of all meant honey and jam hereafter.

He did not mean to play in *milles* until he saw which way

prophecy pointed. He would begin small with the five-hundreds. He had been careful to put his five-hundreds in one pocket and his *mille* plaques in the other. Unfortunately, while giving his bets to the croupier, he put his hand in the wrong pocket. He found himself playing *milles* on the first shot. This often happened. He decided to take it as an omen. One of the amiable aspects of roulette was that you could make an omen out of anything.

Now for the wait; the low-voiced, painstaking instructions, the ranging of the bets. The heads and the hands kept coming, the black rakes went forward, the coloured chips moved into their places on the green cloth. The wheel turned slowly under the croupier's hand. "*Vos jeux, Messieurs, Mesdames.*"

It was the moment for invocation. Those who kept track of the numbers on printed cards bent their heads over them as though the cards were prayer-books. Those who stared upward in fixed suppliance, stared. Those who watched the wheel turned to it like pointers, rigid from head to foot. David, who never watched the wheel, began his automatic pacing, away from the table to the left (always keep on the left side for luck), halting at the ash-tray, turning the chips in his pocket, gazing through the windows at the sea, pacing back, but not to look at the wheel, lighting another cigarette, striding to the window again.

"*Plus rien, Messieurs, Mesdames!*"

He kept his back to the table. Now the hush came down and he could hear the ball rattling around the wheel, rattling around its range of thirty-seven chances, taking its pick. He could hear the slower rattle; now was the moment that it came. The one out of the thirty-seven. His Twenty-One. *Vingt-et-Un-rouge-impair-et-passe.* He was entirely certain. The ball clicked.

"*Vingt-et-Un! Rouge, Impair et Passe. Carré, cheval et plein.*"

He never knew how he could be so certain in forecast and still dazed with astonishment by the fact. It was always going to happen and always impossible that it should have happened. The warm sizzle of gratification, the triumphant shout in his head, never varied. He allowed himself, with the control of the mystic, to smile guardedly at the pink woman, who had the *carré* and the *cheval*. This was as good as you could wish. A *plein* with the first spin. Honey and jam. The four *mille* lost on the other numbers didn't count. Not with thirty-five to come, they didn't. (And if there had been twenty of them, they still wouldn't . . . As all mystics understood.)

As the rake slid the neat castle of chips towards David, René's voice beside his shoulder said, "*A la bonheur!*" In looks, René had a harlequin slickness that David found a little repulsive, but his youth, his smile, were disarming. He added in English, "Jolly good show!" and when David told the croupier to double the stake, René leaned over and placed a *mille* of his own on Twenty-One. "*Vous allez encore toucher, j'en suis sûr, Monsieur Neilson.*" Unable to reconcile this comradeship of lunacy with the things that he said to René on the telephone ten days ago, David covered the Three and the Twelve again. René followed him. The croupier, who knew David's game, invited further stakes. "*Et le Quatre Premier? Et le Dix-Douze? Mais, Monsieur, vous n'avez pas joué le Vingt-et-Un Vingt-Quatre.*" Grinning, he took another *mille* from David and flipped it on to the *cheval* between Twenty-One and Twenty-Four.

René stood, pallid and tense, watching the wheel.

"It is," David reminded him, "highly improbable that Twenty-One will come up twice. Not the sort of thing it does. Mark you, other numbers do. Four, for example, and that monster, Twenty-five."

René was apparently praying. He did not reply.

This time, the wait was longer. And from the slowly turning wheel, the inimical Nineteen was shimmering and leering at him. "Shall I? Shan't I?" David said to himself. He didn't really approve of placating the Nineteen. *Dix-Neuf Vingt-Deux* perhaps; *Vingt-Deux* was something of a chum. No. Be firm . . . the hell with it. He put the *mille* back in his pocket, congratulating himself on his strong-mindedness.

He quickened his pacing on the left side. Superstition made him do all the same things a second time, even to the dropping of his half-smoked cigarette in the ash-tray, the pacing back, the lighting of another cigarette. Rigidly he kept his back to the table as the whirring rattle of the ball began. He looked at the sea, drew a deep breath because

97

tension could wreck everything, and thought simply, trustfully, 'Now!'

"*Vingt-et-Un! Rouge, impair et passe.*"

The thing that couldn't happen, had. Twice running, with the stake doubled and, thanks to the croupier, the *cheval* added to the *plein*. Carillons in your head. Standing, like Colossus, while they paid the lesser winnings, warm and pious and in love with the whole world.

René, obviously no mystic, had lost control. He had summoned his gang with a yell; about him the gang leaped and applauded. All the truly faithful looked at them with cold, hostile eyes. Not even the young could be excused for such behaviour in the sacred edifice. The young did not care. René's hands shook so much when he grabbed his thirty-five *mille* that some of the chips spilled off into the bosom of the pink woman. She salvaged them, unsmiling, returned them to René and took her recurrent twenty-three *mille* complacently, ranging it beside the last.

Eighty-seven *mille* slid down the cloth towards David.

Over his shoulder, he saw the gang still rejoicing: René in a mock-swoon in the arms of Tucker van Merren, the Austrian embracing her beau, the chips scattered among the glasses and Joe van Merren lifting a glass in his direction. Joe bowed and grinned. Relaxed to the point where he could allow himself a breather between spiritual exercises, David acknowledged the salute. The others waved their arms. "*Millionaire en deux coups!*" René called to him, and added, "*Grace à vous, Monsieur, je suis riche aussi.*"

"Champagne, sir?" Joe van Merren spoke as formally as a waiter, but his eyes were amused. He was obviously registering the fact that the stern father could fool around with this sort of thing.

"No, thanks," David said, "though I take it kindly."

"*Il attend la troisième,*" said René. "*Moi aussi. Jamais deux sans trois.*"

"Which rule," said David, "applies to everything else in the world but the Twenty-One."

"Mean it *can't* happen again?" Joe van Merren asked.

"I don't mean it can't. I mean it won't."

"Because it's the Twenty-One? but excuse me, I do not

98

understand," said the Austrian beauty. "I do not play myself."

"Your state is the more solvent," David said.

"Then you have not backed it this time—is that right?" she asked.

"Oh yes, I've backed it. I couldn't not, but it won't come."

She shook her head. "Darling, roulette is a disease," the Spaniard explained—"I have told you."

"Did you double again, Mr. Neilson?" Tucker van Merren had the face of an angel and the voice of a Kansas City telephone operator.

"I didn't double the double. I put one more *mille* on the *plein*, and the *cheval*, just for the hell of it. And left the others alone. But I feel Nineteen in the air."

"You can feel numbers in the *air*?" The Austrian was fascinated.

"Certainly," said David, "all thirty-six of them. And Zero. That's my undoing."

"I love to watch you play," said Tucker. "The way you pace and spin on your heels and keep going. I always expect to see you cross yourself."

"There's a Russian who crosses himself every time around," said Joe.

"*Plus rien, Messieurs!*"

René and all the others except Joe rushed to the table. Deliberately, David sat down next to Joe. The two-in-a-row sequence had thickened the crowd; it was impossible, even at this short range, to hear the ball rattle around the wheel. A solid wall of backs, a solid murmur of voices, cut off the sound. It might have begun; or it might not; he decided on another tested spiritual exercise, of pretending that he wasn't playing.

"Silly game——" he said to Joe.

"Lot of fun, though, when it works."

"It's a vice."

"Well," said Joe, "a lot of vices are a lot of fun. Don't you want to keep an eye on your stake? Plenty of light-fingered characters here."

"It's all right," said David, "the croupier's watching them. In the unlikely event——"

He was interrupted. A turn repeated and applauded

99

frequently at the bar during the next few hours was Joe van Merren's rendering of Mr. Neilson's face when the Twenty-One came up for the third time.

3

The waiter brought two more bottles of champagne; the party seemed to be growing. Most of the names escaped him.

"What nobody will realise is that between the Americans and the British there exists a profound *natural* antipathy, as between cats and dogs."

"I know a cat who's crazy for dogs and hates cats."

"I know a dog who hates dogs."

"I think the Middle Dozen's coming up."

"I hate the Middle Dozen."

"I simply hate the free nations."

"Are there any?"

"Let's abolish nations."

"But keep the French."

"Whatever for?"

"Food, wine and fun."

"Give the Americans control of all measures for comfort and convenience. All gadgets. Nothing else."

"The British must be prevented from catering for tourists."

"They mustn't cater at all. In no circumstances must they be allowed to cook."

"The Scots can make a very *few* baps and scones."

"No cooking South of the Border."

"I'm for abolishing the Irish."

"No; they can go on being Irish provided they never mention it."

"And Jews may go on being Jews provided they don't say they are."

"And Scots."

"*Nobody* must say what they are."

"The Irish must stay in Ireland."

"And the Italians in Italy."

"*All* travel should be banned. It narrows people. Deterioration begins with a passport. No tourists."

"And no immigrants."

"I think the Middle Dozen's coming up."

"I think the British should be allowed to produce leather goods."

"And literature."

"Possibly."

"No Americans must be allowed to write."

"And no Scandinavians."

"May the French write?"

"On occasion. Even Cocteau."

"Anything for the Germans?"

"*No.*"

"They can make lenses and maps."

"Not music?"

"No, darling; they've done enough."

"*No* American politics."

"The Russians can do the politics."

"But not the atom-bomb."

"Nobody can do any atom-anything. Atomic research banned. We'll use up the stockpile getting rid of Asia."

"*All* of it?"

"Certainly. And that revolting Near East."

"In which sense revolting?"

"In both."

"The British must be allowed to control the postal system."

"But *not* the telephone."

"Telephone, to America. All post offices banned except when run by the British. British forbidden to make women's clothes."

"America forbidden to make men's clothes."

"Or movies."

"Do we want movies at all?"

"No."

"Magazines? Advertisements?"

"None."

"Newspapers?"

"Out."

"Radio? Television?"

"Banned."

"Keep the theatre."

"The French and the American theatre."

"No critics."

"No police."

"A few English policemen for quaintness and comedy."

"I know the Middle Dozen's coming up."

"It couldn't, it would be so unfair."

"What about Spain?"

"Infiltrated by Methodists."

"And armed bulls."

"Who takes over religion?"

"Nobody must."

"The Catholics, provided they let up on sex and politics."

"*I* think that Eastern one that means everything's really nothing. I've forgotten what it's called."

"Education must go."

"Except a very few Universities for Indians."

"Persons of artistic temperament and neurotics to take over the public services."

"No Stock Exchange. Or Wall Street."

"No speculation of any kind except Casinos, horses and greyhounds."

"Casinos everywhere."

"Compulsory Casinos."

"Civil Servants for croupiers."

"What about the Army?"

"Banned. Highly-trained troops drafted into the choruses of musicals."

"The British can keep the Life Guards for prettiness."

"What do we use the Swiss for?"

"Cheese and mountains."

"I hate mountains."

"I hate all scenery."

"I love everything and everybody."

"When I'm happy I bounce up and down."

"All sidewalks to be made of foam-rubber so that when one felt happy one could bounce up and down."

"And a world-wide ban on custard."

4

It was two o'clock when David left the Casino. He drove very slowly along the Promenade des Anglais; past the airport, through Cros-de-Cagnes and up the hill-road to La

Colle. He always drove slowly after too many drinks. He could, he fancied, chart the course of the hangover. It would begin with heart-thumps when he lay down; it would rise up into the bones of his skull and clamp itself there in time to wake him early; it would weigh on his head, his limbs and his stomach until evening. His pen would crawl and cigarettes would taste hideous and there would be long minutes when his ill-focused eyes would stare at the ash-tray as though the ash-tray were some new and unidentifiable object.

He changed pedantically into second gear. The town was asleep; the hills were asleep. He was beyond the pleasure-belt and back in the country where everyone was wise.

Wise they might be, but they were not bringing their sheaves home with them, as he was. They could not say, "We are the Jasons, we have won the fleece." He gave a pitying nod to David Neilson the loser, a poor relation who had often driven this way after a disastrous run, knowing that everything said by sane people about gambling was lapidary, true, and unanswerable. However bad the hang-over—and by all odds it would be a stinker—he must wake to happiness. He had won. He had not only won a ridiculous sum on the first three spins, but he had won on each brief, drunken return to the tables. He had been remarkably intelligent. The secret of gambling wasn't, as sane people said, in knowing when to stop; you had to know when to go on.

He came to the restaurant called the Toque Blanche and the turning; this was the narrow road down to St. Etienne, the road home. He stopped the car, climbed out and stood looking at the hills and the moon. He heard the frogs croak in chorus. Nearer than that, his ears buzzed uncomfortably, making a chorus of their own.

There was nothing to be proud of; a sudden run of luck, no more. When he turned out his pockets the money would look like fairy-gold; it always did. There was nothing to be afraid of; only the silliest of all gambling superstitions, urging that if the luck came easily, then there must be a compensating doom ahead. There was nobody to thank, except the wheel, so why did he send this childish 'Thank you' up past the moon to God? Why add the childish 'I'm sorry' because he had overdone the drinks? And it was,

surely, the most pernickety of scruples to feel that none of it
ought to have happened in the presence of Anne's restricted
friends. Already he found himself rationalising this as though
he were on trial for it; reducing the time that he had spent
with them at the bar, storing the names of the other people
for liberal use. 'Will you never grow up?' said David to
David.

He got back into the car; he crawled down the steep,
narrow road, scanning the rough surface ahead for cats. The
local cats, the white cats with the faces designed by Marie
Laurencin, were a hazard at this hour.

So, come to that, was the garage, at any hour. Backing
this car into this garage was like threading a needle, he
thought; no night for threading needles. He made it, at the
third attempt, but the garage floor sloped down and his
slipping foot allowed for a brisk bang as the bumper hit the
back wall. He feathered across the moonlit terrace, well-
assured that he had woken Linda.

There was no need, of course, to drop the half-bottle of
Perrier water squarely on the stone floor of the kitchen. It
exploded like a grenade. Extraordinary, what a lot of Perrier
there was in a half-bottle when you saw it spread out; he
began to mop at it with his swimming-trunks. It was the
work of a moment to cut the ball of his thumb on a glass
splinter. The wound bled impressively. He was holding it
under the tap when Linda came to the kitchen door.

"I seem," he said, "to be giving an awfully good imitation
of a drunk coming home."

"Looks like the real thing to me," said Linda placidly.
"I thought you shot somebody."

"No, it was the Perrier."

"I see it was."

"I'm sorry, darling."

"Plenty of time for that in the morning," she said in her
sunniest voice. "Just stay where you are and I'll get a
Band-aid."

5

It was just the morning for a hangover; the stifling grey
stillness that awaited a thunderstorm. After one look at it,

David returned to bed and lay face downwards under the sheet, praying that Linda would show mercy and take her typewriter downstairs. Not that he deserved it. In terms of penitence he was fully entitled to three hours' clacking from the small study that opened out of their bedroom.

Linda and Anne were breakfasting on the terrace; the sound of their voices came up with the irritating quality of a radio playing in the next room. Penitence qualified him for this too. But was there any need for the motor-*cultivateur* to drive its dentist's-drill across the valley with quite such rhythmic precision? A fly with very cold feet landed on his bare shoulder. He pulled the sheet up to his forehead. After a moment the fly landed on his forehead. He got out of bed and began to look for the fly-swatter. He was stalking a drawing-pin on the wall when Anne appeared, saying, "Would you like some coffee?"

"Oh dear no," said David. "Coffee . . . what a notion." He scrambled into bed and lay helplessly gazing at the young, clear-eyed face with the dazzling grin.

"How do you feel?"

"I'd rather not say."

"But you had fun?"

"Alas, yes."

"And won a fortune."

"And won, as you say, a fortune."

"Can I see it?"

"Sure. That's it, on the dressing-table."

"You won all that?"

"M'mm."

"And brought some chips home. Is that a superstition?"

"No; that's just not turning out enough pockets when you cash in."

"Do you have to give them back to the Casino?"

"I don't have to. I probably will."

"Why this visiting-card? Who's the Comtesse de Pourvilliers?"

"Your guess," said David, "is as good as mine."

"Well, she's written Thursday, 17-30, on it, so you'd better find out. Can I count this and see how much there is?"

"Just so's you take it away and do it downstairs. I couldn't stand the rustling."

"I do think you're clever," she said.

The thunderstorm was still standing off at noon when he came downstairs. Quiet reigned. He moved shakily, wondering whether, by a dispensation, the two of them had gone to the beach. No. They were putting in some work on the rose-beds, just below the lip of the terrace. Their heads bobbed into sight at intervals, the round fair head and the dark curls. Creeping like a thief to the kitchen, he took the bottle of Pernod from the new refrigerator, poured a drink of curative size and tilted the contents of the ice-tray into it. He carried the glass through the arch to the living-room, where the next reproach, his desk, awaited him.

All was in order; the scribbled pages in a neat pile on the left; the blank foolscap at the centre; the bare space on the right. The two fountain-pens were in the pen-tray and the inkpot was newly filled. In a symmetrical halo about the clean foolscap, there lay his winnings, clean, folded ten-*mille* notes going on and on. Anne had stacked the chips and set his writing-mascot, the small leaden frog that she had given him years ago, on top of the chips.

David put the money aside, without counting it in case he began to think about starving widows. He unscrewed the cap of his pen; he gazed sourly at the last sentence that he had written. It looked very fancy and peculiar. He swallowed a gulp of Pernod and began to tinker with it.

The telephone rang.

Its rusty shriek was entirely audible in the garden, but neither Linda nor Anne came to answer it. At the third shriek, David lumbered through the arch to the ledge where it stood. There was the customary explosion in his ear and a voice screaming "*Parlez!*"; then a blocked silence; then a high, ghostly whistling followed by some apparent morse code and two people telling him, in French, not to quit. Presently, small and far-away, he heard an American voice blaspheming.

"Mr. Neilson there? David? Clyde Brewer."

Oh no, David thought, oh no, oh no, oh no. Not Clyde and Menella; not today. Not any day. He found that he had said, "Just off to a luncheon-party over at Antibes; well, I don't quite know; there was some talk of going to Monte Carlo later for a dart at the Casino. Haven't gambled much lately." "How about dinner tonight? We'll be coming your way." All the charm, all the sensitivity of a concrete-mixer, David said to himself. "We have a dinner date, terribly dull British, Lord knows why I let us in for it." "Well, wait a minute—how would this be? We'll be at Vence anyway; why don't we just take a chance and——" There was a new type of explosion; he had been cut off.

David returned to his desk. Anne and Linda came up on to the terrace, carrying their garden tools. They were arguing blithely and energetically about '*Le Trèsor*', the relics in the crypt of the church; it was a recurrent battle.

"I don't *mind* your believing all those things are what they're said to be, darling. Any more than I *mind* your believing in ghosts," Linda was saying.

"Well, but I just want to know why *you* don't."

"Because the relics are just about as genuine as fake antiques. For them to be what they are claimed to be is historically and factually impossible," said Linda.

"Is it? The thing I find hard to believe is that *I* can be in their presence. My scepticism, you might say, applies strictly to myself, not to them."

"Did you get that from David?"

"No," said Anne. "And if he said it, he got it from me."

"Anyway——" Linda's voice was loving, "I wouldn't have either of you different."

They were beside the window now; cleaning the tools.

"How would *you* describe Christianity?"

"As the name that history has given to a certain code of ethics."

"Then what's God?" said Anne.

"Just good. An image of good."

"Didn't you mind having me baptised?"

"Heavens, no. David wanted you to be."

"I couldn't get along without God," said Anne.

"That's all right. That's fine. I've told you; I don't want to impose my belief . . . or lack of it—on you. I never did, did I?" There was the sound of running water; they were washing their fingers under the outside tap.

"Were you always an atheist?"

"Atheist . . . Don't know that I care to be as positive as

107

that," said Linda, laughing. "Not before lunch, at least. Call me an unregenerate and unbaptised agnostic."

"Didn't either of your parents want to baptise you?"

"I should say *not*. They called themselves Freethinkers; which, when I look back, is exactly what they weren't. They had to make a life-work of their disbelief. Fearful waste of energy, *and* a confession of weakness."

"Weakness . . ."

"Certainly. If there's no God, then there's no God. What's all the fuss about? Surely it only suggests you aren't quite at ease with atheism if you have to keep banging away at it; keep standing up and testifying from tubs."

"Bath-tubs? Is that what your father and mother did? Stood up in their baths and said there was no God?"

"You've heard of tub-thumpers, fool."

"Did they hold meetings?"

"They went to meetings."

"Did you have to go?"

"No, they let me alone; they let me decide for myself. And rightly."

"But if they never taught you any religion how could you have anything to decide?"

"One to Anne," said David, drinking some more Pernod. He could see their profiles framed in the tangle of bougain-villæa at the window. Linda was laughing.

"I read Theology. More Theology than most clerics. And I found no evidence. And I still find none. But, as I say. I've not the slightest objection to other people believing in God."

"That's big of you," David muttered, "I'm sure God feels much better." He finished his Pernod and wrote savagely on the foolscap, "Atheists, agnostics and sceptics should refrain from approaching the subject of Theism, just as tone-deaf persons should refrain from singing in public." It had nothing to do with the novel and he ringed it round before going on to the next narrative line.

The telephone returned to the attack while Anne was laying the table. David called through the archway, "Don't answer, it's Clyde Brewer," just as Linda called through the other archway, "Answer it, Anne, there's an angel; I'm up to my elbows in olive oil." Anne said, "I find myself in a quandary." The rusty shriek came again. David strode to the ledge, unhooked the telephone-receiver and covered the whole instrument with a large raffia hat belonging to Linda. Thus extinguished, it could still be heard, croaking faintly and reproachfully.

"Who's Clyde Brewer?" Anne asked.

"It isn't the sort of thing I like you to know about."

"Mean he's a homosexual?"

"No, an editor. He and his wife both edit. Don't let's talk *or* think about them."

Anne looked at the hat on the telephone. "It's still making noises. Can't I just say you're out?"

"Why?"

"Well, I just thought . . . It mightn't be them at all. It might be René."

"All right, go ahead," David told her. "But if it's that fine upstanding Republican bastard——"

"Language, language!" said Linda, bringing the paté. Anne danced at the end of the telephone, "Hullo—*oui*, *j'écoute* . . . René? . . . Well, I'm sorry, chum, there was a mix-up on the line. How's my *father*? . . . He's all right." She looked questioningly towards David; then she pulled a chair up to the telephone and settled devotedly, crossing one bare leg over the other, while the saga continued at the end of the line. "You *didn't*? . . . He did? . . . How heavenly . . . How absolutely enchanting . . . I love it . . . Go on . . . No, honestly?" So she continued while Linda, having brought the salad, said, "We might as well begin."

Through the consoling lens of the Pernod, David watched Anne, her profile tilted, her short nose wrinkled in laughter; the narrow body doubled over and the long brown leg waggling the foot in the espadrille. She seemed to have acquired another dimension since he heard her arguing with Linda. "I couldn't get along without God," he repeated, and then, "The thing I find hard to believe is that *I* am in their presence." How did that thought come, at seventeen? How had he acknowledged God at seventeen? He couldn't remember. Staring at the brilliant, ragamuffin face, he decided that, much as she resembled him, Anne had something that he had never known, a congenital lightness of heart. As though to challenge him, the expression of her face changed at once, becoming awed and grave. "I don't know.

109

I really don't know, René. I'll ask, of course. I'll ask now. Let me call you back."

Her movements as she replaced the receiver, came to the table, pulled out her chair and sat down, were solemnly deliberate. Then she sent a giggle in David's direction, "You didn't say *they* were there last night. . . ."

"Didn't I? Well, a lot of people were there."

"It seems," said Anne, "to have been a riot. They're all crazy for you; Tucker and Mitzi fell in love with you."

"That's just the grey bits at the sides of my hair," he said quickly.

"And René getting two *pleins*. He *never* wins. You were sweet to buy them all that champagne. Bottles and bottles, he says."

"He exaggerates."

"Try to be more tactful, Anne darling," said Linda. "Save it for when I'm not here."

Anne's grin departed. "Look . . . I have a request to make. A solemn request."

"Let's have it," said Linda.

"If I swear to be home by eleven o'clock, may I have dinner with them tonight?"

Linda said "Reasons?" lightly and amiably.

Anne ticked them off on her fingers, "One, they're all going to Venice tomorrow; I shan't see them again. Two, René wants to celebrate the first money he ever took out of a Casino. Three . . . well, three, I want to go. Terribly."

Linda helped herself to salad. "What's the party? One of those hit-and-run jobs along the Corniche?"

"No," said Anne, "I promise. The party's quite static. On the Cap. At Mitzi's villa—I mean her parents' villa. They're going out and Mitzi's giving the dinner for all of us. There's a butler. Positively stately, it'll be."

Linda looked at David. "What do you think?"

Anne said, "Please."

David struggled not to say an immediate "Yes". He grunted. Linda took it on. "You've been very good. I give you full marks for these two weeks; you haven't mentioned it and you haven't sulked. Even so . . . I do hate these roads at night, I don't want you driving with those kids when they've been drinking."

Anne said, "Joe's the only drinker; I wouldn't let Joe drive me."

"That crazy Spaniard's just as much of a menace when he's sober," said David.

"Oh, *Daddy* . . . he's the best driver in the world. And René drives beautifully."

"Would it shame you in their sight if I came to fetch you?"

"Yes, frankly, it would rather."

"Well——" David began just as Linda said, "Well . . ." Each stopped for the other. Then Linda laughed. "I own," she said, "to one obvious inconsistency. And I can see it's in your mind, Anne. You're asking 'Is this a disciplinary measure or is it a safety precaution?' Aren't you now?"

"No," said Anne, "I was just thinking I could come home in a taxi."

Without the hangover, David would have found the retort less funny. As it was, he gave a yelping giggle. His voice still shook as he said quickly, "Why don't we toss for it? Heads you go, tails you stay at home."

"*Ow*——" said Anne.

"What an immoral suggestion," said Linda.

"What's immoral about it? Come on, darling. Be a good gambler, like your father."

"I never," said Linda, "heard a worse way."

David rose, collecting the dirty plates. "Why? You can't, in justice, say a flat 'No' any more than I can. If we could, we'd have said it."

"Why not just say 'Yes'?" Anne pleaded.

"Because we can't make up our poor, ageing minds." He carried the plates into the kitchen, set them by the sink and came back, bringing the fruit and the cheese. Anne's grin was now precarious; Linda looked, as usual, tolerant and composed. David looked down from one to the other.

"We toss, eh?"

"We do, *eh*?"

"It's up to Anne," said Linda with a shrug.

"Agreed?"

"Agreed," said Anne, shutting her eyes tightly.

"There's a brave girl." He took a ten-franc piece from his pocket. Anne kept her eyes shut; Linda was helping herself to fruit from the dish. David flicked the coin into the air, caught it neatly and laid it on the back of his hand.

"Heads. You win," he said—"and if you aren't here before eleven has finished striking, you'll return to England tomorrow alone, travelling third-class all the way."

6

The storm broke with violence as lunch was ending. By four o'clock the sky was clear and the drenched garden shone. At six-thirty, while Anne was still dressing, René came, pallid with good behaviour; kissing Linda's hand, refusing a Dubonnet, calling David 'Sir' with every sentence, brandishing his lighter in advance of every cigarette. His talk was of international affairs. Anne did not hurry. David's hangover had now settled into a solid chunk of neuralgia above his right eye. It seemed to him that several weeks passed before Anne appeared, wearing a lime-green dress and carrying the new scarlet bag that Linda had called vulgar before she knew David had chosen it.

David watched Anne with René. She talked to him as she talked to everybody. Along with her considerate manners, she had inherited Linda's ability to go on being the person she was at all times and in all places; neither shy nor noisy, unaffectedly and comfortably the same. It was a rare quality, he thought, in adolescence. Adolescence was—wasn't it?— the time of the chameleon; when you changed your colour to suit your company; the time when you subscribed to the likes and dislikes that were fashionable, when you hid your ignorance, soft-pedalled and shammed. He thought so. But not for Anne, now placidly admitting to the shocked René that she could make no headway with Proust.

She picked up the scarlet bag, kissed Linda and said to David, "Is there a bonus for getting back at ten-forty-five? One of those ten-*mille* notes, for instance?"

"Certainly not," said David, instantly deciding to award the bonus. She grinned at him. René did jack-knife bows. The bell on the door jingled its clapper; there was the sound of the car's engine going away up the road.

"She's a good girl," Linda said.

David grunted. He had the impulse to keep Anne to

112

himself today. He was still disliking himself for this when there was the sound of another car, the bell jingled again and Clyde and Menella Brewer came on to the terrace.

Over nineteen years, David had observed that there was nothing like a shared social adversity for uniting Linda and himself in the closest bonds of love. It was so now; while to the beauty of the evening upon the valley Clyde and Menella brought their verbal cargo: sinus trouble, colour photography, travelogue, political forecasts, dietary hints, strikes, and the Brewer's-Eye-View of Europe's degeneration. They moved on to David's future, which was assured once Clyde had taught him just how to put his finger on the American pulse and keep it there. Clyde thought well of David's last book; Menella too, but she found it a little over-sophisticated. She blamed his editors for not making him tone that down. Bigger sales would have been the result. It was extraordinary how quick the average reader was to resent what she called Clever-Cleverness. Did he know what she meant by that?

He knew there was no more ice. It was a small refrigerator.

Inspiration-type stories, home-interest stories, human-value stories. Interest-triggers, simplicity-appeal, character-involvement, reader-reaction, audience-identification. And it was all, really, just a matter of remembering Clyde's old maxim—he wouldn't know how many best-selling writers had learned it at his knee (where the American pulse seemed, in defiance of anatomy, to be situated). The old, old maxim, "Don't be bright; be right."

It was dusk when the Cadillac squeezed its way up the narrow road.

Linda spoke first. She said, "I think my American pulse just stopped. D'you suppose there's some ice by now?"

"Undoubtedly. Horror froze it. We'll have two sizzlers and then I'll take you to the Colombe d'Or."

"Suppose they go there for dinner?"

"Then we walk out in reverse and go across to the Résidence. You know, you've aged by ten years," he said, looking at her.

"And you," said Linda, "were the young Achilles at noon compared with now."

"I love you."

"And I love you. But if you ever sell them a story, it'll be divorce, see?"

"Put your mind at rest; I shan't."

"Those *words*——" Linda said.

"Those hyphens. This terrace is knee-deep in hyphens."

"Don't be bright, now; be right."

"Can you," he asked, "imagine them in bed?"

"I'm thankful to say not."

"I can. All too easily. Home-interest-type sex rather than inspirational. Simplicity-appeal by Clyde and absolutely no reader-reaction from Menella."

Linda said, "Anne had the luck . . . How would she have taken them?"

"She'd have asked them what all the jargon meant. Very politely, seriously wanting to know. Thank God she wasn't here; I'd have got giggles."

"You were very good; very restrained."

He kissed her.

"Confession coming," he said.

"I'll buy it. Something that happened last night?"

"No; this afternoon."

"Goodness," said Linda, "when did you find the time?"

David said, "That coin didn't come down Heads. It came down Tails."

"Coin?"

"The one I tossed for whether Anne should go or not. It was Tails, meaning she didn't go."

Linda frowned. "And you pretended it was Heads?"

"Well, she's been so awfully good . . ."

"You're a rat," said Linda lightly—then she frowned. "But if you felt like that, what was the point of tossing at all? I wasn't saying No; I was in two minds."

"Well, so was I. Until I saw it come down Tails. Then I knew what I wanted to happen."

"You are the most sentimental fellow." She pulled his ear. "Nice of you to tell me, anyway."

When they came back from the Colombe d'Or, the stars were brilliant and thickly-strewn. The frogs were making their chorus. The valley had retreated and the hill town picked itself out in lights above the Roman wall. They sat on the terrace, alert for a shooting star.

"There he goes. Did you wish?"

"Sort of——" said Linda, "I was late. They never come where I expect them."

"If the wish came true, how would you account for it?"

"Just that I'd been lucky. Like you with the Twenty-One."

"I suppose one could define a wish as an act of faith," said David.

"Not me . . ." She chuckled. "And I had plenty metaphysics from our daughter this morning."

"I heard a bit of it."

"We take a crack at it," Linda said, "quite often."

"I know. She doesn't, much, with me."

"She doesn't need to. I'm the damned, after all."

"Don't," he said sharply—"Anne doesn't think that; any more than I do."

"Well, maybe not. But she'd like me to have a faith as well as a credo. And for her sake I wish I had. No . . . not only for her sake, for my own."

He was shaken. He could not see the look on her face. He said, "You wish you had . . . But this is something new. What's happened?"

"Oh, I just find it rather enviable," said Linda. "Maybe I'm getting old."

David looked at his watch. Ten-forty. He was divided between his longing to hear more of this from Linda and his hope that Anne would win the ten-*mille* bonus.

"If you want faith, you know you can have it. Just go on wanting it," he said tenderly.

There was a long silence—then Linda murmured, "Comes of being grateful, really. Liking one's life. Wishing there was someone to say Thank You to . . . for all of it."

That made him want to weep. As he rose to go to her side, they heard the roar of a car's engine over the wall. David looked at his watch. "She's won her bonus," he said— "bless her. Just under the wire. But that idiot—whoever he is—drives too fast."

The car stopped. One moment he was looking at the wooden door with the lighted lamp over it and the cloud of night-moths flying about the lamp. He was waiting for Anne. The next moment the door pitched open violently, jingling the bell and scattering the moths about the lamp. Two gendarmes in uniform came on to the terrace. The second of them was carrying the scarlet bag that David had chosen.

115

THE COURT-ROOM

DARKNESS came; and on the darkness Neilson could still see the ownerless frivolity of the scarlet bag. He went on staring at it in his mind until the voice of the guide aroused him from the memory.

"That brings you to the court-room."

His voice sounded tired. Neilson looked at him and thought, 'But how much older he is than I had realised.' It was the suspended and horrible moment wherein any deflection of thought came as a relief; so he forced his mind to stay on this problem; the sudden ageing of the serene and knowledgeable face.

"Is it long after?" he asked foolishly. "Where we are now, I mean?"

He thought that they must be in the alley; it was a straitened, shadowy place, with high walls. The guide said, "Oh yes. But the court-room doesn't change."

"Where is this room?"

"That door will take you in."

"Will they call me?"

"No need," the man said.

"I can go in now?"

"Yes."

"It is I who am on trial. . . ."

"Oh yes."

"May I ask who judges me?"

"Don't you remember, Neilson?"

"Why should I remember?"

"Because," said the guide, "the trial has been going on for years."

He held open the door for Neilson to pass through.

At first the court-room looked to be so large that he could not see to the end of it. He stood on a floor no bigger than a boxing-ring; it held one empty chair. But stretching away from the floor in endless perspective he saw standing figures. The nearest figures were in sharp focus; the hosts behind

116

were not so clear. Unwilling yet to meet the eyes of the men standing at the edge of the floor (Yes, he thought, his companion was right, this had been going on for years) he looked away from them. Then he saw that they were ranged all round him. The court-room was completely circular, with the tiny floor at the centre of the circle. From this pivotal point, he must see the same perspective wherever he looked; the near figures crowding him solidly, the ranks that stood behind them, thinning away, a shadow-army of unguessable strength.

Still unwilling to meet the eyes of the accusers, he took his seat in the chair. At once the whole silent assembly was seated and the court-room was explained. It was no larger than the floor was. The walls were mirrors, cut and angled so that David Neilson saw only David Neilson, repeated to infinity.

He looked into his own eyes. He grasped the arms of the chair. Thousands of pairs of hands made the clutching gesture. He turned his head, and the repetition of the movement all about him sickened his stomach. He must, he thought, keep as still as he could, and look only at the reflection immediately facing him. He could mask off the side reflections by using his hands as blinkers. But when he raised his hands, he saw the gesture made by the immediate reflection and its interminable line of duplicates until all the cupped hands and faces were like a long telescope trained on him.

He lowered his hands again and shut his eyes. Best to keep them shut, to conduct his own trial in blindness. Surely he could do that. For a moment the dark under his eyelids steadied him and the hateful feeling of claustrophobia made by the mirrors grew less.

Then, terrifyingly, he began to lose himself. Thought and memory thinned out; nothingness came in. He had opened the door to black annihilation. He was vanishing. If he could not see himself, he must cease to exist.

At the pin-point of consciousness remaining to him, Neilson laughed. "That," he said aloud, "is the silliest stipulation of the ego I ever heard."

There was a murmur, like that of a crowd retreating. He opened his eyes.

"And now," he said, "I shall proceed with the Trial."

He looked at the reflection opposite; he met its eyes. He saw David Neilson at the bar of his own judgment, on trial for his life in the court-room of his own head, where the wheels of argument turned and turned. For how many years? He had forgotten, but the years were adding lines to the face as he watched, dulling its eyes, breaking its courage. The words came, mockingly:

"Oh, you can say, if you like, that it was the cruellest of misfortunes; you can say that."

"But wasn't it?"

"Maybe it was. But I can't see it."

"What can you see?"

"What can I see? Myself and again myself. Every fault, every foolishness, every weakness in me—contributing to that moment, leading up to it, ordaining it. I see them all. There's a drunken man, there's a sentimentalist, there's an immature ass who thought, when he spun the coin and cheated on it, he was striking his little blow for fun against authority. There's a father whose pride it was that he'd passed his own temperament on to his daughter; there's a smart-alec stealing a march on his wife.

"Oh, each of them excusable, each of them a venial sinner when you take them one by one. But, you see, life didn't, at that instant, take them one by one. It took them all together, used them all together, to kill.

"That's what his weaknesses were used for. That's what was waiting for him. That was the end of the road down which he'd blundered for more than forty years. His own achievement. That's what he made, along with the name and the money. He made Anne's death inevitable.

"As I look back, I see all the little things that could have helped to make it not happen. The little things I didn't do, all my life. Every discipline I dodged; every self-denial I didn't practise. Every drink I drank when I didn't need one, every chip I threw on the table, every shrug of my shoulders at the sensible way. Every time I whistled the Skye Boat Song and thought I was the lad who was born to be King. All the exuberant, presumptuous moments when I patted God on the head and called him a good fellow, those are in the score too. By these sins and these omissions I was helping to ensure that it would happen."

He nodded agreement with his own verdict.

"You," Neilson said, "you—and you—and you again. Only you."

"Who else? . . . Look, I was a writer. What the writer knows is that the incident must come from the character. He doesn't fashion a plot and fit his people into it afterwards. He thinks of them first; and they make the incidents happen; as in life. Anne wasn't killed by arbitrary chance. I made the man I was; and the man I was killed her. It's as simple as that."

For the first time, in all the æons that he seemed to have passed in thinking this thing out, Neilson sighted a flaw in the argument. Now the face of the reflection twisted as though the flaw were in the glass.

"No," said Neilson.

"No?"

"It isn't as simple as that."

The dull eyes stared back at him.

"I cannot accept any of that as evidence," Neilson said, "I rule it as half-truth. But it explains to me why this room is so small. You have made it small. You have shut yourself in alone with yourself. You refuse to see beyond you." His voice was angry. "But you, David, are not God; you are not the beginning and the end. You are not even a good exponent of your theory. Were you the only man alive in that place on that night? Were you the boy who lost control of the wheel when the car skidded at sixty? Were you the truck-driver coming up the road on the opposite side? There were other characters who made the incident; not just David Neilson."

He moved his eyes along the reflected ranks. "I suggest, prisoner at the bar, judge on the bench, court in perennial session, that you spare, for yourself, a little mercy."

"*Mercy* . . ."

"Yes, mercy."

"You think," said the man in the glass, "that I deserve pity? I, by whose acts Anne was flung through a windscreen on to a metal road . . . Pity?"

"People have pitied you," Neilson said.

"Oh yes; human compassion is common currency. Nobody has ever failed to pity me. Even when I was drunk and had to talk about the way I spun the coin. They pitied me the more. All of them. No, not all of them. One person never pitied me. One kept his verdict of damnation and did not waver. Myself. I've never been sorry for me."

"Proud of that?" Neilson asked.

"Proud . . ."

"Yes, you are proud. What is there to be proud of in self-damnation?"

"I passed that verdict," the answer was quiet. "And I am serving the sentence."

"And the Trial's still going on," said Neilson. "How do you account for that?"

"That," said his reflection, "is part of the sentence."

Angry as he was, Neilson still laughed. "Only a part, eh? What's the rest of it?"

"You know, as well as I do."

"Of course, but I have to hear the evidence."

"Hear it, then. I've always held that a murderer shouldn't die, but should live his life out working for those who had loved the victim. I sentenced myself to live like that for Linda. Never to do anything again for me, only for her. To be only what she needed. Linda was the person to whom I owed what remained of myself. Linda, who said to me long ago, 'Life is all of terror and must be faced with courage.' She had no resource but her own courage; she had no faith and no God."

"One moment. You yourself didn't lose faith in God?"

"I didn't dare," the reflection said to him, "I couldn't have lived without praying; praying God to look after Anne —not let her be lonely, or miss us, or hate me because I killed her. And to let us meet again. If I'd been brave enough, I'd have learned to do without that; to stand alone; without a hope in hereafter. I'd have learned to think, as Linda thought, that Anne went out for ever, like a light, at the moment when her poor little skull was smashed. But," he said, "I was never brave enough to try. I couldn't face the fact of death as the end."

"The fact," Neilson repeated. "You never were much of a one for facts, were you? I seem to remember your saying that you would rather have truth."

"Yes; that was my boast once."

"And now . . .? You aren't the best exponent of a gospel of despair, you know, either. You say you are damned. All you've produced in evidence is a determination to live for somebody else, and a continuing faith. No matter how scornfully you speak of them, that is what they are."

The face in the glass grew desperate, hunted. Its physical changes came more quickly. Pouches deepened below the eyes; little veins broke under the skin and left purplish marks. Turning from it, Neilson saw that he created upon the endless smooth panels, a world of sick, broken faces looking away from their own agony.

He turned back; the dull eyes besought him. "You have heard," said the reflected mouth, "the case for the prosecution."

"Then let me hear for the defence."

"Defence?" The battered face broke into laughter; on the glass panels as far as his eyes could reach, all the battered faces were laughing.

"Go on," said Neilson. "Speak for the defence."

"Oh, but you've got it wrong. There's no defence; there never has been. There is only the prosecution."

Neilson thought about it. "You are content, then, for me to give judgment now?"

"If you like. The trial will go on, whether you do or not."

"For how long?"

"For ever."

"That is your wish? Answer me, please."

The man in the glass leaned forward, as Neilson did, but he said nothing.

"Answer me. Is that your wish?"

Still there was silence.

"But you have not answered. Now you will stand, David, to hear the verdict."

As he rose, Neilson saw the mirrors changing. In the panel of glass immediately before him there stood the weary, broken man. But he was no longer ringed about by his own armies, his own image. The other panels darkened, deepened; and into their depth other figures came walking. There was a child who feared the sea; there was a long-legged schoolboy; a figure in cap and gown; a young man with spaniel's eyes and untidy hair; a private soldier in battle-dress; and a captain with a growth of beard, tired, grinning and grateful, home from the war.

These looked out on Neilson the judge, and Neilson looked back at them.

"Gentlemen of the jury, how say you?"

It was the child who answered, "It doesn't matter what we say. He rejects us."

"Why does he reject you?"

"Because he is ashamed. He sees us all as better than he is."

"And how do you see yourselves?"

The child laughed. "Oh, we don't look at ourselves any more. He's the only one who goes on looking. That's what binds him. That's why he's still here."

"Yes," Neilson said. He met the eyes of the prisoner.

"You have heard the jury?"

"The jury . . ."

"Those who once you were."

"Oh, those . . . No," he said dully, "I can't hear them any more. I've forgotten them. Just as well . . . I couldn't look them in the face."

The panels were darkening again; the figures were walking away.

Neilson said, "You are ready for the verdict?"

"Yes."

"Prisoner at the bar, I find you guilty. Not on your own charges. I find you guilty of conducting this trial and of prolonging it, with stubborn prejudice and without mercy. That is the verdict. Before I sentence you, is there anything you wish to say?"

"Nothing. I accept myself as a criminal."

"Were you always a criminal? Answer me . . . These past versions of yourself, whom you disown and cannot face, were they criminals?"

"Not in the sense that I am, no."

"What is the difference between you and them?"

"Time," said the hopeless voice, "only time."

"What is it that happens, with time?"

The answer was long in coming. While he waited, Neilson glanced to left and right. All the panels of glass, save this one before him, were empty. It was like looking into water; water that had drowned his own image.

He repeated his question. "What is it that happens, with time?"

The prisoner raised his head. "One grows careless of the war inside," he said. "One loses sight of the Two."

"The Two," Neilson echoed. "So you know that."

"When I was young, I used to know him—the other fellow, the antagonist. The one who did the Devil's work. He tried to make everything easy. I could hear what he said and I could hear my own replies. Sometimes I could almost see him physically—behind my shoulder or on the other side of the room. We fought openly. Sometimes he won and sometimes I won. It was routine, the war between us." His head drooped again. "I don't remember just when the fighting stopped. I became aware, gradually, that we hadn't fought for a long time. He seemed not to be there any more."

"Where was he?"

"Oh, where he is," said the prisoner with a grin; his voice was suddenly insolent.

"And where is that?"

"Come close. Look at me, and you may discover."

Neilson stepped nearer to the glass. The reflection changed in a blink. It was as if the beam of a searchlight hit the mirror. He saw the face bathed in this light, bleached and drained by it; the eyes lost their colour and were pale; the lips smiled coldly.

"This is where he is," said the lips, "the Two are one."

"No," said Neilson.

"Yes. Where one is, the other is. They are the same person, one and indivisible."

"No. That is a lie. *No*, do you hear me?"

"Yes, I tell you, yes. Look at me now. Go on looking. Look where you like. This is all you will ever see."

With a new fear upon him, Neilson turned. The glass panels were no longer empty. He was looking across a crowd that had one face; the eternal repetition of the face with the colourless eyes. He saw the pale head weaving in its thousands, the cold smile going on and on down the corridors of glass.

There were no figures any more; no bodies, no shoulders, no hands. Only the myriad face looked out at him, and whether he saw it large, or at the end of the long shimmering tunnel where it hung small as a coin, the smile was still there.

Stony, triumphant, the smile endured.

He felt the mirrors closing round him; the circle of the court-room was shrinking to a globe that would hold him prisoned like a fish, with the pale face looking inward at him. And that would be for ever.

He shut his eyes. Now, truly, he was beginning not to be there. He felt himself shredded and destroyed. It was the lie that lived. There was nothing of him left but an empty shell.

He spoke, pulling his voice out of this last shell of himself as though he were wrenching a sword from a scabbard.

"Prisoner at the bar, I sentence you to freedom," said Neilson.

He heard a high, singing noise, the note of an impossible violin, the sound of the glass breaking. The court-room shattered into pieces. He saw the sky.

NEILSON

I

THE grass under Neilson's feet was soft and he flung himself down. Never had he felt so tired. It was good to lie here, cradled in the grass, looking up at the sky. And he was, at last, untroubled. He could remember all that had happened in the court-room and before, but he was free of it. He thought, 'It is over,' and could move on to no other thought at all. 'It is over,' his mind repeated, again and again.

He was only lightly aware of his resting-place, of the blue, empty sky and the warmth of the sun. He had been here before. If he could make the effort, rise on one elbow and look about him, he would see a remembered landscape. But not yet. Now he could only sleep. He shut his eyes and let all go softly into darkness.

"No," said the voice beside him, "I'm afraid you can't do that."

Dragged back intolerably, Neilson opened his eyes. The guide was sitting on the grass, watching him.

"Oh, let me sleep."

"I'm sorry. I know how tired you are. But it isn't the moment. And the tiredness won't last."

Obstinately, Neilson shut his eyes. The guide shook him by the arm; the grasp of his fingers was hard, compelling and infuriating.

"Why can't you leave me alone?"

The guide laughed as though he had made a very good joke.

"I never have—yet," he said. "And this is hardly the minute for me to begin. Sit up, Neilson, will you?"

Reluctantly, Neilson raised himself on his elbow. As he had expected, he saw a familiar landscape: the upland pasture glittering in the sun, the huge, still panorama of the mountains.

"I've been here before," he said.

"In your mind, yes. More than once. In the exaltation of achievement." He smiled.

"I did achieve something that time, didn't I?" said Neilson.

"Do you know what it was?"

"I think so. It seems clear. The pattern has been the same every time. The sin survived—and the sinner, until I found the moment again. I suppose because they were never resolved in my lifetime; I had to resolve them here. But the last was the worst." He blinked at the sun. "One talks," he said, "of fighting for one's life. I never knew it would be so hard to fight for one's death."

The guide said, "And now you must decide just what you mean by that."

"I know what I mean."

"Well, would you assume for a moment that I don't. And explain to me." He turned his innocent eyes towards Neilson and waited.

"That survivor," said Neilson, "that self imprisoned in self by remorse, had to die."

"Oh yes."

"And only I could do it for him. There was a moment when I thought I couldn't; that he was winning. When he brought in his triumphant, despairing lie. The lie about the Two. He very nearly proved it to me. What would have happened if he had?"

"He couldn't," the guide said, "unless you had wanted him to. And then you *would* have been fighting for your own death." Something in the tone of his voice made Neilson uneasy. But he continued to look questioning.

"What are you waiting for?" Neilson asked.

"For you to tell me more."

"There isn't any more to tell. That's all. And it's over. And now I can sleep." He lay down again.

"You feel no further interest; no further curiosity?"

"None," Neilson said, "or none for the time being, anyway."

"If you'll forgive my mentioning it, there *is* no time being."

"Sorry. I'm too sleepy for the subtler metaphysics."

"You must not sleep, Neilson."

"But it is over."

126

"Who said it was over?"

"I just know it is. I have ceased to want anything at all."

"A more dangerous state of mind than it appears." The guide's voice was receding a little. Neilson heard himself asking drowsily, "What's the danger?"

"Refusal," the guide said.

Neilson's heart gave a quick, uncomfortable beat. He sat up again and when he spoke he was breathless. "What is there left to refuse?"

"That wasn't the last of the survivors," said the man with the innocent eyes.

Neilson stared at him. "You mean—this isn't the end of the journey?"

Gently the guide shook his head.

"Oh, but *yes* . . . It must be. Look at it." He stretched his arms pleadingly to the air. "It's so still. And beautiful. And I know it. It must be the end."

"The peak of exaltation is hardly ever the end. And it isn't so for you."

"But what is there afterwards?"

The guide said, "The journey down."

Neilson looked into the face that was at once pitying and implacable. His tiredness made him weak. He lay down on his face and buried his head in his arms; he was near to weeping; he fought the hopeless tears.

"Is it very far?" he asked.

"It will seem like a long way."

"I have no strength left."

"Try to remember the bridge—and the gate."

"What bridge? What gate?"

"Have you forgotten the three people you were looking for?"

The words meant nothing. He said, sullenly and sadly, "I have faced my life's tragedy; what more is there to face?"

"The rest of your life."

And this, Neilson thought, should, by all odds, be the moment of refusal. All he could say was, "You were right; it was easier when I knew nothing."

"There is more to know."

"And if I do not choose to know it?"

"You have chosen," the guide said.

And that must be true, for he was rising to his feet, asking wearily, "Which way?"

The guide smiled at him, touching his shoulder. "Down," he said, and pointed across the pasture, "down to the valley."

"One question——" said Neilson.

"Yes?"

"What makes me go on?"

"You," said the guide.

Neilson looked back once and saw him there, a lonely, attentive shape, standing in the middle of the sunlit pasture.

2

Neilson walked on, and down; by the track that led to the valley. When he reached the road, he was in a different air. Feeling the oppressive, leaden quality of it, he was more tired than ever.

He stumbled along the hard, broad highway, resenting it. It went on and on. It seemed to lead nowhere. This was not like the other revisitations. Along the beach, into the theatre, across the cobbled pavement in the country town, the event had come quickly. Now it held off. There was only the highway, and the valley flattening out, until there were no more hills; there was only a grey, sunless plain. Nothing happened; nothing came to meet him but the road.

He compared it with the light and speed of the transition phase before La Colle. There had been the turning film of memory that wound off the war-pictures and gave him, on its sound-track, the noise of victory bells. What had come next? Oh . . . the builders, of course, Neilson remembered, with a sinking of his heart.

The builders were here. They were at work on the plain. Faintly at first, he heard the ring of steel on stone and the echo of the deep, wordless chant. He was walking to find them. The noise grew louder with every step. For a while he did not dare to look ahead; if he saw them he might well turn back. He went on, head bent, towards the clamour. The air began to be dusty. He put up his arm to shield his eyes. Now there was nothing but noise. He thought, 'I need not see them. When they have finished their work, they will go.' But the thought of walking blindly into the midst of them was horrible. He lowered his arm and halted.

They were swarming off the walls and streaming past him. The building was done. The army of dwarfish men, still singing, went by in their hundreds. Silent-footed, they passed out of sight along the road. Neilson stood looking at the town that they had built. He remembered it.

Its own light lay over it, the clear, brittle light of a spring afternoon in California, colouring roof and wall, touching up the absurdities of Spanish Rococo, washing the flat white modern blocks with a bluer white. These were the University buildings, an exuberant maelstrom of architecture, with the crass yellow skyscraper in the middle. There was the broad avenue running between the eucalyptus trees. Here was the bridge that crossed the creek away from the avenue. He looked at the town from this side of the bridge before he turned and walked up the lane that led to his house.

The house was there, a small white toy of a house, with a red roof, standing in a neat plot of unfenced garden. Half its façade was the garage, whose concrete strip ran down beside the garden to the road. The mail-box stood at the end of the concrete strip; he saw the name NEILSON painted on the box in uneven black lettering; he remembered painting the letters. The mail-box flag was down.

As Neilson hesitated, a man came from the garden at the back of the house, and walked across the concrete strip to the mail-box. His hair was prematurely white. His face showed the dissipation of good looks; the skin had the drinker's flush on it and there was a thickening of the neck. Moments passed before Neilson recognised David. When he did, he saw that David was accompanied. Just behind his shoulder, watching him, there stood a young man with a dark, brilliant face and hopeful eyes.

129

DAVID

1955

DAVID never knew what magical surprise he awaited in the mail, but the childish belief went on. There was always the same upward beat of expectancy when he saw that the flag was down; always the same slump of disappointment when he had opened the box and sorted the envelopes. This morning Linda drove up just as he had come to the last envelope. She gave him her usual cool "Hello" and asked what he had been doing all morning. Her classes began at eight-thirty and they seldom met until now. The overtone behind her question was, "Just how have you been wasting your time?"

Courteously he tried to give an account of it that would please her. Weeding the vegetable-bed was the only thing that would. She grew impatient with his paint jobs and his carpentry, because she saw them as excuses for not writing, which they were. Nor would he confess that, finding a copy of his first novel at the back of the bookcase, he had spent an hour and a half re-reading it. That was an indulgence to be ashamed of.

Linda wore her inevitable, smiling mask. Her beauty was different in these days. She was thin as a dagger; she radiated an inexhaustible energy, a disciplined fever. The grey eyes with the heavy lids looked larger because her face was so thin. She kept her hair short and bleached white-gold.

"I'll get the lunch," she said, taking her letters and flashing past him. Not for years, he thought, had he seen her move slowly. He followed her, saying, "I fixed some sandwiches." "You did? Well, we can keep those for tonight, for the seminar. I made a casserole. Won't take long to heat." She flashed through the swing-door from the living-room to the kitchen. When she came whipping back, David said, "At what hour of the night did you make the casserole?"

130

"Oh, around six a.m." She stood by the brick fireplace reading her letters. "Nice morning, and I was broad awake; why not?" One wouldn't think, from the speed at which she split open the envelopes and skimmed the letters, that she could know what was there. She put them on her writing-table.

"Want a drink?" she said to him. "No? *No?*" He had expected the mocking twist of the eyebrows. She used those clowning eyebrows for him frequently. She twitched them again, looking at the newspaper in his hand. "A breath of Old-e England instead?"

It was the overseas edition of the London *Times*; still a necessity to him; Linda never wanted to look at it. England, for her, had ceased to exist except as an occasional target for sniping.

He went on reading. He heard the tap of her feet going away, returning, the rattle of china and knives and forks as she laid the table; when he looked again he could see her in the garden, pulling chives for the salad. She turned on the radio as she came back, and the news got in the way of *The Times Overseas Edition*. Lunch was ready, its appearance smooth, sudden and demanding as all the meals cooked by Linda. She resented his smallest delay in coming to the table. She would sit down without waiting for him and drum with her finger-tips. A concert had succeeded the news. When he moved to turn it off, she said sharply, "No, don't; I like it." "I'm sorry, darling." Her frown came, the little frown that was like a note she made to remind herself of something. Presumably it was made now to remind her that he had not wanted the music. She had taken a minute helping of the casserole and she was smoking again long before he had finished.

He gazed out of the window: at the neat vegetables in the brown earth, at the corn and the bean-poles, at the unfinished house beyond. It was a skeleton of new timber, mercifully deserted by the builders until half-past one, when they would return from their lunch to their varied noises. There could be silence now, but for Linda's concert. What had happened to silence anyway? As he recalled, it had, in other days, been plentiful. Now it made slender intrusions through the routine of radio, phonograph, juke-boxes, piped-in music and the war of voices in a room where any two or three Americans were gathered together.

The telephone interrupted the concert. Linda snatched it; he heard the temperature drop in her voice. "Oh, hello; kind of you, but I have a seminar here this evening. I guess David would; hold on and I'll give him to you." Her eyebrows were busy again and he knew who was talking before she said, "The Shriner; Popish-Pals' Department."

No matter how often Janet extended the double invitation, Linda would find a way out. Now she was saying, "You dine with her; you'll like that," still clowning with her eyebrows. David said, "I'll be eating here, Janet; early because of the seminar. May I come for coffee afterwards?" When he hung up, Linda said, "Don't forget to take some incense along." He wasn't in the mood for a slanging-match. He smiled agreeably. She tried another angle. "Your patience with that lady never ceases to astound me." He left her stuck with it. She lit another cigarette and went into the kitchen to fetch the dessert. When she came back she said, "I'm wrong, though. Janet may be death to me, but she's something of a lifeline to you. Isn't she?"

He said quietly, "You know I like her." There was little point in admitting the lifeline.

It was not, he thought, that Linda was jealous of Janet; none of his affections, human or abstract, mattered to her in these days. They were good for targets, that was all. Anything was. While she poured him his coffee, she said, "Morris, the new instructor in my department, claims to have a wife who'd like to audit your course." Effortlessly she contrived to suggest that this was a laughable thing.

"I take that kindly," said David.

"She would appear to be writing a novel. Maybe you can spare us that."

"Maybe."

He could not blame Linda for despising his Creative Writing Course, because there were many days when he himself despised it. They seldom talked of it. When they did, one or another of the old charges would come up. She would say that someone who hadn't put pen to paper for five years should be doing that rather than teaching others how. Or she would remind him, with subtle acid, that it was she who had influenced the Faculty to give him the course. Or she would attack the principle of it, inviting him to agree; and however secretly he might agree, he would find himself defending the principle. Better to leave it alone. He had, he saw, become expert at avoiding controversy, he who had once known the violence of his quarrels with Linda to be a proof of their love. And although she enjoyed needling him, she could be expert too at skating over serious things. They walked a narrow plank, where once they had walked together in space and freedom.

Her public façade was good enough. Here under this roof, alone with her, he breathed a thin, poisoned air.

He looked at the room. He liked the room and the things in the room: their books, their small, careful collection of pictures, the pieces of furniture that they had brought from London and La Colle. He looked at the carved wooden angel that Anne had found in Arles; it had a battered, gentle face and there were still flakes of gold upon the wings. A silver tankard dated from his days at Bristol University. Linda had bought the French soldiers when she was still at the Sorbonne.

The possessions of a lifetime were here, because this was home. Home, yes. But there was no life lived in it; these were memorial objects belonging to two people who had died. He mourned for them; no more for Linda as she used to be than for himself as he used to be. There were insane moments when the sound of his own voice made him homesick because of the things it used to say, the friends to whom it had talked, the places where it had echoed. When that weakness came, it was time for a drink.

And there were long periods wherein he did not look back at all, when he could go through the routine of their days, taking an obstinate pleasure in them. Then he would catch himself in the mood of a well-behaved prisoner, working off a sentence. What he really looked for in the mail-box, he supposed, was a reprieve from Now.

He pulled sharply away from contemplation of these things. To contemplate them was foolish; it could produce in him a sense of isolation so complete that he could only wonder whether madness were much different from this. Think of something else, he said to himself, and quickly.

"Linda."

"Uh-huh?" She was skimming the pages of a quarterly that had arrived in the mail, one of the high-powered capsules of current affairs.

"What's your least favourite line in classical fiction? One that seems to you in really abominable taste?"

"Why d'you want to know?"

"It's an exercise I give them this afternoon—needs a little new blood in it; I've confined it to poetry too long. Poetry's a sitter, really."

"Nice childish game," Linda murmured; she thought for a moment. "You may not agree with this one."

"Go on."

She said, " 'The President of the immortals had ended his sport with Tess.' "

"Good *enough*," said David enthusiastically. The comment was not, he thought, good enough for Linda.

She snapped, "That's exactly how I'd see God if I believed in him; the pompous old President of a celestial Chamber of Commerce. Wearing a frock-coat and a silk hat. And the word 'sport' makes me see him batting Tess across the court in a badminton game."

When he laughed she said, "I'd have thought *you'd* find it blasphemous."

He made the mistake of saying mildly, "Oh no, it's not blasphemous. Got any more? Least favourite lines?"

"What d'you mean it's not blasphemous? Of course it is."

"Oh, it is, eh?"

"Yes, it is, *eh*."

"Okay, if you say so."

There was a pause. Then Linda said lightly, coolly, "Now suppose you tell me just why you think it's not." The smiling mask was on again. "I'm interested, David, I want to know. After all, I have to listen to you jumping on people for saying 'Jesus Christ' when—according to you—they should say 'My goodness' or 'Imagine'. What's the difference?"

"Plenty, darling. But we needn't go into it."

"Why not?"

"Because I'll make you angry."

Her laugh was a caricature of a true laugh. "Angry? How *can* you be so ridiculous?"

"Please, Linda," he said. "Let's skip it. We each know what side of the fence we're on."

She narrowed the corners of her eyes. After a moment she said, "Pity it's impossible to have an adult conversation with you," and carried the coffee-cups into the kitchen, unfastening the stop of the swing-door, so that it shut behind her, the gesture of dismissal. He knew better than to follow her. He returned to his exercise. The afternoon building noises had begun. Linda did not speak to him again until she was ready to leave for the campus.

Cool, taut and still smiling, she said, "Want to ride in with me?"

He looked at his watch. He liked to drink a sizeable brandy before he faced the class at three o'clock. This was a dry campus, and if he went with Linda now, he lost the chance. On the other hand, he should be gentle with her; she was coming to the peak of this mood.

He had hesitated too long. "I see," said Linda. "The plan is to stay here with the bottle. Silly of me. Excuse it, please." Still smiling, she flashed through the door.

David winced; not because she had hurt him. He had hurt her. He turned back into the room and paced, trying to see what he ought to do about Linda. The obstacle in the way of helping her was simply himself. Anything that he did would be wrong. He had become, he knew, the focus of a hatred all the more violent and steady because she banked it down. He could not resent nor fear the hatred; he had lived with it too long. And there was a horrid certainty in his mind that Linda could not live without it; that it was the source of all her energy, the dark river down below that drove the mill.

He went out on to the back porch. The noise that the builders made was less lethal if they were visible. He sat in the white garden chair. He stared at the black tassels and papery green leaves of the corn.

He said to himself, as he had been saying over four years, 'It can't go on.' It went on going on. Linda's energy grew. She needed less and less sleep; she did more and more work. Not content with her class and its considerable demands, she crowded the evenings with extra seminars; she taught summer-school; she missed no opportunity to write, to

135

lecture off the campus, to talk on the air. If there were gaps to be filled, she filled them with the social life of the Faculty. To David these people were two-dimensional; their enforced association with youth gave them a false sprightliness. Linda could use them; and among them she was a focus for worship. At the centre of a group, he would hear her voice going on, see her lucid brilliance captivating the circle. He did not think that they caught the whirr of wheels behind the performance, nor felt the presence of a dynamo rather than the presence of flesh and blood. Linda was a miracle in their lives and they all loved her. She behaved as though she loved them. Only behind their backs did she dissect and decapitate them.

She had no loyalties, except loyalty to her work. When he thought of his own isolation, he would remember hers, that was so much greater. She depended on nobody, needed nobody, used people as she used words, ideas and things, "to bundle time away". She who had said long ago, "Life is terror and must be faced with courage," had put on her own armour of courage. There was no chink in it. She never let up, never looked back. She had not failed in her vow to annihilate the past.

He might, he supposed, be wrong in believing that there must come a breaking-point. The only psychologist in whom he had felt enough confidence to ask advice had disagreed. "They just burn themselves out a little more quickly; that's what they want to do. You don't have to worry. She'll keep going at this pace; it suits her."

Why didn't he believe that? Why did he sit here now, feeling that every day found him less effectual in the face of a danger that threatened her? Why could he not see this breakneck drive as a sublimation, which was how his adviser described it? He heard Linda's voice telling him why not. "You'd like to believe that nobody can be self-sufficient—— Upsets all your sentimental religious theories, doesn't it?"

David looked at his watch. Then he went indoors and poured himself the brandy. He added a lump of ice to it. Drink remained constant, a beckoning temptation, a release from sentry-go, a positive factor in his life. Once a year he put himself on the wagon, for the weeks of Lent, and Linda, who despised the need to drink, despised the mortification equally.

136

Grateful for the small amount of physical happiness, he swallowed the brandy. So as not to walk off the benefits, he called a taxi; one of the extravagances that left him always short of money at the end of the month.

As he straightened his tie before the looking-glass, he tried to dodge the unwelcome facts about his own reflection. After the seven weeks of Lent he looked clear-eyed and the bones of his face came back. Now there were red lines on the eyeballs; the face was puffy.

The taxi-driver, a chum, asked sceptically after the progress of his class. He said, as he had said before, that it seemed to him a screwy idea, teaching people to be writers. Surely writers just happened. David said, as he had said before, that he cherished no hope of teaching anyone to be a writer. What he trusted to find in the class, from time to time, was a potential writer who might benefit from his own technical experience. This afternoon, because of the brandy, he added, "In three and a half years I've found exactly two. The reason I really like the work is that it gives me a chance to talk my own shop."

He stood on the rostrum looking at the class, his friendly enemies. He saw crew-cuts and shirts that were like undervests; he saw curls and lacquered waves and bright blouses. The boys, in their attitudes, threw out a listless sexual challenge to the girls. "Take us or leave us, we don't care," was the message. The girls' communal response was an exaggerated air of gaiety and containment; both sides had fun.

It took Neilson several minutes to crack the class self-consciousness, no less a self-consciousness because it manifested a show of democratic ease. Once they became absorbed by their subject, they turned back into people.

The shortest cut to the transformation was to make a statement that sounded outrageous. He made it. "Ninety-nine per cent of fiction-writers in this country have no use for words," David said, "in which indifference they are supported by ninety-nine per cent of fiction-readers."

It was a new line. The proof that he had no gift for teaching was his boredom at giving the same lesson again and again. The official syllabus of the Creative Writing Course, drawn up by him three and a half years ago, was still on the files. It was the course offered, the course for which the

137

students enrolled. He strayed from it irrevocably. The classes were enthusiastic. Joshua Phillips, the Head of the English Department, was not. When rumour of David's unorthodoxies reached him, there was a warning. Sometimes there was a battle. David tried to be good. Now that his news value was gone, now that the tinny trumpets of best-selling popularity had ceased to echo, he walked on hazardous ground. It would not be long, he judged, before he exploded his own trivial legend here. The numbers who enrolled for the course were shrinking.

The prospect of losing his post hung often at the back of his mind. It hung now, while the bombardment from the floor grew in volume. The young were disturbed.

For all their assertions of non-conformism and the rebel spirit, one had only to shake a lance at something that they assumed to be in a good way (in this case modern literature) and they rose in fury.

The names of all contemporary giants came chorusing out like a Litany. A few colder minds gave him back sarcasm for sarcasm. Would he tell them, perhaps, how a writer could get along without words? Could he say what it was that a reader read, if not words? Could Mr. Neilson (the speaker was a steadfast blonde, classified by David as one of the Great-Granddaughters of the American Revolution) in that case explain away the system of awarding prizes for literature?

David was delighted that she had raised this matter. It needed their attention. What, he asked them, did adults want with prizes? The shame of a supposedly civilised culture, said David. All prizes ought to be abolished. The competitive spirit was more than an absurdity. It was a menace to the arts just as it was a menace to the Christian ethic. A little less noise, please. Every prize awarded for literature was a handshake with the commercial ballyhoo that inflicted upon us photographs of movie-stars simpering above their Oscars. No artist should identify himself with such immature nonsense.

"How did you feel when you got the Book-of-the-Month Club choice?" asked one of the friendlier enemies. There was a roar.

"Crazy for myself," said David. "On top of the world.

138

And very, very rich. That's just what I'm complaining of."
This roar was louder.

It was now a loving battle. Having proved to his own satisfaction, and to nobody else's, that current novels were deficient in syntax, taste and euphony, he went on sunnily to invite their prejudices. He would expose a few of his own. Here, he said, were some of the worst lines in classical fiction. Comments and further suggestions, please. He wrote them on the board. The battle became a series of duels. "It's beautiful." "It's corny as all hell, Mr. Neilson's right." "I say it's good prose." "I say it stinks."

When he reached the example that Linda had given him, introducing the President of the immortals, a lively religious discussion began. The creative writing course had stopped at the Creator. "I'll have to interrupt you, I'm afraid," David said regretfully. "Time's getting short." An impassioned young man in the third row was putting forward the claims of an artistic conscience as an adequate substitute for God.

"Well, but—there's something to be said for that view, isn't there, Mr. Neilson?"

"No," said David limpidly. "Nothing's a substitute for God."

There was a shocked murmur. Somebody drawled, "Isn't a Deity a matter for individual belief?"

"No," said David. He was at his table now, picking out the paper he wanted. The silence made him look up. The air was changed. He said, still sunnily, "The main thing about God is that He is—if you see what I mean. Whereas individual belief may be, or may not be—again if you see what I mean. Arising from the last exercise, here's what I want you to do for me by Thursday."

He came back to the cupboard-sized office that he shared with Bryce Evans and found Bryce there ahead of him. Bryce was a newcomer to the English Department, twenty years younger than David, merry-faced and bland. He was a Rhodes Scholar and his favourite game with David was the exploration of the Anglo-American mysteries. In David's eyes Bryce himself was mysterious, for his youth and his unshadowed quality. He had published one novel. He was set, David thought, for success in two careers. David could not envy him. Envy demanded passion of a sort. He merely stared at him and wondered how it felt to be Bryce Evans.

Bryce was correcting papers.

"This man," said Bryce, his voice sounding a tempered satisfaction, "is a moron." He wrote a neat 'C' in red chalk at the end of the paper and added a minus as an afterthought. He smiled at David. "We mustn't forget, must we, the advantages of the discussion method? Its freedom, its call to awareness, its mission to the democratic unfolding of the personality. We must remember the literal translation of the verb 'educare': to draw out. Can you, David Neilson, draw out the Leviathan with a hook? Can you, alternatively, send a bucket down an empty well and come up with some water? I can't." He drew the next paper towards him. "One with a prayer on it. 'J.M.J.' he's written. Never know if they aim to placate the Holy Family or just me. Poor fellow, I can tell him without reading, it's the only prayer he's got. You look as if you had a good session."

"I usually do," said David.

"Very curious," said Bryce. "The product of pre-war Oxford let loose in this Athens of the West—and enjoying it."

"As I never cease telling you, I went to Bristol, not Oxford."

"Doesn't show," said Bryce. "And, as the President told us at one of his biennial appearances on this campus, we've a grand bunch of kids here. One fine morning I may kick their teeth in, but let it go."

"I like them," said David, heavily and truthfully.

"That's very gracious and lovely in you, a Britisher," said Bryce, mimicking the accent of a Middle West matron. "So in fact do I. But I own to a weakness for those jaded, clipped, stiff-upper-lipped, poetry-reading, cricket-playing, complacent little bastards in your country. Which is very gracious and lovely in me, an American citizen."

"We're exceptions, you and I, to the universal law." Over the years, David remembered his own gay, drunken words in a Casino, the night the Twenty-One came up three times; the night before everything stopped. He repeated, "Between the British and the Americans there exists a profound natural antipathy, as between cat and dog."

"So true; so true. *Why* do you like your students, David? Do you know?"

He said confusedly, "Honesty. Liveliness. No side. Digging after the truth with a pick and shovel. Exaggeration, from the guts, as compared with careful understatement."

"Me, I'm for meiosis."

"Well, Bryce, it has its points. But when somebody says, 'The house burned down and mother died raving and it was all quite a cope,' I don't rate it higher than would-be-genteel."

"You're safe from it here."

"And I like," David persisted, "their being so instantly available with their emotions and their ideas. They bury nothing."

"Bury nothing . . ." Bryce repeated. "From you, that's ——" he stopped. One of the things that he had caught from the British, David observed, was the habit of rationing personal remarks. He grinned apologetically.

"Go on. Finish."

There was the beginning of a blush on Bryce's cheeks. He swallowed. "All right. I was thinking that it was an odd compliment. Coming from someone who buries everything, the way you do."

A small knock sounded on the office door.

"Excuse me; are you busy, Mr. Neilson?"

It was the student with the traceable look of Anne. She could never guess how important she was, simply because she had a wide smile and a bumpy forehead. David said, "Come in." Bryce said, "I'm on my way," rising, collecting his books, sliding from his chair.

"Sit down, won't you, Miss Dale."

Though she said, "Thank you," she remained standing. The reminder of Anne was only in her face. The body was quite different. She was stocky and muscular. In her white blouse, long black skirt and heelless shoes, she looked as though she were training for the ballet.

"Maybe you'll think it's not very nice of me," she began. "But I thought you ought to know. . . ."

"Have a cigarette?"

"No thanks, I don't."

She hesitated. "I love the course," she said. "It's terribly stimulating. And different." She looked down at the floor.

"Thank you," said David soberly.

Still not meeting his eyes, she said, "But it looks as though there'll be trouble about that last thing you said to us. I can't tell you names, but it made some of them quite mad. They want to take it to Mr. Phillips."

David tried to remember what in fact was the last thing that he had said to them. Stupid to have forgotten so soon, but this was inclined to happen.

"What did I say? I don't remember."

The student looked as though she found it hard to believe him. "Sounds silly, I know," he said, "but when I talk I get excited." And this was true. The course, for all its short-comings, was a passion; the only one left; a spark that, three times a week, lit those forty minutes. "It goes to my head a little," said David to the girl who looked like Anne, "and I get carried away."

"That isn't an act?"

"No, I assure you."

"I didn't really think it was. Some of them think it is. How lovely—to feel that way about teaching people." She stared at him.

"You haven't," he reminded her, "told me what subversive remark I made."

"It was when you talked about God."

"Oh . . . yes . . . always a controversial subject, God," said David lazily.

"They didn't like it."

"I'm sorry. Never mind." Seeing that she seemed to be on the verge of tears, he said, "Didn't you like it, either?"

"Well, it surprised me that you should say it—just sit up there and tell us what to believe. But it didn't make me mad. I was interested; I thought I'd like to take it up with you, sometime."

"I told you what you ought to believe . . . How, exactly, did I phrase it?"

She turned the pages of her notebook. "I wrote it down; I always write down the bits I want to think about." She read aloud, "God *is*; whereas belief may or may not be."

"H'm," said David, "yes . . . I do see."

142

"Did you mean it?"

"Oh yes."

"Wasn't it a little——?" she frowned and wrinkled her nose. "I don't have the right word . . . but a little——" She came to a stop again.

"Let me help you. I can give you plenty. Undemocratic. Narrow-minded. Dictatorial. Bigoted. Autocratic. Arbitrary. Hidebound." She looked so miserable that he said, "I'm sorry. Shall we just leave it that the observation was quite outside my province as an English instructor in this University?"

The girl said, "That's the way they'll slice it. For the Head of the Department." There was a pause. Then David said, "Oh, well; Joshua Phillips and I are old friends." He added conventionally, "You were very kind to tell me; I'd rather know." He expected her to go now, but she waited, regaining composure because she was thinking hard.

"God is . . ." she repeated. "God exists, and that's final. What is your religious denomination, Mr. Neilson?"

"None," said David, "or all. I wouldn't really know."

Her stare said, as plainly as words could, 'But surely, at your age, you *must* know. You must have made up your mind.' Then, sounding a little relieved, she asked, "It's just a hunch, then, a feeling?"

"No," said David, "it's a conviction."

"A conviction. Really? You mean that?"

"Yes."

She turned shy again. "Then . . . I know these things are very personal . . . but I would like to hear how it comes . . . What it was that convinced you . . . Not just from curiosity. I'd *like* to be convinced, you see. But I can't be."

David looked at the bent head. He wished that memory would not hold up to him the moment on the terrace at La Colle; the moment before the police car came down the road; his voice saying to Linda through the dark, "Keep on wanting faith. If you want it, you can have it." He could never make himself say that again.

He said, "Whether this can help you, I don't know. As far as I'm concerned, it's simple enough. I'm aware of God's presence. I think I have been, always. There have been times in my life when I haven't wanted it. There are those

143

times. It isn't, always, a comfortable Presence to be aware of. And, other times, it's the only thing that keeps you sane."

She looked as she looked when she sat in the front row and took notes of his talk. "The presence of God . . . All the time. Like—like the weather?"

"In a way, yes. In a way, as unlike the weather as possible. The weather doesn't prove that it *was* there by a sudden and drastic period of absence."

"I don't get that. God can be absent as well as present?"

"When He chooses to be, I think."

"What happens then?"

"Look," David said, "I can talk about God any time, with the greatest of pleasure, and go on all night. But haven't you a biology class pending?"

"I could cut it."

"I wouldn't if I were you."

"Well then—could we go on—another time? Just you and me?"

"Sure. If I'm not sacked meanwhile. Good-bye, Miss Dale."

At the door she said, "It was nice talking to you."

David sat on, thinking about it. When the time came, he felt more than the usual reluctance to fetch Linda from her office and drive with her to the President's house on their way home. Not a Faculty party, she had said; they were invited to meet the presidential house-guests. The privilege included him only because of Linda. He was used to this. At least there would be drinks. (And jokes about the dry campus and the technical breach of the Charter rule. Like the Army, the University was hard on its jokes.) At least they could not stay long, because of Linda's seminar.

The second highball brought him peace of mind and a privacy from which he could look out, undisturbed, at the party. Only eight people, with Linda in the centre and himself on the side. He watched her, trying, as he had tried before, to know the technique of the game that she played. It was not an elaborate technique. She talked well and not too much. She listened with an air of arrested movement, as though the speaker's words, charged with magnetic power, had galvanised her into stillness. She never drank. He saw the stimulant that was the group taking its effect as palpably

144

as alcohol would; the rising light in her eyes, the more fluent gestures of her hands; the readier laughter. Always, as they left a party together, he was aware of the hush coming down on the end of a performance; he half-expected a round of applause. As the door shut, the voices would rise behind it to talk rapturously of Linda.

In the car she began to tear them all down, one by one. This, gaily, in no need of agreement or contradiction. The President was an insult to the University; a catch-penny business man with a talent for the worst sort of public-relations. His wife had all the allure of Scotch tape. The Senator—if indeed he was a senator and had not, as might be assumed from his grasp of national affairs, come to fix the plumbing—was, she supposed, sleeping with the unexplained red-head. The steel-magnate with the wife who looked like a toad reminded her of a Mormon bishop who had once tried to seduce her on a train. The identity and purpose of the other two remained a mystery—one which, she trusted, she need never unravel.

Listening, David glanced ahead in his mind to the seminar where seven young women, differently rapt, would sit at the feet and hear the word; not these words.

She was still maliciously aglow when they began their rapid meal. Now the malice pointed his way. She drooped her eyelids and cooled her voice as suddenly as though she had added a lump of ice. "And our class? Just what went on in our class today, huh?"

The grapevine, he thought, must have carried the news of battle remarkably quickly. Had it not been for the third high-ball, he would have recognised the tone; it was routine patronage; the routine sneer; no more.

He said, "Oh, storm in a tea-cup. I'll hear the angle fast enough from Phillips. On reflection, I suppose it was rather too thunderous an affirmative for the kindergarten."

"What was?"

Then he knew that she had heard nothing. Now he had given himself no choice but to tell her.

The ensuing frozen silence gave him the signal. So did the pinching of her lips and the flare of her nostrils. She did not speak again. This silence would last out the fifteen minutes remaining before the students arrived. And, knowing Linda, he could guess that it would last twenty-four hours, or more. She was expert at this; and it was the thing that he found hardest to bear, the most refined of her tortures. It was the suspending of all communication, so that only the "Pass-the-salt" variety of domestic exchange survived. He never knew how she could keep the mood and the silence without breaking down; how she could remember not to laugh when something funny happened; preserve her own injury and his guilt in her mind all through the working hours when they did not meet, so that the same low temperature prevailed when they met again. It had, on occasion, lasted a week. He had never been able to induce a thaw. The moment of thaw came at her choosing. Now for the deep-freeze, he said to himself, as he helped her arrange the chairs in their half-circle.

Suddenly he lost patience with it. It was too silly.

"Linda———"

She answered him with her eyebrows.

"Would this be the great frost setting in, by any chance?"

Still the eyebrows.

"Because I think we're both getting a little too old for it. Don't you?"

She replied, in the airy head-voice, that she didn't know what he was talking about.

"As you know," he said, "it happens to be my worst thing; and at this moment I'm not prepared to put up with it. If you want to quarrel with me, fine. Say anything you like. But this schoolmistress, putting-in-Coventry, terrorising act is just too damn' silly for speech and I'm not taking it. So you'll kindly stop being Miss Priss with a grievance, darling. The house is too small. If you don't stop, I'm packing a bag and going to an hotel."

The pallor of her face and the rage in her eyes were the only answer. While he was struggling with the impulse to shake her and slap her and shake her again, the door-bell rang.

Linda reached the door ahead of him. She was, at once, transformed into affectionate liveliness. Of the two girls, one greeted him as though he did not exist; she was the dark slender child with the burning eyes; he had overheard two of the others discussing her under the name of The Present Incumbent. He knew what they meant.

He waited until the seven had arrived. Now he saw no

trace of the woman he had wanted to slap. He saw somebody who reminded him of the girl from Dijon. He saw a glimpse of her magic, which was, though the young women did not know it, as much their gift to her as hers to them. It was their company that took the years from her, gave her their own luminous and hopeful quality. She might not be their middle-aged teacher at all. She might have been of their generation, their chosen leader.

As he went to the car, he looked through the window into the room that was beginning to be shadowy. He saw her there, leaning back her elegant, boyish head to laugh with them; the stillness of her body, her restless hand that waved the arguments on; the spellbinder and the spellbound. He went on remembering the picture.

While he drove, his thoughts travelled to the place where he did not want them to go. This aspect of Linda, above all, gave to their shared life a feeling of peculiar insanity. It was foolish to make much of it in his mind; the tendency had been there always; from the beginning. (Far off, he heard her voice saying, "All intelligent people are bi-sexual anyway," and his own voice replying, "Oh pooh.") For twenty years of their marriage it had troubled neither of them. Sometimes he had been aware of its overtones; in her tenderness towards women, in her utter lack of the feminine competitive spirit; it even showed itself a little in her strong, affectionate way of looking after him and Anne. But in all that time, he knew, he was her only love.

And now, over these five years, hating him, she could love in this way again. She would not deny it, if he challenged her; she never denied anything. What he most disapproved was her compulsion to light up the worshipping fires, to beckon the hysteria. It was not merely that she allowed the young women to tie themselves to her with emotional bonds; she invited them. Oh, subtly enough, delicately enough to deceive the worshippers; but deliberately all the same. Here his moral judgment began. She had no right to initiate the young. That was a sin, as he saw it.

'Do I care—from my own point of view? Do I feel, as other husbands, I think, would feel, that it makes me look ridiculous? No. I think I'd feel more of a fool if she were busy enslaving the young men. This thing is too remote, too

foreign, for me to be able to resent it at close range.' Linda
had told him years ago that he was deficient in masculine
pride. 'Better so,' David thought, 'God knows, however
abundantly I'd possessed it, she would have beaten it out of
me by this time.'

Still, the picture that he had seen through the window
stayed on his eyes, all the way across town and up the hill-
road that led to Janet's house. It should not, he thought,
give him a greater sense of solitude. Like Linda, he was surely
at home with solitude by now. He did not believe that the
obsessive passions gave her any true relief from solitude.
They made one more channel for her energy, that was all.

He parked the car at Janet's gate and walked through the
twilit garden. This was one of the older houses on the hill, a
grey frame house with white shutters, more reminiscent of
New England than of California. Janet's cat, a silky and
reserved Maltese, stepped lightly to meet him, then, dis-
concertingly, lost interest and remained in the middle of the
path with its back to him, twitching its tail.

The door was open. The living-room door stood ajar. It
was a high room, walled with books to the ceiling. Living, as
he lived, in the neatest of boxes, he was comforted by the tall
windows and the floor-space; he strolled around at ease.

From the far end of the room, behind the painted screen
that hid her desk, Janet was calling. "Hullo. With you in
five minutes; I'm having acute scansion trouble."

Contentedly he waited for her. She was, as Linda had said,
his lifeline in this place and sometimes lately he had been
ashamed of it because he could see that he was gaining in
importance for her. Her importance to him remained static.
It had begun when he found somebody whose life, like his
own, had been split by sudden death, somebody who liked
him to talk of England and of Anne.

Janet's husband had died at fifty; that was four years ago
and she lived here quite alone, remembering. When she
spoke of him, she still used the present tense . . . "Vernon
thinks—Vernon likes . . ." When the Faculty spoke of Janet,
they deplored the unnatural determination to live on in the
same house, doing the same things, without Vernon. She
ought, they said, to Get Away, Snap Out of It, Start Again
Somewhere Else. Why not, for example, go back to England

148

where she belonged? They spoke of grooves, of ruts, of morbidity and melancholia. There were others besides Linda who spoke of the house as The Shrine and called Janet the Shriner—though Linda had said it first.

Linda had three quarrels with Janet: one that she was immune to Linda, two that she was a Catholic, three that she had money. (It was easy, Linda said, to live a dedicated life, writing your little verse and brandishing your melancholia, if you had money. No need to remarry for security's sake, just a lover or so when you felt inclined, and the confessional afterwards. And everybody saying how brave you were. You must have a wonderful time.)

David admired Janet for doing the thing that he had never given himself the chance to do; for standing fast to live with sorrow on the site of bygone happiness. She had not been afraid of the empty place. She had taken the long journey back to peace of mind. He saw her as one who had travelled, and arrived.

Now she came from the screen, looking ruffled, and tired. Janet was in her early forties. For a woman poet her appearance was almost a cliché; she had dark hair, a pale skin, good bones and the demon-haunted look. When he first met her, he had found her astonishingly gentle and humble; her placid temper was at odds with the cliché. One did not expect a poet to have a sunny disposition.

"Oh, goodness me," Janet said, "let us have coffee. The *hair-line* between writing passable light verse and what that lady used to call Rippling Rhymes—what was her name, David? A funny name—English."

"Wilhelmina Stitch," he said. "Have no fear. You're not in the Stitch bracket."

"Jolly nearly, sometimes." She smiled at him as she poured the coffee; then frowned.

"Linda been putting you through it?"

"Not more than usual." There was no solace in talking to Janet about Linda. In the convention, perhaps, there should be. But he had not found it. It was like trying to describe your headache to somebody who never had one. And it aroused in him afterwards a sense of disloyalty and shame.

"But I dropped a brick in my class today. A full-sized brick."

149

"What was the brick?"

"God."

"Good show," said Janet. "I trust it fell on the right head or heads." When he told her the rest of it, she was silent, not like Linda, but pacing as he did when his thoughts went down deep.

"Queer way to be martyred," she said at last. "A clutch of eager beavers selling you down the river to Joshua Phillips."

"I *may* not be . . . But I rather think that if he needed anything more to decide him not to renew my contract, this'll be it."

"Ow!" said Janet, grimacing.

"I've seen it coming. I don't really care."

"Yes, you do."

"Yes . . . you're right, I do. Silly. Such a little thing."

"But it's all you've got."

"H'm." As usual she came too close to his thoughts for his comfort. Not that he resented this for himself; she was never tiresome; it awed him to think that he could matter to her so much.

"Of course," she said, continuing to look demon-haunted, "it *oughtn't* to be all you've got. I do wish you'd try to write again."

"It's gone. You know that."

"It never really goes."

"If you let it, it does."

"Can't you stop letting it?"

"Five years," he said, "is a long time. And the rust, as you know, accumulates."

"If you could get away by yourself—right away."

"I never could."

But she was crusading. "And I know where. It doesn't sound right, but it is. In up-state Connecticut. Just a road-house, really. The woman, Mary, used to work for us in England. She married an American; I helped them start it. They run it well. It's cheap and comfortable and lonely and perfect." She looked at him again, hopefully. "For people who want to get away—to be alone—uncoil their nerve-ends."

David considered people who could do that. He stared at

them as he stared at Bryce Evans, not with envy, simply wondering how it felt to be one of them.

"I went there myself, at the beginning," Janet said. "I had to. I couldn't write after Vernon died. There was one miserable poem that I picked at from time to time, like a piece of knitting. It never got finished."

"But you fought to get it back. I didn't. I tore up that novel I was working on; the day of Anne's funeral. And I said, 'I'll never write again.' And I meant it."

"Silliest of vows. Understandable, but entirely misguided. And you won't be able to keep it, mark my words. If you did keep it," she said in a growling voice, "it would be a sin."

"And what is it now, may I ask?"

"A weakness," said Janet, grinning at him. Her hazel-green eyes were lively and curious. "Anne liked what you wrote, after all," she reminded him.

"Yes, she did. Never thought she would. I remember giving her the first one to read when she was fifteen and she said, 'It brought tears to these jaded, cynical eyes.' "

Janet laughed. "Well, she wants you to go on with it again, take it from me. She's probably praying for that."

He said, "Don't!"

"Sorry, David." She put her long thin hand on his.

"All right——" he said after a moment, "I'll take it. It just made me feel guilty; which is, I guess, the way I should feel."

"Oh *lord*——" said Janet, throwing back her head. "The man with a load of guilt. Think, if you began writing again, you'd stop blaming yourself for everything under the sky?"

"I don't know."

"You'd have less *time* for it anyway. Look, David, can you never get it into your head that you're doing more for another person than most men would find possible? You've given up everything you had. Cut off your career, torn up your roots, left the places you loved, all because Linda wanted to smash the past to pieces and start again here? You've walked beside her all the way. And in all humility. You're so cursed with guilt *and* kindliness that you can't see straight, that's your trouble." She rose and pushed both hands through her hair, standing it on end. "I admire you for sticking to it, but it's beginning to make me damned angry. Don't you see, I'm not only thinking of you as a writer, but as a person. Nobody's given *carte blanche* to destroy himself as you're doing. That *is* what you're doing. And that's a sin, too."

"In your terms of reference, maybe," David said. She made him feel precarious. She had never tried to convert him and he thought that she was now going to begin.

"I want you to promise me something. Will you? Before you know what it is?" She faced him like a duellist.

"No, certainly not."

She said, "It isn't a difficult thing."

"Talk to a priest?" he hazarded. Janet began to laugh. "Oh, poor David—no. Because I used the word sin . . .? It's your word too, darling. And I'm no proselytiser, you should know that by now."

"Well then, what?" he asked a little sulkily. He thought that a drink would be nice. Janet said, "You'd like a drink, wouldn't you?"

"Yes, please."

"Help yourself. And then promise me."

He waited for it, glass in hand.

"Will you please—tomorrow morning—sit down at your desk and try to write again? Anything. It doesn't matter what. Just give it a chance. A serious chance. And do that every day—till it comes back."

He looked at her mutinously. "Make an act of Will. That's all it amounts to," she said lightly and lit a cigarette, looking at him now with an Olympic assurance that reminded him of Aunt Rachel and set him in the mould and the mood of an obstinate little boy.

"What is it I'm making now? An act of Won't?"

"I'd say it began as an act of Won't and has turned into an act of Can't."

"Why do you care?"

She hesitated. He knew the look of her body well enough, a slight, well-made body, the shoulders always hunched up towards her ears; the waistline was narrow and the breasts were deep. Something in her meek yet defensive pose suggested that she wanted him to look at her as a woman.

"Because you are important to me. And you always will be." She sounded amiably truculent.

He honoured her too much to make a conventional reply. When he did not speak, her face coloured and she said, "I know you'd rather go on thinking that you're not important to anybody." She seemed much younger now; she must, he thought, have talked like this long ago; he saw her with no lines on her forehead, troubled and burning, yet ready to laugh at herself, the lover with the vexed profile and the violent hair.

It was, he thought with a simplicity that stunned him, nice to be loved.

"Hullo, Janet," he said to her eyes.

"Hullo. Are you going to promise?"

"I'll try," said David, not thinking about it at all.

"Tomorrow morning, as ever is?" But she wasn't, he judged, thinking about it either.

"Yes."

"Thank you."

A silence came between them. As he said to himself, 'But it would be unforgivable; I don't love her,' he knew that it would happen. She smiled at him and came back to sit on the sofa. He took her hands. He could say of celibacy, as of his abandoned work, "Five years is a long time."

"But this," he said laughing, "comes easier."

It was, for the time being, the end of loneliness. He kept believing that the closeness of their two bodies making love must change everything, that because his flesh was in hers and the climax made her cry out and press her face to his throat, they would be close when it was over. Surely now he loved her and would go on loving her. He would awake from the drowsy peace that followed to find the magic waiting for him. He slept for a little while, holding her in his arms.

But when he awoke, and saw her watching him steadily, there was no magic. Nothing was changed but the physical senses, relieved at last. He looked at her with gratitude and tenderness, not with love.

"Do not say, please, David, that it oughtn't to have happened."

"I loved it," he said, "but it still oughtn't."

"I'm glad it did. It'll happen again too," she said— "and for the time being I'll have to stop gunning you about *your* sins." She laid her head on his shoulder. "This is a sin for me, as you know."

(Linda's words came back. "A lover or so on the side, and the confessional afterwards.")

"And you are the first—since Vernon, as you must have realised."

(He had made Linda's words true.)

He said, "I cannot think that this makes God angry."

"Well—have it your own way. But the only sins that really weigh on my neck are the enjoyable ones. I get the same freedom when I defeat my own sensuality that you get when you go on the wagon. Had it a long time now." She turned into the young woman again. "You mustn't let me become a responsibility in your mind—or a nuisance—or a demand. I can only love one way. And I'll love you that way. As I loved Vernon. And I'll understand perfectly if it gets too much for you. You won't have to lie to me. I'll know. I almost know now . . . Time you went home, my darling."

It was after eleven o'clock; the stars were bright. As he went, David saw that the last three hours had driven out the rest of the day. He echoed Janet's comment, "Stop blaming yourself for everything that happens under the sky." No good. He was guilty this time, too. He had known, before it happened, the kind of person she was; humble and whole-hearted; he had known that he was—assuming too great an importance in her mind. Lust and loneliness were not good enough excuses for tearing another person's life-pattern across. He would fail her in love; he was failing her now.

And, despite his last protest, he thought that she was right about the sin. Why else should he feel that he failed God too?

He drove across the bridge at the end of the town; along the road beside the creek. As he reached the toy house, he saw that the curtains were drawn at the living-room windows, but that the lights still shone behind them. He put the car in the garage. Passing the window he could hear the quiet voices. They became quieter still. When he came into the lobby there were no voices sounding at all. Passing the shut door on the way to his bedroom, he knew, as if the door had been transparent, that there was only one person there with Linda. He knew who it was.

He went through the bedroom and bathroom to the

154

dressing-room. He was heavy with sleep when he lay down, but the dressing-room was built out beside the porch and the lights shone from the back windows and their voices kept coming through. There were no words that he could hear, or wanted to hear; only the low echoes of a seemingly endless dialogue. David drifted slowly into sleep.

He awoke once, suddenly, thinking that he had heard Linda call. He sat up, listening. He had the symptoms of nightmare, the thumping heart, the sense of doom, the question-mark in his mind. Nothing happened; there was no sound; the teasing shaft of light no longer lay across the rail of the porch. After a time he slept again.

The queer dream of Anne was the next thing that he remembered. At first she was Janet, reproaching him sadly because he did not love her, but then she turned into Anne; and Anne was crying and saying, "Do write again. Please do. Otherwise you make me think it's my fault—and you know what a one I am for a sense of guilt."

He said aloud, "Oh, darling. That's not you, that's me," and awoke himself. The sun was strong; the noises were beginning outside the window. Eight o'clock and after; the builders came at eight.

He said his morning prayers, lazily, aware that he was more comfortable physically than he had been for a long time, and knowing why. He tried to think of Janet, but only a kind of arrogant gratitude came with the morning mood. He could feel no emotion about the coming show-down with Joshua Phillips. When he turned his mind's attention to Linda and the start of the cold war, he felt positively bored. She would be breakfasting without him. Or perhaps she had already left for the campus. He sat up and looked at the clock. Eight-forty-five. Certainly she had left. "Thank God for that," said David, getting out of bed.

While he bathed and shaved, he recalled, with a groan, his promise to Janet. 'Tomorrow morning. Sit at your desk and try to write again. Every day until it comes back.' 'Oh, pooh,' said David. 'You promised,' said the voice in his head, the voice of the one who, always, made everything sound as difficult as it was. He tried to ignore the voice, but it went on talking.

Coming into the kitchen, he saw that Linda had gone

without breakfast. Only a cup with some dregs, and a jar of instant coffee, stood on the draining-board. Linda ate a solid breakfast and continually advised him to do the same. It was unlike her to oversleep, to leave herself so little time.

David squeezed his oranges and made his coffee. As a concession to the threat of a working-day (though he wouldn't, he knew, sit at the desk for more than half an hour) he scrambled some eggs. It surprised him to see the newspaper lying on the sill of the front window, where the boy always left it. Linda took the paper with her when she went. It was nice to have it to read with his breakfast. And he liked the scrambled eggs. Really, he thought, he would be at peace with the world this morning were it not for the voice that nagged, 'You promised to try today. You promised.' 'Shut up,' David said to it. 'Leave me alone, there's a good fellow.'

He carried his tray back to the kitchen and washed the dishes. He lit a cigarette and prowled around the vegetable-bed. 'All right; in a minute. No hurry.' He looked at his watch. Ten o'clock, now, would make a nice symmetrical time to begin. He would do a little weeding and start at ten.

Then he laughed. He might have lost all the habits of a writer, but the old temptation not to begin at least remained. This reluctance was familiar, unchanged, exactly as he had known it in the days of industry. The same postponing devil who was the enemy of all creative work took his same weapons from the wall.

For the first time in years, David felt the impulse to fight him. Was this what Janet meant by an act of Will? Did it come because of her, because of his dream about Anne? Or had the eternal guilt attached itself at last to the buried and rusted talent? He did not know. Nor had he any idea what he would search for in his head when he got to the desk. But that must happen now; without waiting for ten o'clock.

As he went to the desk, that stood below the living-room window, he glanced out at the mail-box. Too early for the mailman yet. No; the flag was down. Well, he could afford this one concession to the postponing devil; he would get the letters first.

Strolling across the concrete strip, he heard the builders launching a new salvo. The jagged rattle of the concrete-mixer, the whirr of the buzz-saw, began. The hammering grew louder.

He lifted the flap of the mail-box. In the small tin tunnel there was only one letter, a blue envelope. He drew it out. It was unstamped, addressed to him in Linda's handwriting. She had scored a thick, angry-looking line under his name. Puzzled, he opened the envelope.

"DAVID,

"There is no explanation that I can give. I didn't expect things to break this way, but they broke last night—more accurately, at two o'clock this morning. Not very important, to find oneself unloved, but somehow significant. I have come to the end of my life here. And I must start another life somewhere else.

"Alone, of course. I don't want any questions, or fuss, or people. The Department has a message that I've had to fly East because of family illness. In fact I am driving across, taking my time. They won't expect me back for a few days. I'll write to them, signing off. I think there comes a time when the machine breaks down.

"Please don't attempt to find me or follow me or write to me. I couldn't stand it. I know just how intolerable I've been to you. Believe me, I have spared myself even less. You and I should never meet again. We have nothing to give each other, ever, any more. I take full responsibility—and you'll just have to take everything else.

"Sorry,
"Linda."

David stood still, reading and re-reading it. The volley of noise that the builders made seemed to be inside his head. Presently he folded the letter and put it into his pocket. He saw that the flap of the mail-box was still hanging open. As he shut it, he realised that the thing he had been waiting for was here at last. This was the reprieve from Now.

NEILSON

THE sound of hammering grew quieter, ceased and there was silence. At first there was still the sunny road and the toy house; David still stood by the mail-box. Then, as Neilson watched him, he turned away.

'I see him differently,' Neilson thought, 'I am closer to him. I know this man better than I know the others. And in growing closer, we lose the need to talk, to discuss together. So, at this moment, we are, paradoxically, separated. We part, tacitly upon my judgment that he understands; my judgment that held him here and that now sets him free.'

He could see that David walked as a released prisoner would walk, looking trustfully ahead.

"Yes, he goes free," Neilson repeated.

"Why did you hold him?" the guide asked. Neilson looked at the guide. His face was ageing still, but in the lined face his eyes were more innocent than ever; the only youth he had left was in his eyes. Behind him, the Californian landscape dipped and dimmed. This was just a road somewhere, Neilson didn't know where. The sun was still shining.

"Why did you hold him?" He spoke, Neilson thought, in the tone of the examiner, knowing the answer as he asked the question.

"Oh, there were more charges than one. I held him for sloth. It was a kind of fatty degeneration of the soul that set in over those years. He'd grown lazy and half-hopeless. And I held him for his adultery; less for the act itself than because no compulsion of love went with it. Simply for his body's sake, he chose to disturb that person. He could give her little or nothing. And he knew he couldn't. All very well for him to judge Linda because she aroused other people's emotions deliberately. That's what he did himself, that evening."

The guide was drawing a pattern with his staff in the dust of the road. "Any more charges?" he asked equably.

158

"One more. I held him for that moment of blinding, over-whelming relief when he stood with the letter in his hand, knowing Linda was gone. There was nothing in his mind but relief."

"Hardly surprising, was it? Not that it's my business at this stage, or any stage, to cross-examine you. But it was surprising?"

"No. And perhaps, as he grows older, I grow harsher to him. But it did seem to me that he might, even at that second, think of all they'd shared in nearly twenty-five years. No matter how hideously things had changed for them, she was the one love of his life. And he might have pitied her. He'd condemned her emotional course as a system of selfish plundering. Was it? I wonder. I think she looked for love and that she broke at last because even that meaningless child who had seemed to adore her didn't want her after all."

The guide went on drawing in the dust. "From your silences," Neilson said, "you'd appear to disagree."

"Not entirely. But if you expected him to have room for those thoughts at that second, then I'd say you expected much of him."

"I did," said Neilson.

The guide picked up the end of his staff delicately from the dust.

"Naturally I expected much of him. Because, in spite of what he'd become, the other one was there. I couldn't see him all the time in the survival, naturally. But he was there. He was about."

Looking down into the dust, he saw that what the guide had drawn was a perfect circle.

"The other . . ." the guide repeated. It was not a question; it was a peaceful statement. It sounded, Neilson thought, as though honour was satisfied and he was tired. He did not lift his eyes to Neilson's face but went on looking at the full circle.

"The dark, glowing one, I mean; the hopeful one who stands beside him. *You* know, because you told me I should see the Two again, but differently."

"It is well," the guide said, "that you understand."

"How could I not? The balance shifts as he grows older;

the angle of vision changes. Once, he could see clearly what was wrong, what was evil, what was, as the survivor said in the court-room, the devil's work. It was alien to him. It was visible. And now—he sees cloudily, through middle-aged eyes. It's a long time since good and evil began to overlap. In these days, with experience behind him, the issues are hardly ever clear. More's grey than was ever black and white when he was young. When he looks through the settling greyness, he does, occasionally, get a glimpse of absolute good; a flashing glimpse. It surprises him, I think, when it comes . . . When the voice speaks in his ear, when he realises that there are two of him still. It takes him unawares, just as the antagonist used to; and sometimes he fights. But sometimes the other wins, and works for him."

"So." The guide's voice was sharply authoritative. "Will you look at the other now."

Neilson turned. He saw the dark and brilliant face, the eyes with hope in them. He did not think that the bright, untroubled spirit would speak, but the lips moved.

"I worked for him. And so you come now to a different survivor. One who is not yourself."

"Who is it?" Neilson asked him.

"Somebody on a journey where you could not follow. You've forgotten your sorrow and your sense of loss, your endless anxiety for her."

"For Linda."

"Yes. What was that one instant of relief compared with this? Your prayer in the silence was to know. You lay awake and prayed to know. The best of you prayed to share in her unhappiness. And the prayer went unanswered. It is answered now."

The air was changing; the sunlight had gone and there was a pale mist coming about them.

"How can it be answered?" Neilson said.

"You will see her as she was, alone." The bright image began to fade. "And afterwards," it said, its voice growing fainter, "you have summoned the man to whom she turned for help."

As Neilson asked, "Who was that man?" he knew that he dreaded the reply. None came. The image had faded and there was nobody there.

160

"Who was it?" he cried again to the closing mist. It was the guide's voice that answered, "Go and see."

"Now," said Neilson, "I am truly afraid."

"Not yet," said the man with the innocent eyes, "true fear is still to come."

Neilson stepped forward into the mist and it shut him in, like the walls of a room.

LINDA

1955

I

THE room was clean and anonymous. It was hard, on waking, to remember which room this was; which of the first-class motels, with wall-to-wall carpets, television and kitchenette. But there was no need to remember. At morning, most of all, it was important not to remember; the only important thing was to get up and be gone, get to the car. Driving helped your head. At the wheel, for the first hour, you could fool yourself. Almost you could believe that you had left the load behind in the anonymous room with the rumpled sheets, the room that was now stripped and made ready for the next transient. But of course you had not.

The load lay at the bottom of your mind, like a cache of rocks. The rocks awoke you at morning when they began to hit against one another, so that the echo came reverberating up. All night the sleeping-pills kept you from hearing them. Because of being tired, because of taking the pills, the evenings were never as bad as the mornings. And the mornings, once you were out and driving, could be handled. By afternoon, memory took over; you simply drove and remembered. Sometimes you were afraid of that; when you looked at the mileage and saw how far you had driven, an automaton with another landscape in your head. The absorption in memory made you deaf. When you stopped for coffee and a sandwich (How many cups of coffee? How many sandwiches since you started?) you always had to say "What?" to the waitress.

You heard other words all the time. There was the refrain that said, "Keep going, keep going, keep going." Sometimes it got into the wind-shield wipers so that they said it as they swept to and fro. And there was a line of Browning: "Ours is a great, wild country." Why should that line keep you company? It was beginning to acquire the fearful flavour of the journey, so that afterwards, if there was an afterwards, you would only need to say it aloud in order to bring back all this. You talked to yourself about the Browning line, trying to be funny:

'Ours *is* a great, wild country, yes, indeed, goodness me, yes; just look at it, now. How it does go on. America is very large. A *great*, wild country.'

You made it greater and wilder by the route that you took. And you took the route because you were in no hurry to arrive. Why should you be? You had arrived in Oregon, in Wyoming, in South Dakota, in Minneapolis, in Madison, Wisconsin. You had only to keep going and you would arrive somewhere else. Who wanted a terminus, anyway?

Other people, perhaps, had driven across the Continent when they were insane and knew that they were insane. It was not difficult, so long as you knew. You had to know all the time, know what to guard against. Against the desolation at night, against the morning, when the rocks shifted; against the terrible absent-mindedness that could make you do silly things, as on the day when you drove back seventy miles because you had left your wallet on the lunch-counter. You had to keep an eye to the sign-posts; and to the fuel-gauge; it was no use looking just once and trusting yourself; you had to look again and again. And you had to bear the deafness in mind; otherwise people began to bellow. What you could not explain was that if you didn't see them, then you didn't hear them, didn't realise that they were talking to you. Difficult to see them, when you spent so much of the day looking inward, at somebody who wasn't there at all.

You needed to remind yourself to eat; the pain in your head grew worse if you did not eat. All foods tasted alike. 'But we don't, do we——' you said to yourself, trying to be funny, 'want to get into a groove of tuna on white, toasted?' Dinner was easier. The two drinks before it helped. Never more than two, because of wanting to cry.

Despite your careful eating, you were getting noticeably thinner. Your face when you saw it in the glass (you never looked for long) was quite bony; and there was something else disturbing about it; you could see how different the two sides of the face were. One eyebrow was a little higher than

163

the other, giving one side of your forehead more lines than the other side had; your mouth was quite crooked.

There were always too many mirrors in the motels. You caught unwelcome glimpses of yourself at your little labours. ("Electric iron in locker in kitchenette.") It was important, in this madness, to be very clean and very tidy. And to wash and iron in the new room kept you busy, instead of spying for horrors, a snake or a big spider, or a face looking in at you through the window.

You always locked your door as soon as you got inside. Never before had you been so physically afraid. Why were you so much afraid when you only wanted to die? That was an odd one. Here you were with every opportunity. A turn of the wheel at sixty miles an hour would do it. But you didn't do it. It was waiting for you all the time, somewhere ahead. But not today.

When you stopped driving early and there was not enough washing or ironing to keep you busy, you wrote letters. Letters to her and to yourself. You tore them up before you went to bed.

At the motel on the outskirts of Buffalo, where the wall-to-wall carpet, with the curtains, was an unhappy shade of magenta pink, and the pattern on the coverlet humped in the middle, like a spider, you were writing.

"I shall get to New York tomorrow. I must, because, although this was useful at first, it has been going on too long; and it doesn't help the pain in my head as much as it did. What was useful was the feeling of safety, of enclosure that came from moving along all the time, from nobody knowing where I was. Nine days (only nine . . . feels like ninety) has worn that solace out.

"So, time to call a halt. Time to examine my own head. I know, from the symptoms I've observed, that I'm well on the borderline now, if not over it. I must be. Look at it.

"I am Linda Neilson, aged forty-seven, principal instructor in history at Brand University, California; author of two books and God knows how many other publications, theses, articles, surveys, in my own field, nineteenth-century Europe. Up till ten days ago, I was living a full, active and apparently successful life, back in the place where I began.

"I had cut the intervening past, according to my credo.

That is still my credo. A part of one's life that ends as completely as a part of mine ended with my child's death, must not be remembered. It must be annihilated. That way, the pain is killed; that way, life does not defeat one; one learns to defeat life; and to go on.

"If you are strong enough, you can do it. Weak and sentimental people cannot do it; they cannot even try.

"I did it.

"All right. Now it looks to me as though I am doing it again. It is too soon to turn off memory. Driving, one remembers all the time, but I am letting it have its head, letting it wear itself out. It will do that. I shall succeed. I shall forget. I shall never go back.

"In the evenings I think that I will leave the car at the airport next day and fly to her, but in the mornings I know that I shall not. There are two sides to my head (this begins to show in my face now) and I can live in either side, moving over when it suits me. I cannot rest for long in either.

"So, tomorrow, New York. To my friend Reisman on 61st Street? Reisman ready with the couch and the diagnosis that will never be a cure? Reisman first, of course. What other hope have I? My analysis, as he has told me, as I have told myself, was never complete. He has claimed he can complete it. I don't believe a God-damned word of it, but it's the only answer I know. I'll have to give it a chance. Just as long as the money holds out. If the bank acted on that letter I pushed under the door at 7.40 a.m. the day I left, there'll be nineteen hundred dollars waiting for me in New York. Unless David stopped their cashing the bonds on the grounds that I'm insane. As though he would. Poor David. Why do I feel as though he is running after me? I keep seeing his eyes. He will be so much happier without me. I hurt him so. Why can I never stop hurting him?

"Because, my friend, you are, as you have observed, on the borderline, if not over. Tear it all up now. Pills. Bed. Lie down in darkness."

2

This room too was clean and anonymous; a New York hotel room, with everything that one could want, particularly the television-set, which occupied the corner where the best light was, and where Linda would have preferred the dressing-table to be. There was no dressing-table. There were a number of birchwood boxes with ledges that pulled out; there was a bed that halved itself into a neat, narrow divan, with the aid of two sliding ratchets, two roller-cushions and a tightly fitting cover. At night the bedroom looked like a living-room and all day the living-room that it had become hinted at a bedroom.

She went every day to the couch in the room on 61st Street; she returned every night to the divan. All was orderly. The money was there. The letters, from David and from the University, came to her care of Reisman. Reisman opened them, read them and put them in his desk. He gave her their messages about practical things and said that she must soon make up her mind to read them. Linda felt that he was less sympathetic to her on the days when there was a letter from David. She had to tell him this, because she must tell him everything. "I feel you're on his side. I hate you both equally." But it wasn't true; she couldn't hate David, because she felt too sad and guilty about him. Reisman assuring her that she still hated him helped a little.

The explanations were all there, in the unconscious mind, and in the room on 61st Street. They were doing something for her, perhaps. At least her head hurt much less; and she had stopped writing letters to herself. And she dreamed less often that she was still in the car, still driving across the Continent. But the grey limbo endured.

She stood by the window, watching the lights that began to tower up the evening sky; this was a different New York from the city that she had known. She made it so. She was drawing a new map of it, deliberately. The old map was still available. Scattered variously over Manhattan, from the 'Eighties to the Village, there were friends out of the years; people who would be glad to see her again; doors that would open. Familiar restaurants waited. Theatres waited. She had only to pick up the telephone and the old map would begin to unroll.

She left the telephone where it was. She went on drawing the new map, here in the Lower Thirties; she found shops and restaurants where she was unlikely to see a face that she

166

had seen before. Sooner or later, it must happen; this luck couldn't last. Sooner or later some face would split into an incredulous smile and there would be the voice crying, "Why, Linda!"

Sometimes, more than anything in the world, she wanted that to happen.

The television-set, although she cursed it, was becoming a part of the day's programme.

Linda looked at her watch, then turned the knob of the television-set, adjusted the antennæ and sat down before it in the square arm-chair. The ripples broke over the screen.

The commercial was ending and the lush voice and smiling face of the announcer told her, as she had expected, that this week's guest in the 'My Life and Faith' series would be Richard Jay Powers, famous novelist, world-traveller, uffle, uffle, uffle. Linda despised Ricky heartily for the ten years that had gilded him.

At the start of his sky-rocketing, she had been jealous on David's behalf. David never was. She had to hide her opinion that Ricky was only by a hair's-breadth the worse writer of the two and that David, by taking just a turn for the smoother, could have cornered the same market.

Ricky now was a title that stayed at the top of the best-seller list for an indecent number of weeks. Ricky was a record price paid by M.G.M. for the Novel of the Year. Ricky was serials and syndicated stories. There was a continual persecution of gravure pictures that showed his large, grinning face ever larger and grinning more widely. The domed forehead was now quite bald, the soft pagan mouth a whole lot softer. Sometimes the gravure section sent its cameras to Ricky's country home, the model farm in the Hudson Valley, coming up with Ricky in the neighbourhood of a Black Angus. Sometimes the cameras were trained on the Sutton Place penthouse, coming up with Ricky in the neighbourhood of antique furniture, modern pictures and his second wife, who had inherited a million. He had got the divorce from Madeleine when they came back to the United States.

It was impossible, Linda thought, to remember him as he was in England. Had he ever been anything but the All-American Prize Pet? Was it possible that he, who yelled periodically for the dropping of the newest bomb on Russia, had ever been a pacifist? And what had happened to Madeleine and his two sons? "And why——" Linda asked, as the announcer wound up the orgy of Ricky's achievements, "do I have to keep this date with you now? Just out of curiosity and for your irritation value."

And here he was. This week's guest in the 'My Life and Faith' series. Brought to you by . . . (did they have to say it again?) Richard Jay Powers.

The big face shimmered into the frame; sharply lit; domed and jowled; determined with good humour. You could see the sweat standing out on the good humour, Linda thought. Over the years Ricky had worked at his hearth-side manner. "Hello," the face said, twinkling at her, "I'm Ricky Powers." The camera pulled back; a picture of the Hudson Valley Farm filled the screen. "And here's where I live most of the year."

There was the face again, talking about the farm. "Farming's something that's good for a writer to do because it's true and real all the time. Things are happening all the time. Real things." He told an anecdote about a calf. On a farm, Ricky said, the seasons came and went and you were a part of them, not just a part of the publishing season. "But, in my belief, a writer needs the fast-moving life of the city too." And by the fast-moving life of the city (just in case somebody else got the crack in first) he didn't mean the cross-town traffic. What he meant was that Manhattan was a nerve-centre and—maybe here his emotions were a little ahead of his geography—to him it was the centre of the world.

Sometimes a writer needed to be at the centre; sometimes he needed the periphery, which was just a word the Greeks had for the sticks. The smile, Linda thought, was beginning to bulge the screen at the sides.

Now for heresy, Ricky said. This was a heck of a thing to admit and he hoped he wasn't offending any egg-head who might, by mistake, be viewing him, but he, Ricky Powers, was a happy man. He knew it was, by the standards of the intellectual, quite wrong for a writer to be a happy man. Writers, according to that slant, ought always to be agonised —didn't matter by what, just so's they were agonised. "Not me—sorry, fellers."

His recipe for happiness was working regular hours, playing between deadlines, and the pursuit of his avocation, the farm. Did it sound simple? Gradually he turned off the smile until the mouth set in what might, with other equipment, have been stern lines.

"It isn't so simple. It seems so now I've got it; I hardly ever think about it. But I've known unhappiness; deep unhappiness." He leaned forward. "I've known despair," said Richard Jay Powers.

"Now I won't weary you with the details. It all happened more than ten years ago and it's over. But I was down, way down. I'd come to the end of everything; I'd failed. I'd cut the past, and that was right, but I still couldn't face the future. I might say, without wanting to sound melodramatic, that I could see just two ways out. One was when I looked down the barrel of a gun and the other was when I looked down from a window on the thirty-fifth floor. I thought I was through."

"And what did you do?" Linda jeered at the great, awed face. "Take Carter's Little Liver Pills?"

For some minutes, as Ricky began to describe what he called The Climb Back, she thought that he was advocating a religious spell. He talked about being the captain of his soul and he talked about the devil. There was only one devil that plagued a man, the devil of fear.

What emerged was that a doctor, no ordinary doctor, not a psychiatrist either, but a great and good friend, who would cut Ricky's throat tomorrow if his name were mentioned in this talk, had taught him what fear was; and taught him how to master it. "Just so soon as I realised that my fear was simply fear of myself, then it was easy. I found I could skip myself and face the future. The past couldn't hurt me any more; I'd beaten it. I could look ahead. I could go ahead. That's how to be happy, just keep looking ahead. Keep plodding along. Which, as a farmer"—the smile was coming back—"is part of my job. Part of my job as a writer, too. There's rather a beautiful poem—a great favourite of my wife's, by the way. . . ."

Here his voice took holy orders and he began to recite.

169

At Sutton Place the manservant wore the same grey
uniform as that worn by the chauffeur who had called for
Linda in a Cadillac numbered R.J.P. 1. The chauffeur
parked it behind the Cadillac station-wagon numbered
R.J.P. 4. (Two and Three missing, Linda noted; possibly
Five and Six as well. Perhaps they ran into double figures.)

The penthouse was exactly as it appeared in the gravure
section. So was Mrs. Richard Jay Powers. The rooms were
decorated in grey and gold; Mrs. Powers in a vivid make-up,
skilled tailoring and awesomely genuine jewels. Everything
here from the Vlaminck on the grey wall to the collar on the
grey poodle aroused in Linda a sales resistance dating from her
Marxist youth. But Mrs. Powers, who looked all of twenty-
three years old, was not only paying courteous tribute
to Linda's book on the Enlightenment; she had read it. 'The
rich,' Linda quoted to herself grimly, 'are always right.'

"May I say it—you're so much younger than I imagined,
Mrs. Neilson."

(Thank the hairdresser; thank the facial; thank the instinct
that tells me to buy an expensive suit before I seek the company of expensive people.)

"I know you and Ricky have a lot to catch up on. He's
talked of you so often; and I'm going to slide out of the
picture and leave you to it. I've the damnedest committee-
lunch anyway; but I had to meet you. And we both hope
you'll come to the farm for a week-end. And here he is . . ."

He was, Linda admitted, more closely related to the
Ricky of the Devonshire days than the gravure section let
him be. After his wife had gone, he looked all around his
expensive shell and back to her, grimacing comically.
"What d'you know? Honestly—what do you know?" said
Ricky. "And I won't pretend I don't like being stinking
rich. I do. I'm happy, Linda."

"So I heard and saw," she reminded him. He fluttered his
eyelashes. "How *you* of all people, happened to be watching
that. It wasn't *all* crap," he added wistfully. "Some of it
made sense."

"And, as I told you, aroused my curiosity."

"Just assuage mine, will you, please? Why are you in
New York? My guess is a high-powered historians' con-

vention. I always wanted to know—do educationalists get as drunk when they convene as the lower echelons do? And does David come with you, making like Elk's wife?"

"I've left David, Ricky. We're not together any more."

Ricky's plentiful face sagged. "You're not? Is this permanent?"

"Yes."

"You, too. I'm sorry, Linda. I know what hell it is; I should know. Let's have a drink, shall we?"

"Not for me," she said. "I'm not in the best shape for drinking, these days."

"Let me look at you. You're very unhappy."

"Yes."

"On account of this?"

"On account of . . . well, you said it yourself . . . of having come to the end of everything."

He patted her shoulder. "Ah, but you're not like me. You're brave—damned brave; you always were. I know how you took Anne's death. Tell you who told me—he was in France when it happened and——"

"I don't talk about that, Ricky. Or think about it. That thing happened to somebody else, not to me. Like you, I've cut the past."

Ricky made himself a double dry martini, explaining that he made it a rule not to drink in the middle of the day except on special occasions. At the martini's instigation, he began to tell her about his parting from Madeleine. It fitted chronologically with his televised despair, with the gun-barrel view and the skyscraper view. It was, she saw, a story whose anguish was wrapped in the obscurity of one person's psychological trauma, just as her present anguish was.

"And, of course, we were married in a Catholic church; not that I ever turned Catholic, but the kids were brought up as Catholics. And the damnable thing about all that is that when it comes to the breaking-point it suddenly matters. Or seems to matter. I went through hell—*real* hell. I knew I'd lose my mind if I went on living with her and it looked as though I'd lose my mind just as fast if I quit. Well, I did quit and I did lose my mind. It's one hell of a thing to do, to walk out on your children. I couldn't sleep; I couldn't work; I was down to a hundred and forty pounds in weight and I was drinking myself silly . . . Linda, I do know what you're going through. I know what it did to me."

"What," Linda asked dryly, "happened to Madeleine?"

He looked a little shocked; as though, she thought, she had interrupted his story of being run over by asking if the car suffered any damage. "Madeleine—oh, she's fine, she's over it. She went back to Europe and the boys are up at Oxford. But that religion of hers is the very devil," Ricky said moodily. "In her view we're still married and always will be, and what I have with Primula is a bigamous attachment."

When the grey-uniformed manservant and a maid in grey with a lemon organdie apron had finished serving them, they reached the point. Linda led to it by way of Reisman and the couch. Ricky flapped his hand exasperatedly. "Reisman's no good to you, darling; he's no good to any of us. And he's a highway robber. As to which," he said, pouring another glass of the hock that had followed the martinis in salute to the special occasion, "how are you for dough?"

"I'm living on my savings, such as they are. I can keep going for a while."

"We'll talk about that. Or rather we won't talk, we'll fix it. Linda, here's what I see . . ." He pushed back his chair a little way. "You and I are quite a lot alike. We always were. You're a serious person and so am I. The fact that you're an educationalist and I'm just a best-seller doesn't, I quote, signify. We were both crazy idealists, once. Which is right, which is how it ought to be, just so's one matures out of that. We've both thought things through pretty thoroughly since we began thinking at all. I might almost say we've worked at living. . . ."

He savoured the phrase. "Worked at living, studied the art of it on more than one map. Our patterns are alike, too. Pulling up the European stakes and coming home. I really do feel that the United States is home. That isn't just crap for the public either . . . It's a crazy country, but we're Americans, you and I. We think violently; we feel violently. Violent things happen to us and we make violent things happen . . . Turbulence is our heritage."

He paused. She could see him thinking, 'Now, *there's* a title.' He repeated it. "It's a natural to us, a natural growth

172

from our volcanic emotional soil." He looked pleased about that, too. "People don't have to fight for their emotional existence in Europe because Europe's half-dead. This is alive; this is our place; this is home—don't you feel it?"

"Nowhere," said Linda, "is home right now. It's all just one damned limbo."

"I know that," he said quickly, "it was like that for me . . . But I'll promise you something. Want to know what it is? That there's a whole new beautiful life ahead—and waiting for you. I promise you. You'll laugh again—you'll fall in love again——"

"God forbid," said Linda.

"You will," said the innocent Ricky. "And you'll work. You'll be the great human being you really are."

"I am not a great human being. Please don't kid yourself."

"Yes you are. And you don't need that monkey-faced Jew to adjust you. Adjustment—what dat? Do you believe in adjustment? All who believe in adjustment—please clap your hands."

"There I'm with you, Ricky. Psychiatry isn't the answer any more. It used to be. Now I've come to the end of it."

"I did, too. When I was down in the depths. I took one last crack at it—didn't help." His smile held a secret now; he was producing his effect by way of the story-line. "In fact I was still in the hands of that smooth son-of-a-bitch when I met Primula. At a cocktail-party. The funny thing was—I was pretty drunk but I knew she wasn't drinking. There stood this beautiful girl not drinking . . . Primula says the first thing I ever said to her was, 'Tell me, are you happy? You look happy.'" Tears stood in Ricky's eyes. "Funny thing," he repeated caressingly, "I don't remember it. But that's what I said." He remained silent for a moment in benediction. "But the next morning," said Ricky, "I was in Russ Jones's office. Primula took me there."

4

The Cadillac was waiting outside Russ Jones's office. It was a three-hour drive from Manhattan to the farm in the Hudson Valley. On this Friday, as on all the other Fridays, Ricky and Primula, having departed in the station-wagon at noon, had left R.J.P. 1 for Linda. They would not let her take the train until she was stronger. Not, they added scrupulously, that she didn't look wonderful already. She looked a different person.

Osborn, the grey-uniformed driver, who was a chum by now, seemed to subscribe to this view. He said it was nice to see her look so well. He was an elderly, Nanny-ish person and he helped her into the car as though she were truly an invalid. Linda wondered regularly whether Osborn had any idea of what went on in Russ Jones's office. Fortunately the distance between the back seat and the driving-seat made talk impracticable: all the same, she pressed the button that raised the glass between them.

It was hot now. The afternoon temperature was somewhere up in the eighties, with a forcible humidity. But the car was air-cooled and Linda liked the week-end drive as much as she liked anything that was happening to her in this new and peculiar world. Osborn had put the evening papers beside her. She glanced through them drowsily as they drove across town. The drowsiness was one of the natural results of the treatment. It was amiable enough when you got used to it. Only occasionally now did she feel a panic of resentment at living in a slight haze. It was, as the Powerses said and as she could see when she looked in the glass, doing her an immense amount of good. (A surprising, an illogical, amount of good, her intellect added waspishly. Her intellect was not an easy convert to Russ Jones.)

She was making progress. According to Russ she had reached the half-way point. Or just about that. He was still careful to be indefinite about the time that the cure would take. He gave her no more shots; and, from today, he was decreasing the pills. And she could, if she liked, stay in the country through Monday; the longest gap between treatments yet. "You can always call me if you want to. I'll be here." Russ worked through every week-end.

Linda looked at her own week-end, lying ahead. It would be, as all the week-ends were, a cocoon of physical comfort. (Cocoon was the word that came to mind most often when thinking about her present life.) The house-guests were usually bearable. Both Ricky and Primula understood that she was immune to Bridge, Scrabble and Canasta. When she wanted it, she had one of the guest-houses to herself. Ricky had built a number of guest-houses. Privacy, Ricky said at intervals, was the only really precious thing that money could buy. When he said that, Linda found herself looking at Primula's diamonds. One had not, despite the new life, lost one's confirmed disapproval of the very rich.

It was kept alive—in part—by the company of Russ Jones's patients. Russ, as Ricky was never tired of reminding her, charged his patients exactly what they could afford, which meant, Ricky said, that a third of them paid seventy-five cents a visit and another third came for free. 'So, talking to them in the waiting-room,' Linda thought, 'I plug the fact of being a teacher and soft-pedal the penthouse.' She was embarrassed when the Cadillac came right up to the door and the patients could see it through the waiting-room window. She made punctual references to "These old friends of mine who are looking after me—who are so very good to me." And why not, after all? It was true.

Hence the cocoon, spinning as the days passed, and swaddling her away from memories of California; softening the horrors of the nightmare drive; mellowing the smaller box-nightmare of the hotel room, Reisman's couch and the television-set; which became, in this perspective, merely the prelude to relief.

The thought of David was now almost manageable. She read his letters and saw him through the haze of wisdom given to her by Russ Jones. She no longer feared the letters. At the sight of his handwriting, she did the exercise that Russ recommended. He said, "Don't fight the feeling; let it come; let it come all the way up to the top of your mind, and then slide over it."

She took from her wallet the letter that had come this morning.

"Yes, I must accept what you say; that you are firm in your decision to cut the past completely. Since I'm included in the past, I'll try not to write to you any more. (I do worry about you, darling; I can't not; and I wish—though I know it's an idle wish—that I could help you—some way—somehow. You are always in my prayers. I am grateful to know that you are being well looked after.)

"But, Linda, I have to say this, at the risk of infuriating

175

you. Cutting the past is an impossible piece of surgery. You can move on from the past; you can plough it under so that good things grow; but the cutting is beyond human power.

"I know that this is what you have tried, with great courage, to do ever since Anne's death. Because I was never able to try with you (I could not have fought to annihilate those memories even had I wanted to) we have ceased to be companions. There is no 'us' any more. But there *was* an 'us'. You cannot annihilate that. Please don't try. It might, in your view, be brave to try. But it is the brave effort of the last five years that has, in your phrase, made the machine break down. I cannot bear to think of you fighting to forget the person whose name you ask me not to mention, the love that has hurt you this year. Must you? Time will deal gently with this, as with all things, if you wait."

Linda folded the letter and summoned the voice of Russ Jones, saying, "Cut the past . . .? Good idea. Most of us carry too much of that luggage around . . . After all, you, as an historian, ought to be able to pigeonhole it easily enough."

Poor David. No, she thought, I will not let him be poor David. He begins to be free now, just as I am on my way to freedom.

She glanced again at the opening of the letter, giving her the last of the practical details. The sale of the house was complete. She had given him *carte blanche* to sell their possessions with it. The letter said, "I have kept a few books, and one or two things that we liked; among them your French soldiers; tell me if you want them." The statement and cheque would reach her from their accountant. He himself was moving East. Would she write, if she needed him, care of his literary agent in New York? As to the divorce, he asked her to wait another six months at least, so that she should be sure.

Why did that run a knife under her ribs? Because she was not yet sure? She thought back, to the Registrar's office in the Euston Road, the man in the blue suit saying, "I pronounce you man and wife." Aunt Rachel frowning below her flowered busby and asking, "But *are* you married? He mumbled so."

'Not back to there; it is foolish,' Linda said to herself. She put the letter in her wallet again. David implied that Joshua

176

Phillips had cut short his contract. Or perhaps he had handed in a tactful resignation. It was no trouble to think about the University; she could look back to there across the solid bridge that Russ had begun to build for her; she could recall, deliberately and without emotion, the local newspapers reporting her retirement; the paragraphs that talked of complete nervous prostration; the stately letters of regret.

All over; all gone.

And inside the cocoon, Russ promised, as Ricky had promised, a new and useful person was being made. "And I promise it, too," said Linda.

The high resolution endured through the haze.

It was, her flickering sense of satire informed her, a little more difficult to keep the high resolution in sight from the windows of an air-cooled Cadillac. She drowsed until they reached the farm. The car came past the careful fields, the creamy-white buildings and the black cattle, to the white-walled house with the rounded and turreted towers. Ricky's architect had taken the design of a *château-ferme* in the Loire country. There were pink and blue hydrangeas growing around the house; there were tall elms; the sprinklers kept the grass green.

This week-end, the manservant told her, Mrs. Powers had thought that Mrs. Neilson would be more comfortable in the blue room; the air-cooler in the guest-house was only a little one.

Better, she thought, to face the party at once. Not because Ricky or Primula expected it of her; they never did; she was testing herself. She went through the stunning coolness of the high rooms to the veranda and the indoor pool, where they were drinking and sounding like a dozen. In fact there were only three guests, in the usual ratio, two of Primula's friends to one of Ricky's. There was a steady uniformity about Primula's friends. The men were well-dressed and civilised, players of golf and the markets. Many dry martinis had gone to the making of their complexions and the tinge of their eyes. Linda did not know whether she had met this one before or whether he was just a duplicate. The wife followed the pattern of the wives, sleek and shrill, fluent enough to sound as though there were a brain below the bleach. The third guest, Ricky's friend, was a man. (The week-end parties followed the mating rule; Linda never found herself unprovided for.) He was a lanky and shaggy creature, with solemn blue eyes. "This is Job Vale," Primula said, and she was none the wiser. Ricky passed her a beaker of tomato-juice. She sat, as usual, silently looking down the slope of the garden towards the river. She never made the centre-piece of a party now; nor did she want to. The haze made them all into a brightly-coloured panel; people in a coloured movie. She stayed with them only a few minutes before she went to her room.

Looking with a hazy but ruthless eye upon the sum-total of luxury here, she began to do the Russ Jones exercise again. She let the feeling come all the way up to the top of her mind and prepared to slide over it. It was not, in itself, important; but he encouraged her to do the exercise with any feeling that recurred; and this recurred obstinately. It did not scream, 'I must get out.' That compulsion, Russ told her, need not come again. But it asked coolly, distinctly, 'What am I doing in this place—where I don't belong?'

Before she made the answer, 'I am staying here, as in a convalescent home, until I am well,' Linda stared at the source of doubt. That wasn't in the Russ Jones drill-book; he discounted the source; the feeling alone was the enemy. Linda stared at it all the same.

To come into this room, as into her room at Sutton Place, finding her clothes cared for and put ready, finding in bed-room and bathroom everything that a sybarite could conceivably ask, was to be at once shocked and beguiled. Much as she enjoyed the peak of luxury, she could not settle for it. Why not? A perverse social instinct? A worker's reaction? An inherent belief in the moderate? Or just a natural inability, since she was not born to this, to take it for granted? In another time she might have said, "Spoil the Egyptians," have taken their gifts and jeered at them inside. But the pills left her too gentle to jeer. So she stood, uncertain, rejecting the word Mammon because of its enforced association with the word God. After a while she completed the Jones exercise and slid over the feeling.

She was bathed, powdered, scented and in her dressing-gown before the looking-glass, when Primula knocked at her door.

"Just to say Hello. You're not too tired? Ricky thought you might like to eat up here."

"Heavens, no, darling. I'm not tired at all."

"You don't look it. Russ is pleased with you, I'll bet. . . . How was it today?" Primula asked. "Talk—or just treatment and out again on the conveyor-belt?"

"We talked. He gave me a good report-card—cut down the pills and all."

"Oh, wonderful," Primula said.

"He made me laugh a lot, too. I really do like and admire him more every day." (Would you say, by any chance, that he was slowly wearing down your integrity? Not to Primula, you wouldn't. . . .)

"I believe he's the only really great man I ever met," said Primula. "And I know he saved Ricky's life. I mean it. Ricky was damn' near suicide, nearer than he himself realises now, poor old sweetheart; and naturally. Bad enough to be tied to somebody you don't love without having religion thrown in. Nobody but Russ could have gotten *those* feelings out of the way. At least you're lucky there, darling."

"I know it. I'm always so thankful. Thankful I've no religion to clutter me." She had said it before; there was no need to recall David replying, "I'm always sorry I've so much me to clutter my religion."

"Not," she added, "that I wasn't plenty cluttered without it, two months ago. Dear Primula . . . I am so very grateful to you."

"That adjective's out; house-rule, remember?" The vivid mask flashed a smile at her. "Linda, just brief me about something. Ricky doesn't know the protocol either. This fellow Job Vale . . . quite an old buddy in the publishing world—though we both feel he's getting too highbrow to live . . . Apparently he's just changing his——"

"Sex?" asked Linda.

"No, darling. I don't believe he has one. He's changing his firm . . . going to David's firm of publishers."

"Fortunately for him," Linda said, painting her lips, "they've other authors besides David on their list or they couldn't afford to pay him a salary."

Primula giggled. One of her endearing qualities, Linda thought, was to greet your thinnest comedy-line as though you were Bob Hope.

"When we told him you were coming, he got all excited on account of he has a passion for David's work."

"*Eh?*"

"And he longs to talk to you about it; he pines for David to write again—admires him so much—thinks he's much underrated. D'you care? Ricky asked him to lay off; he said it wasn't liable to be your favourite subject."

"Oh, he can talk," Linda said indifferently.

"It won't rattle you?"

"Those who frequent Russ don't rattle, as you should know. Not," said Linda, powdering the sides of her nose, "that I can tell him much. Except that, from the way things have gone for the last five years, we're all likely to be spared David's next book."

Primula's laugh was not enough to stop her hating herself for the compulsion to pan David. She saw his eyes. As a rule now, the haze hid them. Primula was saying, "How can a writer *live* without writing? That's what I don't understand."

"How can anyone live without working?" Linda said. "That's what *I* don't understand. . . ."

It was a tactless remark to make to Primula, or any of Primula's kind. She would have given much to take it back. Worse, it seemed to her that here, in the cocoon, she had lost the right to think it.

5

Linda came out of Russ Jones's office and walked east. She passed the church, where at any hour of the day there were people going up the steps, or coming down. She went on walking. It was the first cool day of this September. 'Change coming,' said the thought in her mind, and she felt young and adventurous. The tremor of anticipation for the talk with Ricky was no trouble. She was alive again. She had said that to Russ.

Ricky, her sense of satire informed her, would take her news well, because he had come to look upon Russ Jones as though Russ were Everest and he, Ricky, was Sir John Hunt. She herself, doing this thing, would also become Ricky's personal achievement. But there were words that must not be said. And she would not say them. She could hope only that he would not see her thinking them.

She took a taxi to Sutton Place. Cadillac R.J.P. 1 was outside the door. Osborn, standing beside it, said, "Good evening, Mrs. Neilson." The doorman said, "Good evening, Mrs. Neilson." If the last five months had not made her feel, as Ricky and Primula wanted her to feel, that the farm and the penthouse were her two homes, they had at least induced a habit. The thought of breaking out of the cocoon (the gilded cage, the doll's-house, or what-have-you?) set up a disproportionate alarm. How would it feel to live alone again, in a place that belonged to oneself, remembering to buy groceries and put out the garbage? 'One may find,' Linda said to herself, 'that one's housekeeping instincts have atrophied.'

She went through the grey and gold rooms, with the poodle following her plaintively. Primula was away and the poodle grieved like a widower. Ricky, on the other hand, emerging from his study half an hour before time, did not. Ricky seemed to have swollen and to emit luminous rays. With reason. Clyde Brewer had bought his new novel for serialisation. On six chapters and a synopsis. Clyde and Menella would be here in a little while to discuss some changes suggested by their team of editors. "Only *tiny* ones," said Ricky. He careened about the room, singing, "Oh, what a beautiful morning." He pulled her out on to the terrace, where he stood under the striped awning, waving his arms at the sky and threatening to turn a handspring on the parapet. "Come, come," Linda said; "this is no moment for indulging the skyscraper view." She thought that it suited Ricky to be crazy for himself. Utter simplicity came down on him.

"Literally the biggest price they ever paid. No kidding. I said what about Maugham, but Clyde said it was ahead of Maugham's price and I think he's playing straight. No point in his not. I could easily check. Let's open up the champagne." Champagne splits were lined ready on the drink-table.

Linda accepted the glass. There was need for a change of gear, when you had something to tell the person who got in first by having something to tell you.

181

"Ricky, I want to get this said before the Brewers come. I think it'll please you. I've been plotting it a long time. Only I didn't feel I should talk before it was a *fait accompli*. And it is now. I'm going to work for Russ."

It was all right. It was as she had expected. Here was all the noise, here were all the adjectives that she had expected.

"He's very sweet—he insists I say 'work with' and not 'work for'."

She might, she thought, listening to Ricky, be going to marry Russ Jones.

"It is the thing I want to do and I think I can do it. When I'm in my senses, which—thanks to him—I am, I'm pretty intelligent with people."

Ricky reminded her, among other things, that she was a great human being. Russ had no such illusion; he had said solemnly that this was a generous decision, coming from somebody of her achievements; and added, "If you find it's driving you to drink you'll tell me, won't you?"

"You see, Ricky, of all the answers I've tried to find, this one makes the most sense to me. I was sceptical at the beginning. But I do know now it's a thing I've been looking for since I was seventeen and started crusading against the sellers of fear. Russ is a seller of courage; *and* a seller who'll give his product away." She stopped and laughed. "Me—telling you what Russ is!" she said. "Anyway, I know I'll be happier helping with that work than with anything else I could do."

"I'm terribly glad, Linda. Terribly, terribly glad."

Now there had to be the rest of it. In her mind she shuffled and discarded useful clichés: 'Living my own life.' No. 'Preserving my independence.' No. (And nothing about one's old chum integrity, either, because that would bring one close to saying the words that must not be said.) The truth was simple. And the truth would hurt him.

Could she speak truthfully, she would say this:

'I'm taking an apartment of my own; a walk-up in the village that I've seen and that I can afford on the salary from Russ. I have to leave you. Not only because it will feel all wrong to live here and be driven to the office in the Cadillac, to work among those shipwrecked people all day and come back to find my evening-clothes put out for me. Not only because, at forty-seven, I oughtn't to be living with you and Primula like an adopted daughter.

'If I could be detached about it, I'd settle for it because you're both genuinely fond of me and you get pleasure from my company. That's true. It is vulgar, isn't it, to go on noticing the material assets I receive in exchange, the free board and bath-essence? But I do go on noticing them, thinking about them, worrying over them . . . Lord knows how many weeks it is since I paid for a drink or a telephone-call or a dress come back from the cleaners.

'But even that's not all of it. I have to leave you because, for some reason I can't fathom, I cannot take the society of very rich people indefinitely. I know it isn't their fault they're rich; and that being rich needn't stop anyone from being nice, but they aren't my kind and I am not their kind. And I never lose that feeling. I suppose it is bourgeois and foolish. But it means I mustn't go on living here.'

Since she could not say it, she said that she could now afford an apartment of her own, and Ricky had begun to bellow that neither he nor Primula would hear of it, when the Clyde Brewers arrived.

Linda had seen them more than once, in California. She saw that, for the first moment now, they did not recognise her. "Out of my context, you see," she explained smoothly, while Clyde and Menella insisted that it wasn't that; it was that they never saw anybody so much changed; so young and beautiful—and with a sort of (did Linda mind Menella saying this?) a sort of new, wonderful awareness.

'I might be sick,' Linda thought. Listening to the hyphenated talk, she decided that she was indulging Brewer-resistance. Clyde, she observed, still had the smugness of Little Jack Horner, and Menella still looked like a big, laughing rocking-horse. "And I hear David's down to a new book—that's wonderful," said Clyde. "Young Job Vale was telling us only last week."

"That little hideaway hotel sounds a wonderful place for creative work," Menella frothed and clashed. "How do you like it there?"

Linda was sorry for them now. (But what was this cold, creeping discomfort in her mind, this sensation of a string that pulled and hurt her?) She said, "Don't let it embarrass

183

you; David and I have separated," while Ricky joined in heartily, "Linda lives with us now; she'll tell you about the wonderful job she's just taken on," and the Brewers plunged up and down like dolphins in seas of apology. Not content to apologise, they sympathised. Deeply, as though David were dead.

This, Linda decided, was a reader-reaction. The Brewers themselves moved in the world of matter-of-fact divorce. But in a Brewer magazine story it was a tragedy that never happened. A marriage, in a Brewer magazine story, must endure. It might show mistaken signs of cracking half-way through, but it was always riveted reliably again by the last paragraph.

She found herself saying that she and David were still good friends. "But we never were good correspondents, either of us." (Another lie. And why this violent compulsion to know where he was? It didn't matter where he was. She would never see him again. No reason for this pang because he was writing a book and she not there. No reason to remember the yellow foolscap, the two pens, the leaden frog sitting beside the inkpot; his voice saying humbly, "Want to hear?" and his profile turned from her while he told it, as though he watched the story happen in the air; no need to remember, "You're the only person I can ever tell them to. You always have been. Thank you for listening.")

The Brewers were now straining considerably to change the subject, but she kept on. Where was the hotel?

Menella thought that Job Vale had said Putnam, Connecticut. The place belonged to that woman poet who lived in California: what was her name? Janet Something.

DAVID

1956

I

THE snow lay deep. The colours changed with the coming of late afternoon. He watched the blue shadows of the trees turn to grey; the sky behind the trees glowed and the fading sunlight struck the last flashes from the ice-puddles on the path. He had helped Hunter dig the path through to the road; it was a deep trench and the edges of it, sharply sliced, were frozen solid. On the eave of Hunter's white-capped toolshed the long, hanging icicle glinted like a diamond blade; a moment more and it would be dull glass. The garden was a world of silence; and a world of small movements, the wings of the catbirds and towhees who came to Mary's wooden table for food; a wind-flurry swaying the trees; a lurch of snow from the branches.

At this hour he saw the garden cloudily; the inner windows were steaming up. Double windows, storm doors, the pipes and the oil heater made the porch impenetrably warm. The thick air smelt of his cigarettes. When he came down here at morning, Mary hoped that he would not be cold. When she brought his tea she hoped that he wasn't suffocating.

David looked at his watch; the minute-hand had again performed its trick of swinging around the face with the rapidity of the needle on a compass. An instant back, it had pointed half-past three; now it pointed half-past four. Between then and now there lay five rewritten pages.

He switched on the lamp. The fresh light sharpened the table, with the yellow foolscap, the leaden frog and the inkpot. He collected the new pages and laid them face downward, without reading. From the other foolscap pile he pulled off the top pages, the old scribbled sheets, and began to read; he was already unfamiliar with these, written last November. He went down and in.

"Excuse me. I did knock, Mr. Neilson," Mary said apologetically; she stood just beyond the lamplight, carrying the tea-tray. David came up out of his smoky stupor. ("If I exploded a firecracker behind you," Hunter said, "you wouldn't hear it." Hunter enjoyed telling the story of coming on to the porch to ask David if there were anything he wanted in Putnam. When, according to Hunter, he came back on to the porch with David's mail, David had said, "Oh, I forgot—could you buy me some razor-blades while you're there." "While I'm where?" "In Putnam." "David, I'm back. I've been back nearly an hour." "Oh, sorry, I thought you said you were just off." "That was four hours ago," said Hunter.)

Mary would always knock and always expect him to answer. She kept all her English deferences, including the habit of calling him 'Mr. Neilson', where Hunter had called him 'David' from the beginning. Mary was a pretty woman, fair and placid as a cow. She reminded him of an A.T.S. corporal who had been his clerk before he went overseas.

There were, in this life, other reminders of war. There was the severance from a past pattern; familiarity coming down upon the new pattern and the new company, until they assumed a look of permanence, as though they had been there always. There was the routine that made a rhythm. There was the strangely comfortable and solid feeling of being essentially alone. Because there were no longer any close ties, any emotional demands from outside, the reserve-tanks of energy, strength and peace were filling.

Mary poured out his tea. She sniffed the dubious air and asked him if he would like her to open something, for example the door into the hall. She told him that more snow was on the way, and hoped that the train would not be late. "The train?" he said vaguely, his eyes on the page in front of him.

"Miss Janet's train from New York . . ."

Guiltily he met her reproachful eyes.

"Today's Thursday, Mr. Neilson."

"I thought it was Wednesday. It feels like Wednesday."

Mary said patiently, "I thought perhaps you'd both like to have dinner in the sitting-room?" For her it was always the sitting-room, never the living-room. "The fire's nice, and you'll be cosier there."

"Thank you—yes—nice," he said vaguely. It was unkind of him to wish that this evening were going to be the same as last evening, as all the evenings since October; eating his early dinner alone; going to his room; in the routine he shifted his ground at eight and worked upstairs till midnight, or after. There was a break at ten o'clock, when Hunter brought him the last cup of tea; Hunter put a can of beer for himself on the tray and they talked a little while.

'Nice to have Janet to talk to,' David said to himself and then wondered if he meant it. With Mary he talked of England, or of the birds and the garden. With Hunter he talked of war and peace, of the fighting-fields that they had in common, the desert and Italy. He could talk of religion with either; Mary was a steady Catholic; Hunter's Catholicism was tempered with the suspicion that God winked an eye at the rules. What else did one need, really, in the way of conversation? David thought that this was now enough for him; he felt a reluctance for more. A curmudgeonly mood began to creep on him. Meaningless irritations danced into view. Peevishly he supposed that he should change his sweater for a shirt and a jacket. That meant putting on a tie.

"Shut up," he said aloud; he gulped his tea, lit another cigarette and resumed the process like putting on a diver's helmet and going under.

An hour slipped past and he came up again; stretching, rising on his cramped legs to empty the butts out of the ashtray. Now, because he let it, the echo of a shapeless music came in. Hunter was playing the juke-box in the bar; there were windows between the bar and the porch and when the regulars began arriving Hunter would draw the curtain to screen him off. At the moment, the bar was still deserted, save for Hunter, large, blond and lonely, playing the juke-box. David looked through the glass, into the long room where the log fire crackled and the pine walls shone. Since he was not drinking, he saw the bar more often in this perspective than in any other.

From the juke-box, the crooner, as usual, was moaning "Ha-aa-app-y". The crooners patronised by Hunter always sang about being happy; either they were, because some-body loved them, or they were not because somebody didn't. Hunter despised them, "but with me it's a reflex," he explained, dropping the nickel into the swollen, coloured machine. Mary called it "that nasty thing again".

A regular came in: Mike Field, who owned the garage on the corner where the road joined Route 101. Hunter came to draw the curtain; not before David had seen the look on Mike's face that made him feel as though he were a rare animal in a zoo. Once, when Hunter left the window open, David had heard Mike saying, "You'd think he'd use a typewriter. Wouldn't you? Wouldn't he be able to go much faster on a machine?" and Hunter replying, "No, he wouldn't."

"Why wouldn't he?"

"Because he can't type."

The crooner moaned "Ha-appy" for the last time, scraped and subsided. David picked up the pen. Hunter was controlling his reflex; there was no more music, only the two voices, low, receding—gone.

2

Janet's considerate message kept him safe until seven. As always, when he had set the table in order, switched off the lamp, and shut the door, he felt that he left a piece of himself behind on the foolscap. He walked down the hall, moon-struck and incapable.

The living-room door was open. It faced the bar, on the opposite side of the hall. Tonight this made a blue-print of the Golden Dragon in the Devonshire town of Harloe; with the war talk in the saloon and the Jewish family smiling at him as he came out. Since he wrote of the past all day, he was subject to confusions of time. Alone, he would think often that time was surrendering, that soon he would be able to step from Now into Then, walking in wherever he pleased, appointing the place and the hour. It was one of the fantasies that he could not indulge tonight; one of the games that he might not play.

The room, all the same, had an obstinate look of the past. Due, he thought, to something in the pattern of Mary's chintz, besides her pictures of Corfe Castle and Winston Churchill. Mary won out over the pine walls, the New England wheelback chairs and the Cape Cod lighter. In this room he might be excused for misreading Time. But Janet, standing before the fire, reminded him sharply that he was here and that this was now.

"Good evening, David."

As in October, she was trying not to look too pleased. Still she contrived to suggest that all the light had come on suddenly in a dark place.

He felt mean for noticing how palpably her soft, wild hair had been set and lacquered; it made blue-black curves that would soon be lost; she must have had it done in New York today. She wore a scarlet suit and a white sweater. The sculptured face was pale with the poet's cliché, but the lips matched the suit. He wondered for how long she had stood here, tense and tidy, awaiting the sound of his footstep. Her drink was untouched; the jigger of whisky, the Club soda and the ice were ranged beside the ginger-ale that she had ordered for him.

Once she had taken a swallow, she said, "Do you mind my coming?"

"Oh, honestly, Janet . . ."

"No need for honesty, chum. I didn't do it because you might want to see me. I did it because I wanted to see you. A selfish excursion." She took another swallow and asked, "How does it go?"

"The book?"

"Certainly, the book."

"Oh, better . . . More like an illness than a creative job; sometimes I'm writing it; sometimes it's writing me. But I've almost stopped fussing. I was so terribly slow—till this week. Now I'm past the rough; into the beginning of the rewrite. Half-way-house."

"Good," said Janet.

"That depends on the second half," he said warily.

"But it sounds as though the rust were off the rails."

"I believe it is—most of the rust, anyway." He added, "Thanks to you."

"To me . . . What have I done, except introduce you to this odd blend of roadhouse and English pub?"

"You wanted me to write again."

"So did everybody."

"Not vocally."

"Linda did," said Janet, "I've heard her."

"Oh . . . in a cross sort of way, yes. And equally no. Made another good stick to beat me with, the fact that I wasn't working. Poor darling, that was her state of mind."

"Was . . .?"

"Well, I can only suppose it was."

"I meant . . ." her eyes were afraid. "Nothing's changed, has it? You haven't heard?"

"I've heard nothing. Nothing at all. Since last June. This is February, no?"

"This is February, yes."

"Well, that makes eight months of silence."

"Do you still mind?"

"I still worry." His reply was automatic. A voice inside his head asked damnably, 'Do you? Are you sure? Isn't that a line? When did you last see your worry?' Janet was saying, "How's money? You must tell me."

"Bless you. No, I mustn't, get that clear. But I will, because it's all right."

She scowled. "Seriously—would you not take a loan from me if you needed one?"

"At the risk of hurting you—no, I wouldn't."

"Why not?"

"Blame Aunt Rachel, if you blame anyone. What a gentleman does—or does not—do. It's an early training," he said, "so I've forgotten the details. As I recall, one is a gentleman about women and money, about opening doors and keeping one's mouth shut. Ask me no more, for fear I can't reply."

"It is very stupid."

"Maybe. But I promise you. I don't need money. I couldn't be living more cheaply. I say that to Mr. Vale every time he dangles a royalty-advance in front of me."

"He still does?"

"Oh yes. Every twenty-eight days. Along with a request for the opening chapters, when ready. I wonder," David said, "if his patience is a quality induced by his being christened Job."

"Does he know that it isn't a novel?"

David stared at her. After a moment, he said, "No. And how the devil do you?"

"Hunch," said Janet.

It was, he decided, as discomforting as one of Aunt Rachel's thought-reading invasions.

"Not a novel . . . that's what you know?"

"Yes."

"All right . . . what sort of book? Let's have the results of your divining-rod." In spite of himself, his voice sounded sulky.

"Certainly not. None of my business," said Janet.

"Tell me what you think."

She shook her head.

After dinner, as soon as they were drinking their coffee by the fire, she looked at the clock. "By nine-fifteen I'll be in bed. With a whole new, unexplored thriller. The *beauty* of early bed and a thriller . . . Something one never does at home."

"You're not leaving me tactfully alone—to work—by any chance?"

"But of course," she said impatiently. She clutched her chin and gazed at him, frowning until she had made a vertical pleat between her eyebrows. "What . . . ?" he said to the frown.

"You're *quite* a different person. From the Californian one —the one I fell in love with. And this one," she said solemnly, "pleases me more."

"This one drinks less," David offered.

"That's not important. I'm all for the wagon—as I'm all for any mortification—in theory," she added, beginning to tug at her hair. "But you could still be drinking and be different; different because you're a writer again. A person with a rendezvous. Does it ever occur to you how lucky we are? Because of that? . . . Doesn't matter what God does to us—or love—or money—or the weather. If work's all right, then everything is. And if work isn't, then life has a hole in it —and nobody can stop up the hole for us . . . nobody."

"It is, as you suggest, a selfish trade."

"But I don't believe," said Janet, "that it was ever selfish enough for you. Till now. I just don't."

"You don't, eh?"

"No. You've always let love in—and let the world in. Till now." She was wrecking the New York hairdresser's achievement. "Isn't that true, David?"

"I wonder."

"I'll swear it is." She leaned towards him, in the young thrusting likeness of herself twenty years ago. "Look . . . only five minutes past nine and I could be very embarrassing. I could put the direct question. I could ask, 'Do you need me in your life at all?' and add that I wanted a truthful answer. Which would make you freeze and shut your mouth, opening it just enough to murmur that of course I'll always matter to you. To which I might, with reason, retort that at this moment I mean less to you than Hunter and Mary do. So better not. It would be unforgivable to start this one if I weren't going somewhere with it, too. You see, my love, my love, my love, I know what's happened. I saw it beginning in October; tonight I saw the process completed."

"The process?"

"Insulation. When I asked if you still minded about Linda, I knew. You said, 'I still worry,' and then you looked shocked, because you realised that it wasn't true. You've stopped worrying."

"You know too much, damn it," David said.

"Only because I love you. You don't need me, or Linda, or anyone." She looked at him with bright, drowned eyes. "All you need is you, and Time remembered, and the ink and the paper. And I rejoice for you. And—you may not believe this—I rejoice for me." She stood up. "Because, you gave me back pain. Never believe it's a bad gift it's a good gift. One of the worst things, after Vernon, was to believe that nothing could hurt me any more. '*My heart all winter lay so dead*'—you know . . . Good night, David. I love you."

When she said good-bye to him the next day, she called from the train window, "And remember I praise God for you," causing some interest among his immediate neighbours on the track.

3

David pushed his chair from the table, and stretched and let the sounds come back. There was the whirr of the electric fan, the frogs croaking in the garden, the buzz and bump of the night insects against the screen, the far, thick hum of voices and music from the floor below.

His watch had played its trick; the time was a quarter to ten. At ten Hunter would bring his iced tea. It was better not to go down deep again before the next interruption. He went across the hall to the bathroom and took another shower, standing gratefully under the cold water, though in ten minutes he would be sweating again. The darkness had not yet brought the night breeze. All the heat of the day was still in the room. The porch was a hot-box now and he worked here from morning, stripped to the waist.

The shower did nothing to help the hot stirring in his head, the childish excitement. 'Oh pooh—just because you think you can finish tonight . . . No reason,' he told himself, 'to stand here with your heart dancing.'

He stared into the dark; at the dim shapes of the crowding trees and the sparks that were fireflies; beyond the trees there was the sense of a large land. In the room, between these four walls, the land was larger.

He looked at Anne's carved angel, standing alone on top of the highboy; the shadow of the wings towered behind it on the white wall. It no longer made an echo from the past because the past was recaptured, was here; all of it, in this room, nearer than the big white moth, blundering against the screen outside. The shadows with whom he lived had put on flesh and blood. Anne was in the room.

He went back to the table and stood reading the first page. He had named the book *A Pause in the Conversation*, and it began as though he were talking.

"It is more than five years, Anne, since we last met. Am I, perhaps, in danger of forgetting you? I tell myself that I am not, that all is distinct and remembered. I can put back the times and the places; I can recall, accurately, the most trivial dates."

(Linda has teased me for this, for keeping what she calls anniversary accounts in my head, as in a ledger; for my habit of saying, "This time two years ago, we were just

stopping for lunch in Castellane." It is true; I have a head
that records. I am not pleased about it. Indeed I find nowa-
days that it has certain disadvantages.)

"I have your photographs, and I stare at them. They
fall short of you; they always did; but they are better than
nothing. As I stare, I protest that I can improve on them,
that I can still remember you perfectly.

"But I am afraid that if you did walk into my room at this
moment, my memories might prove to have fallen short, like
the photographs. The sound of your voice would almost certainly take me by surprise. I have tried hard not to lose it; I
practise hearing it in my head; but voices are more easily
forgettable than faces. Not only this. I believe that the impact
of you in flesh and blood might bring me to my feet, crying,
'But how much I had forgotten. . . .'

"So I must set out in search of you, now, before it is too
late. I shall follow you as far as I can. I shall go down deeply,
like a diver, past my conscious memories, to the sea-floor
where there is buried treasure. And I pray that when the
search is done, you will be here for always, in these pages."

It was a bold prayer, and he could not know yet if it was
answered. You never could know. No matter what you
wrote, you were, after all these months, so close to it, so
entombed in it, that you could not tell.

'I think,' he said to himself, 'that I need two more
hours, maybe less.' Less, if it were one of the times when the
daemon took over, when you yourself had only to hold the
pen; it should be like that, he said, it shouldn't be you who
writes the end.

Would he, this time, write the words 'THE END' in block
capitals at the foot of the last page, as he had done all his
life? This had made Linda giggle. She said that it was sentimental. So it was. All the aspects of finishing a play or a
book were sentimental. Including the moment after you had
dashed down the block capitals, when—from standing on
top of a mountain and shouting at the sun, you became
suddenly bereft and desolate. And the next morning, when you
awoke to anti-climax, with nothing left to do. And you were
sentimental now, thinking, 'Two more hours—maybe less.'

Hunter was late. The iced tea would help—just as, a long
time ago, a drink would have helped. (Pernod at twilight,

with the shadow walking up the other side of the valley till it reached the Roman wall.)

Waiting, David kept himself obstinately from going down again. He read his bank-statement, unopened after a week. He did not need the reminder that he was one hundred and eighty dollars in credit. There was just one war bond after that.

Though he did not feel like a gambler any more, he was, he supposed, still gambling. If he were not, he would have taken the unanimous advice given to him in California last summer, and set about his re-training with an eye to the markets. (Clyde Brewer and the American pulse, God forbid.)

He looked at the future as he looked at the past, finding that it had no power to frighten him. He could imagine a letter from the faithful Job Vale regretting, between garlands, that this sort of book would not sell. He could imagine a letter of congratulation and acceptance. Either prospect seemed shadowy, unimportant, a thing that would happen anyway, that was there already in Time ahead of him outside this room.

Another resounding proof of happiness, that you could not, would not, look ahead.

Happiness, David said to himself, the great over-simplification, the world's will-o'-the wisp; Hunter's song in the juke-box. Always he had pitied the world's conscious search for it. Sometimes he had argued against its existence, save as a cliché in the mind. He might still argue that, were it not for Mike Field in the bar last Saturday night.

David had gone down late, for some more ginger-ale, an order that was good for a laugh on Saturday nights. Mike Field, at the discursive stage, drooping affectionately on the shoulders of his neighbours, had said, "Here's Mr. Neilson, now, he'll tell us. He's a happy man."

"Eh?" said David, still in his working-trance, meeting Mike's red, good-humoured eyes.

"I said you're a happy man. Isn't that the truth?"

"Yes."

As he said it, he knew that he could have given no other answer. But it came as a revelation. The truth from God. And Mike, with a skinful, was an odd choice for an angelic messenger.

Mike's voice, other voices equally blurred, had asked what his secret was. He had said, "Give me time . . . I never thought about it till now," and the blurred voices had said perhaps that was the secret, never to think about it.

And still, David thought, it remained the truth and he could not know why. Nor was he sure that he had the right to be happy. If the thing that Janet had told him in February were true, this happiness came only from insulation. He thought of the reserve-tanks filling, by the cessation of human contacts, by the release from daylong compassion and anxiety. He did not like to think that this alone was the cause. Work was a cause. And in writing this book he had turned to face his ghosts; if he had not freed himself from remorse, he had at least set the remorse within a frame, appointing what he had done, for judgment.

What need he do about happiness, after all, except thank God for it? He felt a new warmth towards Mike Field, though Mike went on looking at him as though he had two heads.

Now Hunter's feet came up the stairs; the large blond shape appeared at the door. Hunter's shirt was black with sweat. He had put his can of beer on the tray with the iced tea.

"Orf'ly sorry I'm late with your tea, sir," said Hunter in his routine misconception of a British accent.

David said, "Doesn't matter, ta ever so," and the routine reply had its usual effect. Still laughing, Hunter slumped in the basket-chair. "I don't know why that gets me every time. It did when I was over there. Say it again, David."

David said it again.

"Ta," Hunter repeated. "Ta . . . it's wonderful. Sorry to be late, though. There's a bunch on their way to Boston cutting it up. Too much noise for you?"

"I don't hear it."

"And that's wonderful, too. All the same, I'll have to throw them out; close down in a little while. Mary's needling me about Mass tomorrow. You're a lucky guy, you know, not to have a religion."

"Eh? Come again?"

"I meant a religion that gets you out of bed in the mornings. Sorry, David; I know you believe in God—

and everything. We talk about him enough, that's for sure."

"Well, just you pray for me, there's a good fellow."

"I always do; so does Mary, you know that." Hunter drank his beer, grimaced. "Yours is the better drink, this kind of a night. Ever get bored with the wagon?"

"Punctually at six every evening."

"That's my time, too," said Hunter and looked suddenly agonised. "Gee, David, I forgot. Somebody's calling you from New York. They called twice; wouldn't leave any message. I said you were working; that's right, isn't it?"

"That's right. It'll only be Job Vale, anyway; agitating for me to bring the manuscript in before the ink's dry."

"It was a woman," said Hunter.

"His secretary. What are you looking like that for?"

"How do I look?"

"Shall I say vicariously lecherous?"

"You can say it, I wouldn't know what it means," said Hunter.

"It means you think I've got a girl."

"Well, but I know you don't have a girl," Hunter said plaintively. "You can't do that if you feel the way we feel; that when you're married you're married for keeps. But it's tough when it doesn't work out and there you are stuck with it." Tacitly, David thought, Hunter and Mary had accepted that this was why Janet didn't come East any more.

Hunter said, "You never have any fun, do you? You're just happy without it, like you said to Mike. Mike's gotten a new theory about you. He says you weren't born any place, you just dropped from the moon. That's why you're happy and why you aren't homesick. I said you were homesick, just a little."

"True enough. Does no harm," David said, "but I believe I'll go home next time I see some money."

"You'll see that fast enough when you deliver the book, won't you? How near the end are you?"

"Well, don't look now, but I might finish tonight."

"Yippee!" said Hunter. "But that means you'll be leaving us."

"Not yet. I'm in no hurry."

"You should be. What Mary and I'd like to see would be

this book of yours on top of every best-seller list and you sailing home in the *de-luxest* suite on the *Queen Elizabeth*."

"Yes, you would, too," David said musingly. "I believe the reason you both do your job so well is that you really do like other people to have a good time. This is rare."

"Why is it rare?" Hunter asked. "People who don't have a good time are just a pain in the neck to have around." He cocked his head on one side, listening. "Sounds to me as though some of the good-timers downstairs are getting a touch out of hand, though. Here's Mary." He plucked open the door. "Trouble? I'll be down."

"No," Mary said placidly, "there's no trouble; it's the New York call again, for Mr. Neilson."

"Job Vale? Late for him to call."

"No, it's a lady who doesn't want to give her name," said Mary.

"Then she's no lady," said Hunter.

"I did tell her that you were still working, but she said it was important. And I thought she sounded a bit sad and lonely, so I said I'd see."

The words 'a bit sad and lonely' repeated themselves in David's head as he went downstairs. They sounded a tocsin. He did not know why they should. Why, after all this time, if she were sad and lonely, should she turn to him? He was still thinking, 'No, it isn't Linda,' when he picked up the telephone and heard Linda's voice.

4

The sound of the voice was too familiar to trouble him. Ten minutes or less might have passed since he heard it; not the voice of the Californian Linda, who had ceased to exist, but the voice of the woman whom he had brought, with other ghosts, into the room upstairs; Linda as she used to be. He had re-created her, lovingly, with Anne. He had, though she didn't know it, been living with her recaptured image for months.

He felt the queer glow of affection that came from dreaming vividly of a person and seeing the person next day, still haloed in the magic importance of the dream.

Mary had said 'sad and lonely', but she sounded to him

light-hearted; she spoke as the woman in his book would speak.

"Hullo, darling. How are you and how's work?"

He said, "Both in good order, God be thanked. Nice to hear you. Tell me what's been happening to you."

Linda said, "Well—roughly everything."

"Oh, it has, eh?"

"Yes, it has, *eh*. David, I'd like to see you. In fact I've got to see you. Is that a hell of a proposition?"

"No—no, of course it isn't."

"You sound a little stunned."

"Well, I am."

She laughed. "Your Mr. Vale says you won't see anybody."

"Certainly I won't see my Mr. Vale, till I take him the manuscript. But that's quite soon now."

"D'you ever take a week-end off? There's rather a nice farm I go to. Ricky Powers's farm. I thought," she said vaguely, "we could talk there. There are three things, really . . ." her voice trailed.

"Three things you want to talk about?"

"Yes."

"Did you say Ricky Powers's farm?"

"Yes."

"Truly? I've seen pictures. King-size cattle," he said.

"Certainly. And pigs with platinum nose-rings. But they're away."

"The pigs are?"

"Depends how you look at it. I meant Ricky and Primula. They've gone to Europe. I'll be alone there—as of tomorrow —taking a bit of rest."

"You've been working?"

"Pretty hard," she said, "from September till today. . . . Could you come there, David, d'you think?"

"Maybe I could; on my way to New York. I'd like to see you."

"You can get to it in about three hours," said Linda. "I've just worked it out on the map. You go through Hartford— and over by Torrington and Sharon. It's cool, air-conditioned to the hilt. Stay all night and drive on to New York next day—why not?"

The tocsin was sounding again. 'You would be better——'
the tocsin informed him—'to say No. This is jumping into
deep water.'

He said, "If I can borrow Hunter's car—I could do that.
Look, Linda, it sounds silly, but I'm out of the habit of going
places and seeing people—I haven't got any decent clothes;
I couldn't come if it were a Powers party."

"I've told you," she said, "there'll only be me."

('Say no.')

He said, "Darling—give me the number there—I'll call
you. I can't be definite about the day, yet."

"But you will come?"

"Yes, I will."

"Promise?"

"Promise."

After he had written down the number, she said, "Good
night, darling. Thank you for being so sweet to me. . . ." She
sounded a little shy when she added, "God bless you."

She hung up. David came out of the booth and walked
through the bar and on up the stairs. He felt moonstruck, as
after the hours of writing when a piece of him stayed behind
at his table. Now a piece of him stayed behind in the booth,
still talking lightly to Linda.

When he came into the room, the room was changed; its
peace was disturbed; it was he who disturbed it. He stood
by the table, drinking the rest of the iced tea, his head
crowded by the vivid pressure of the moment.

Now there was the delayed shock of hearing her voice;
there was sharp wonder and speculation; there was an
excitement that he could not explain to himself.

He sat down at the table and read the last lines he had
written. He found that he was figuring the road from Hartford through Torrington; he was wondering whether Mike
Field would rent him a car cheaply, so that he need not
borrow Hunter's car.

"This won't do," he said aloud. He turned the pages back
to the point where he had begun this morning. He should
not, at this stage, need the process of reading himself in.

Here on the ruled paper, he said to himself, was the only
thing that mattered; the thing that must be kept safe. But
he, who alone could keep it safe, had let it be invaded. Now

it seemed colourless and shrunken. He was reading the same page twice over, not taking it in; not caring. All his thoughts were busy, like telephone lines; the book couldn't get through to them.

Half an hour ago, he had stood here with a heart that danced, trusting in the daemon.

He began to be angry.

He put the tray outside the door, lit a cigarette, dragged his chair closer to the table. He wrote the first sentence that made a shape in his head. He crossed it through, wrote it again. No daemon would take over tonight; no magic would come. He had only his stamina and his technical resources. These would, if he kept at it, prevail against the arid, striving brain that had to fight for words.

He sat on, toiling, conscious all the time, held back by his anger with himself. The floor began to be littered with crumpled sheets of torn-off paper. This was like the grim early weeks of his re-training. This was a hell of a way to write the end. He kept saying, "Why go on? Why not leave it till tomorrow?" and going on.

Presently, as he had known that it must, a faint impetus returned. The room was cooler now with the night breeze. His watch pointed half-past twelve. He felt as though it were four o'clock in the morning. Time and the minute-hand played no tricks.

"But I'll finish," David said. Even if he had to reach the last line by conscious effort, without a spark striking, he would finish. He had to. Because, the tocsin said, here comes the end of peace; you will not live alone with happiness again.

The minute-hand moved on; slowly, to one o'clock; to half-past one; to two-fifteen.

He wrote, "I remind myself, Anne, that we believed the same thing. You know, and I know, that we shall meet again. As I walk alone, I am aware of you walking a little way ahead. I shall catch up with you. This that has happened to us is only a pause in the conversation."

He thought that it was the end. He was too tired to read the ten pages back. He stripped and flung himself down and turned out the light. He was not alone. Just at the beginning of sleep, he saw Linda's face vividly. The face was sorrowful and the eyes reproached him. He wondered why.

LINDA

1956

I

The day, for Linda, had begun like the other days; with the alarm clock, the heavy heat lying in the room, the sunlight on the plane tree outside the window. The apartment was on the top floor. 'Another twenty-four hours at this temperature,' Linda thought, 'and my resolution will melt, along with everything else. Back to Sutton Place. This morning's quiz question: When is a penthouse a climb-down?'

Illogically, she decided as she made the coffee, it would feel less like a climb-down with Ricky and Primula gone. She had taken a drink with them yesterday, among their shining luggage labelled for the Cunard and some equally shining friends who were going too.

Though she was careful in these days to keep up an act for the Powerses, she thought that the act had failed a little.

She had not meant to say, "Lord, I'd like to be sailing tomorrow." It had slipped out and one of the poised friends had taken it up, saying, "But do you never go back now?" She answered with a quotation that she looked upon as David's property, "*The gates are barred on the summer side.*"

Primula's face had shown an anxiety over and above the usual American baffle induced by quotations: "Darling Linda, I do wish you'd move in here again—be comfortable; you wouldn't get so tired." Ricky had said, "It's crazy, working as you do, to go home to that hot-box every night." She had felt herself putting a shadow upon them. Nor had it been polite to shout with laughter because one of the poised friends said, "We always skip Dijon, the hotels are so lousy." (But why, she wondered, had they chosen to bring up Dijon, of all places? It was just another of the magic insanities that had begun to happen around her.)

When she left, Ricky had come after her, saying, "You'll

move in, won't you—promise?" She had made vague and grateful noises. Then he had said, "You're all right, aren't you? Happy?" and she had made strenuously positive noises.

They would be away two months. When they came back, there would be nothing to explain. It would be done. 'And that,' Linda thought, 'will be the end of my friendship with them. And they have been so kind to me.'

She put on the thin black dress for which Primula had paid three hundred dollars before deciding that it didn't suit her. "But lovely on you, darling. Do have it."

She looked in the glass. The face that looked back at her was awed, yet serene. "Today?" she said to it. "Perhaps today."

When she went downstairs, the door of the apartment below stood open; the girl who lived there was bringing her terrier back from its morning walk. The girl said, "Hello; it's hitting ninety outside," and stood smiling at her. She wore a buff-coloured shirt and trousers, a pair of sandals. She was dark-haired and blue-eyed; her tan made the eyes look paler. In the eyes Linda could see the look of a shared secret, the high-sign. "I'm still waiting for you to come and have a drink with me, you know," the girl said as Linda stooped to pat the terrier.

And in another place, another time, Linda thought, another person would have been interested. That other person would have noticed the body because the shoulders were straight and the legs were long.

All that she saw now was the attitude, the casual, show-off pose, visually arresting but rousing no more curiosity than when one saw in a show-window well-cut clothes that one had no wish to buy.

That impulse, Linda knew, was spent. Perhaps the last wild aberration, seeming now both shameful and absurd, had killed it finally. Or perhaps one's body, with one's mind, acquired a belated wisdom. 'I don't condemn it,' she thought —'except in myself, because for me no true love ever went with it—simply desire, excitement and possessiveness; the limited fevers that should belong only to the very young.'

As she walked to the bus stop, she was certain that the thing must happen today. When she got off the bus, she

203

halted for a moment outside the church, trying to make herself go in: but an early Mass was ending and she felt as though the crowd who came down the steps pushed her from the door. The church was easier at night, when they had blown the candles out and all was shadowy; when the one red lamp burned beside the altar and in the empty place she could think that there was somebody there. She would go in tonight. The visits that had begun from curiosity (Russ saying, as they walked past together, "Grand Central Station, isn't it? Ever been in?") were ending as a need.

Linda always arrived at the office before Russ Jones. The elevator doors opened on to the waiting-room; a long room, crowded with chairs. There was a table in the middle, with books on it: copies of the two books written by Russ, *Time To Be Happy* and *The Meaning of Fear*.

This was the only moment of the day when Linda saw the waiting-room empty. From nine until the late evening the room went on filling with patients who were in no hurry to move. Some of them sat on all day after their treatment; and the room would feel hot and wet with them, thick with the drone of their voices. It was a kind of Ellis Island, this room, a detaining-ground where washed-up, broken and still hopeful people waited for their release.

Linda went through it into the small surgery; she took off Primula's black dress, hung it in the closet and put on her white nylon overall. She went down the hall to the room where Russ received the patients. He refused to call it an office. It did not look like an office; it looked like a study or a library, with the bookshelves, the solid furniture and the grandfather clock. There was a magic of quiet here; and the room felt cool. As she stood by the massive desk, sorting his letters, she could hear the tick of the clock, sounding hushed and tentative. When she opened the window, the New York noises were muted, here as nowhere else. Outside the window there was a roof-garden, with little trees in tubs. Russ would, on occasion, walk the patients up and down the garden while he talked to them.

Hearing the elevator doors, Linda thought that he, or the nurse, was unusually early. Instead she found a woman standing alone, looking helplessly about her. She had soft dark eyes, good features and a spotty skin; she wore a mauve dress that was a mistake.

"I'm Mrs. Beale," she said, "Mrs. Beale from Philadelphia. Doctor Jones is expecting me. He has a letter from Mrs. Rogers—Mrs. Rogers advised me to come early. Now I'd like to say——" her voice trailed . . . "Well, I guess I'll wait and say it to the doctor."

"He's usually here by nine. Would you let me take your particulars? Name, address, age and such?" When Mrs. Beale looked sullen and alarmed, Linda said, "It's only the ordinary routine for new patients."

"I'm not a patient yet," said Mrs. Beale. "And I don't know if I'm going to be—I don't mean to sound rude, but I'm very nervous."

"Well, don't worry. Just sit down and take it easy. We'll skip the preliminaries till you've seen Doctor Jones."

Mrs. Beale remained standing. She said, "Can he really cure people?"

"Yes."

"You've seen cures?"

"Plenty. Including my own."

Mrs. Beale blinked. "You were a patient?"

"Yes. Last year."

"My goodness——" But the look of suspicion came quickly as though this were sales-talk. "How did you come to hear of Dr. Jones, Miss—Miss——"

"Platt. Linda Platt. I heard of him from a friend of mine, Richard Powers, the writer."

"Richard Jay Powers?"

"Yes."

Mrs. Beale said, "My goodness," again.

"When he told me about Dr. Jones," said Linda, "I mistrusted the whole thing profoundly. Just like you."

"But you tried it just the same."

"Well . . . it seemed worth trying. I'd come to the end of everything."

The phrase struck a chord; Mrs. Beale whispered "Yes" and looked despairing. "D'you mind my asking——"

"Please ask anything you like."

"You—didn't feel a psychiatrist could help you?"

"I'd tried that. I've been a student of Freud for years."

205

The arrival of Russ and the nurse together interrupted them. Linda saw the new patient look warily at Russ and be reassured, as all were reassured the first time. Russ was in his early forties, tall and broad, with a tan and tufty brown hair. He wore sporting clothes, tweeds and checks and home-spun ties when the weather was cool; seersucker and an open collar and loafers on a day like this. His appearance was part of the act. Every day at this time, Linda saw two people come in, Russ and Russ's act. As the day went by the two merged into one and she was again convinced.

She followed him into his room. He flipped through the letters, said "All yours" and handed them over. He had long ago given up asking "How are you?" and it disquieted her that he should ask her now; not formally but in the deep, exploratory tone reserved for the patients; he followed it with the long stare. His eyes were bright blue.

"I'm fine, thank you, Russ."

He went on looking at her, silent, and leaning his big brown hands on the desk.

"Why? . . . What?" she said to the look.

"I don't know," said Russ. "Better bring the new gal in first."

In the surgery the nurse was measuring out the little pills in paper cups. The waiting-room was filling as though by a siphon, all the patients greeting one another in a gabble of Christian names, chorusing "Hello, Linda", as she came through. The motherly type from Brooklyn was bearing down upon Mrs. Beale. Linda detached her and led her in. She sat down at the table by the wall to take the notes, while Mrs. Beale was protesting, as all the new patients protested, that she wanted to see the doctor quite alone.

"You don't have to look at Miss Platt," Russ said. "You can take it that she's the other half of my head or just pretend she's a dictaphone." With her back to him, Linda knew that he smiled, that his attitude in the chair was lazy and relaxed, that he was sending out waves of ease. He asked the questions softly, as though affection made him want the answers. Age? Married when? Marriage okay? Children? Sex-life normal? Physical health? Drink? Drugs?

They always stopped on drugs. Russ always laughed. "No, no—I'm not suggesting you're a dope-addict, Mrs.

206

Beale—I'm talking of medicines—laxatives, aspirin, sleeping-pills . . ."

The fluttering voice made its dazed answers, until he paused and said (always in the same deepened, affectionate key), "Now . . . just try and tell me."

There was no need, Linda reminded herself, to listen carefully. Whatever the story, Russ would treat this patient as he treated the rest; and he never asked her for the notes of a first interview; he filed them in his head as she filed them in the register.

But today the new mood was here again; the mood that made Mrs. Beale of singular importance, Mrs. Beale as she was, the incoherent creature with the dread of death.

"Sometimes I lie awake and wish we could all die together now, just so's I needn't think about it or be scared any more. And I know that's wicked, but I pray and pray and the feeling just goes on."

"Well, of course it does," said Russ gently, "because it isn't something you can pray about."

"Oh, don't say that, Doctor. I pray about lots of things."

"Sure; that's all right. I meant it won't get you results; prayer couldn't cure the feeling and I'll explain why not. It's just a physical sensation, that's all."

"Oh *no* . . ."

"You don't think so . . . of course you don't. But I can prove it to you if you'll be kind to me and listen. Now—suppose you just tell me again what it is you're afraid of?"

Mrs. Beale hesitated.

"No trap," Russ said. "Just tell me."

"I'm afraid of dying."

"Uh-huh. And how does it feel to die? What's dying *like*? Can you tell me?"

"But of course I can't, Dr. Jones; that's just silly. I've never done it."

Russ said, "So, when the feeling comes over you, you don't know—do you?—precisely what it is about death that makes you so afraid? You're not specifically afraid of one kind of death—of being drowned or burned or killed in an automobile . . . You've told me that. It's the thought of dying; of knowing suddenly that you're going to stop, not be here any more, that brings the feeling, yes?"

"Yes."

"Well, it's the feeling that matters; not what brings it. And in fact, though you won't see this for a little while, it's just a feeling, that you're afraid of. That's the common denominator of all fear; no woman's really scared of her husband, or of spiders, or of a thunderstorm; she's scared of the way that they make her feel. And since the central nervous system—that's to say the mechanism with which you feel—is a purely physical matter, there's a physical cause for your fear. And a physical cure. Just as there is for every fear that exists."

Now, as before, Linda could feel the change in temperature. This was not an answer that the new patients could believe. It disappointed and offended them. No matter how clearly Russ expounded it, their stock reaction was mistrust. "You mean it's just a *physical* treatment you give?" Mrs. Beale was complaining shrilly. She went on arguing. After he had made her lean back and shut her eyes she sobbed a little. Russ stood behind her chair, stroking her forehead.

Linda assembled the routine gifts that she would take away; the résumé of case-histories, the diagrammatic explanation of the nervous system, the reprint of an article Russ had written for one of the Brewer magazines. From the nurse, Mrs. Beale would receive the shot, the first dose of pills, the phial of pills to be taken at evening and the tonic in the bottle, to be taken twice a day. "If there wasn't a bottle of something," Russ said, "they'd never believe I was treating them."

The quiet was greater in the room; he managed somehow to increase it with his laying-on of hands. The nurse took Mrs. Beale away; after the shot, Mrs. Beale would be told to lie down in the cubicle. It was the same beginning for all of them. Linda remembered her own first day, her reluctance to go into the long room and join the others after she had slept. Russ did not insist, the first day. He knew that it took time for them to understand and appreciate the benefits of discussion, of sharing symptoms.

Russ said, "Just give me Dysart Haddon's letter again, will you please?" He read it and murmured equably, "Well, damn his eyes. I'd like to see Catherine Haddon. If she isn't there yet, tell one of them to send her in just as soon as she comes."

Catherine Haddon was there. She had been coming to Russ for only six weeks. She was an intelligent, wild-looking creature who reminded Linda a little of David's Janet. Catherine had no taste for the social life of the waiting-room. She sat in a corner and read a book. "Me? Oh, wonderful," said Catherine, and followed Linda, with the book under her arm.

"Hello, Catherine." Though Russ's treatment never varied, his manner did. When he talked to Catherine, he brought up special reserves. Catherine had a formidable education. She was not in love with him. She showed a reluctance to report progress. He didn't say, "How are you?" He said, "What's the book?" and they discussed the book for a time.

"Treatment?" Catherine asked briskly, laying back her head.

"Wait a minute. Look, honey, did you ask your husband to write to me?"

"I didn't ask him to. He said he was going to, and I didn't try to stop him."

"You saw him over the week-end?"

"Yes," said Catherine. "He came into town."

"Was he a nuisance?"

Catherine scratched her head and said, "Not more than usual, no."

"Well, he is now. He says here that he finds you perfectly well, that you admit to being well, and that he sees no reason why you shouldn't go home."

"Yes, that's his view," said Catherine indifferently.

"In the ordinary way, I'd put the letter in the trash-basket—I've told him clearly enough already. But since it's you, I thought you'd like me to answer."

Catherine rose, put her hands on the desk and leaned towards him. "You don't have to answer, Russ. Because I *am* going home."

Linda waited for the quiet monosyllable. It came. "Why?" Russ asked tranquilly. He gave her a cigarette. Though he had taken pains to teach her to sit still, he did not protest when she began to pace the room. He watched her, still lazily smiling.

"You see," said Catherine, "I know all the arguments.

209

I know he can turn me into a nervous wreck. He has before and he'll do it again. But the fact remains I married the guy and I'd rather go back and sweat it out."

"Why?" said Russ again.

"Because he's miserable without me. And I'm sorry for him."

"Listen, Catherine, nobody's said you're not going back to him. You can do anything you like once you're cured, you know that. All I ask is that you complete the cure. You're a lot better, already."

Catherine shook back her hair; she had a long neck and Linda thought that she looked, at the moment, like a half-crazy deer.

"I'm not, really, Russ. Physically I'm in better shape; I'm steadier, and stronger, and I'm sleeping all right. But that isn't what counts. Inside I'm eaten up with guilt, and *that's* what counts. You'll never cure my conscience; so I'd rather be back in Cambridge with Dysart and going crazy. That's the way I'm made and I must settle for it."

"This isn't a matter of your conscience, darling. I've told you what it is; it's a compulsion-neurosis . . . a mental disease. As soon as you've been with Dysart for a week, it'll come back. All you'll want to do is run, just as you did two months ago."

"Oh, sure," said Catherine, grinning at him. "That's what I'll *want* but I won't do it again. Because now that I've done it I know it's worse. And I'll remember. When he's driving me round the bend, I'll remember how this felt; and then I'll stay." She pointed a tremulous finger at him across the desk. "Mind you—I'll admit that if I stuck this out for a year or more, you might win. I might get used to the idea of being mean to Dysart. And that would be a sad pity."

Linda watched Russ, who was leaning back with his hands clasped behind his head and an expression of courteous sympathy.

He said, "So you want to put the chains back on . . ."

"Yes, please," said Catherine.

"What'll you do if I say, 'Okay; off you go and pack your bag'?"

"I packed," said Catherine. "I checked out of the hotel this morning."

"Well, that makes it easy, doesn't it?" said Russ amicably. "And if I put it to you that you're making the same compulsive pattern in having to get back to him that you made when you had to get away? You're intelligent enough to see that, surely."

"Oh yes . . . I see it."

"And you trust me enough to know that when I tell you it'll be worse the next time around, I'm speaking the truth."

Catherine darted her head from side to side. "You're speaking *your* truth, Russ. It'll *feel* worse; but it won't *be* worse. I'm sorry. And I'm more than grateful to you. And I'd like my bill."

He shook his head, smiling at her. "You know the house-rule. No cure, no bill."

Outside his door, Catherine said to Linda, "Just tell me where he banks and I'll pay the cheque straight in."

"That's against rules, too."

"He doesn't have to know."

"Give a thought," Linda said, "to *my* conscience."

She shook hands with Catherine and longed to say something more than "Good luck to you". She put her head round the door of Russ's room: "Who next?"

"Nobody for a minute. Come in." He was looking more shaken than she expected. He said, "What mistake would you say I'd made with Catherine?"

"No mistake at all."

"Yes, Linda; I dropped a stitch somewhere."

"I don't think you did."

"Well, what do you think?"

It was impossible to tell him what she thought. She tried to imagine the look on his face if she said it aloud. Yet his wave-length was so keen that she was afraid, while she stood silent, that he might pluck her thought out of the air. She assumed a conscientious frown.

"I guess," he said, "I was deceived by the fact that she's got more brains than all the rest of them rolled together. I thought she was too intelligent to lie to me."

"Oh, she wasn't lying."

"Yes, she was. She said sex didn't mean a thing to her; the real trouble is that she has to sleep with him."

Linda had known him to misunderstand before; never, she thought, so completely, nor with such vulgar simplicity.

"Oh, Russ—no. Catherine's a person with a conscience."

"I'd use another word, same initial," said Russ, laughing.

She went to call the first of the waiting line. The line came on; smoothly, rapidly, with scarcely a word spoken beyond the "How are you?" and the answer; each to lay her head back in the chair and feel his hands on her forehead. These were all old patients; they did not need to tell him again about the compulsion to wash every half-hour, the fear of the subway, of the department-store, of the cancer campaign. They loved and trusted him. And with reason, Linda thought; he performed miracles for them. When he decided that they were becoming too cosy about it all, he cursed them and they loved him the more. She heard it begin now:

"What are you doing here, Jeannie? I told you not to come back for a month."

"Oh, I had to, Russ. My mother was so terrible to me last night—you've no idea. I just couldn't sleep; and I woke up with all the old feelings."

"I'm too busy to clean up emotional hangovers. If you're silly enough to spend an evening with your mother, you know how you'll feel next day. Run away and don't waste my time." He paid no attention to tears; he knew that there were sympathetic shoulders in the waiting-room.

Sometimes he would decide to hold up the line and take time out for a debate.

"Mrs. Carrick—I told you before—you can worship any God you like; it's no concern of mine."

"But *you* don't believe in a God."

"Well," Russ said sunnily, "I'm open to conviction. Just prove Him to me—that's all I ask. It's not unreasonable. You felt the same way about the central nervous system till I proved it to you."

"You can't prove there isn't a God."

"Of course I can't; I never said I could. I'm not a damn' fool, Mrs. Carrick. What's your worry?"

"You've made such a wonderful difference in my life and I'd like to think the way you do."

"Oh no, you wouldn't," said Russ gaily. "What you mean is you'd like me to think the way you do."

"You're *quite* wrong," said Mrs. Carrick, "God's part of my trouble." Linda had her written down as one of the chameleon cases; she would change her trouble any time; just so long as she had a trouble, she was fine. "If I didn't believe there was a God, I'd have no feelings of fear. I know I wouldn't. That's what makes me afraid."

"Then maybe, when you're through with being afraid, you will think the way I do," said Russ lightly. "Now—just put your head back."

2

By half-past twelve, the last of the line was out of the door. In the interval, the two of them would work here on the outline of Russ's new book, with milk and sandwiches sent in from the drugstore. It was a time for talk; there would be another time for talk this evening, before Russ gave his lecture to the faithful in the waiting-room. 'Now——?' Linda said to herself. 'Or then? Or after the lecture? . . . Or, perhaps, tomorrow? . . . What I am doing, surely, is waiting for a sign; the thing that doesn't come.'

She saw Russ pick up his rakish straw hat. "I forgot to tell you I've an appointment up-town. Back at two, traffic permitting." He treated her again to the long stare. "Wouldn't do you any harm to get out of here."

The reprieve was consoling. She waited until his taxi was out of sight before she went up the steps and into the church.

This was harder than at evening. She was still self-conscious, still acutely aware of the alien mystery that brought these people in, to kneel alone, to light a candle, or rattle a rosary before the Stations of the Cross. Always she kept as far from the random worshippers as she might.

There was nobody near the high altar; she walked quickly up the aisle and forced herself to kneel down in the front pew.

"Show me. Please show me," Linda whispered through stiff lips. She stared at the tabernacle, the small, shimmering tent that made a question-mark in her mind.

(All the way back to La Colle and to Anne, speaking of the relics, "The thing I find hard to believe is that *I* am in

213

their presence; my scepticism applies to myself, not to them.")

"Am I in God's presence? How can I be? And yet, if all that I've ever fought and scoffed at and denied is true, how can I not be?" She shook her head despairingly upon the answer.

What was the use of pleading 'Show me . . .' when you were utterly uncertain to whom you spoke or what you wanted to see? What was the use of praying at all? No need to tell God that the whole pattern of your life was breaking up; that for ten months now you had travelled through strange places, on shifting ground. If God was there, he knew it; if he wasn't, the journey had no end at all.

What was the use of thinking, yet again, 'If only I could talk to David'? David stood far away, behind a barrier not to be broken.

'But this began with him.'

She found that she was no longer making any attempt at prayer. She was down to earth; still on her knees and in a reverie; an accustomed reverie. She was staring at the pictures her mind made of David and Janet; she went on with it, wondering and curious.

That was the beginning. She could still see Menella Brewer's horsy face champing out the words. "The hotel that belongs to that woman poet . . . Janet Something." She could still bring back the moment; the startling rage inside, the shudder of shock, the furious "Why?"

It had been a long walk from "Why?" to understanding; fighting her own ego all the way; desolate and angry; anger turning at last upon herself and the walls coming down. So that the view gradually widened, showing her her failure towards David and around it a whole grey landscape of failure; nothing else.

She had thought of writing it to him. She had tried to write:

"I realise my selfishness at last. I realise that I took all from you. I even tried to take Anne's memory. I would, if I could, have robbed you of that. But, as it turns out, the only person I have robbed is me. I am sorry, beyond words, for all of it. Be happy, please, with somebody who is wiser than I; somebody who believes in God."

And when the words were written they displeased her; they were so trite and weak. Could one ever come to terms with one's own triteness and weakness?

She was still saying 'Show me' with the top of her mind. Useless. Nobody would show her.

Linda rose from her knees. She wanted to duck down in a genuflection, as the others did, but she was too shy. She contented herself with an absurd social bow as if the tabernacle were a friend of Primula's, met in Saks. That would make David laugh. Wouldn't it? 'Oh, surely, even though I'm getting no place, he would sympathise; he would be glad to know that I was trying.'

No. That was fantasy. In the truth, he stood always behind the barrier, safe and far, with the woman at whom she had sneered.

She went down the steps. The thought of meeting him suddenly, face to face, was a fantasy too. (And there was another fantasy: the clamorous, persistent dream of the thing that she wanted him to write. It was a vision that had shaped slowly in these months of loneliness. How could she be so certain of its worth and so sure that she would never dare ask him to write it?)

'Show me' meant 'I wait for a sign'. And that was all it meant. She had not prayed.

Linda walked to the corner of Fifth Avenue. The young man walking towards her, shaggy and thin, his face luminously white with sweat, was Job Vale.

"Hello, Mrs. Neilson."

There was nothing strange in meeting him; the publishers' office was two blocks away. There was nothing magical about his calling her "Mrs. Neilson". Miss Platt was confined to the Russ Jones territory and to the apartment on West Eleventh.

Vale blinked his solemn eyes. "Do I alarm you? You look alarmed."

"No. No. It is just that I was longing to say something to somebody, and they've sent me you."

Vale said in his lugubrious voice, "I'd think they might have done better for you."

"They couldn't, not really. Have you heard from him?" When he looked blank she said, "From David?"

Vale said yes. He steered her away from his usual drug-store, to the Swiss Tavern in the next block. It was ice-cold, dark and half-empty. "I never eat; I just drink beer," said Vale. "Will you have a sandwich?"

"I don't know. Not yet. Please tell me about David."

"Well," said Vale, looking like something in an aquarium, "he doesn't say much. And his reluctance to see me—or anybody—goes on. But he allows as how he's nearly finished the book. And then he'll bring it to New York."

"Does he tell you what sort of a novel it is?"

"He tells me nothing."

"No," said Linda, "he never does. Look——" she put her hands around the tall glass of beer, clutching it and staring at the gold rim—"I'll have to say this very quickly or I'll never say it at all. Will you please give him a message when he comes. Don't say it's from me. Just ask him if he'd ever think of writing something about Anne—our daughter who died." Her lips were shaking absurdly. Perhaps he had not heard what she said. She couldn't say it again.

Vale said slowly, "I'd be glad to. But—forgive me—I'm always imbecile in this weather—why not ask him yourself? Surely it should come from you."

"We don't talk any more."

His bulgy forehead wrinkled. "Oh . . . I didn't under-stand that, quite. Sorry."

"He is in love with somebody else," Linda said.

"Oh . . . Well, couldn't you write it to him?" His flat vague manner did not disturb her. She said, "I've tried. It's been haunting me for months. I wouldn't want it if I didn't think he'd want to do it. It isn't for me. I've no right to want it—no right at all." Her voice cracked and she was ashamed.

Vale said affectionately, "Drink your beer." He waited for her to recover.

"Sorry," said Linda.

"No, don't be sorry. Wouldn't you be much happier if you talked to him or wrote to him or something?"

"I don't know."

Vale said, "In my view it's a mistake to cut off com-munication. It's false—if the communication's still going on in one's head." He blinked at her again. "I guess the fact of the other person makes a difference, though I don't see why she should. But then I'm awfully stupid about those things. I can't get angry or jealous. I suppose," he said thoughtfully, "it's because I'm so very ugly."

3

The quiet room was shadowy now; they had paced the roof-garden for a long time, Linda thought; the sunset was turning smoky and in the tall flat façades the lights came on.

Russ turned up the lamp on his desk; when he deserted the chair behind the desk and sprawled in the patients' armchair, leaning back his head, Linda laughed, "I never saw you sit there before."

"Make you feel I should be standing behind me, stroking my own forehead?" He looked at her tenderly. "All right, Linda. I understand. And I accept. And I'm glad you told me. In fact, though I hate to lose you, I know it's time. Time you were back in your field. All success to you. Where's the job?"

She hesitated.

"It would be no good my lying to you, would it, Russ?"

"None at all."

"Okay, then. There isn't a job. I just feel it's time to be going."

He was silent for a moment. Then he said, "No, Linda; sorry; that won't do. Try and tell me the truth."

"That is the truth. I swear."

Russ laughed. "If I thought it was, I'd be worried. Realise what you said . . . 'I just feel.' It's impossible that you, of all people, should give way to your feelings."

"Why is it impossible?"

She heard his voice change tempo, soften, become the authentic voice of Russ Jones dealing with a case. "Because, thanks to me, you've learned how to understand your feelings and conquer them. Not only as a patient but as my partner in this work."

His, she thought, was the most reputable type of ego; his work was his life and his creed; all were bound up in himself. Even now she did not know whether he was a charlatan or a miracle-worker. And there were times, she guessed, when Russ himself did not know. He was doing the best that he

217

could with his gifts. And that was all that anybody could do. Nor had he failed her. It was simply that she had come to the end of him.

"Russ, as I've said already tonight, I admire you enormously. I think your work does a magnificent amount of good. Please don't be hurt when I tell you that I don't believe in it any more. And that's why I can't go on with you."

She saw him waiting, hugely attentive and still. "To you," she said, "it's the answer to every human problem. But I can't believe, any more, in a human being whose troubles begin and end in his central nervous system. That framework's too small to hold all of him. That's why I sympathised with Catherine Haddon this morning."

"Tell me more about that." His voice was gentle and drowsy; he was sending out the waves of ease.

"I thought she was wiser than we were. When she said, 'It will feel worse but it won't *be* worse,' she hit a nail on the head for me. It's the antithesis of your teaching."

"Certainly," Russ drawled.

"You want to cure the exact feeling that she's prepared to suffer. Because she thinks it would be right to suffer it. You want——"

He interrupted her, "I want people to be happy, Linda."

It was not in conscious imitation that she gave him the gentle monosyllable, "Why?"

He did not answer; the lamplight made his eyes frosty and pale; his mouth still smiled.

"Russ, after you built me up, and cured me, I was happy. First, because I was at peace; then because I was alive, and could be useful again. The day I told you I wanted to work with you, and you accepted the offer, was one of the really happy days of my life. And it was on that day, that evening, just as I thought I was strong, I had it proved to me I wasn't strong. I heard something that disturbed me profoundly; that made me wretched and furious; a whole new cycle of unhappiness began."

He said, "Then . . . on that day?" as though he could not believe it.

"Yes."

"Why didn't you tell me?"

"I didn't tell anybody."

"What was this thing?"

"No," she said. "It's over; or my resentment of it is over. And I'm deeply grateful for it. Because it set me off on a voyage of discovery that I might never have taken."

He said, still motionless and attentive, "Can you tell me what you found on this voyage?"

"Some of it. I found myself for a start; not a person anyone would care to meet in the looking-glass. And from there I've gradually come to see my whole failure. I've learned a lot, very late. And I'm glad I know. It's the first time in my life that I've ever had my nose rubbed in the truth. I'd rather have truth than happiness, see?"

It was his turn to use the "Why?"

"I couldn't tell you why. There's no logical answer to that. There's not much logic about human beings, anyway. Just because they are human, they consist of something more than an intellect and a central nervous system. Your theory, Russ, leaves out the soul."

"And what—————" asked Russ—"do you mean by the soul?"

"That," said Linda, "is what I have to find out."

There was a silence between them. Outside they could hear the elevator doors, the voices rising again; the faithful returning for Russ's evening lecture.

"You must go—————" she said.

"And you. Don't stay for this." He rose and put his hands on her shoulders. "What I want you to do is take a holiday right away; as of tonight; go down to the farm and take it easy. And remember I'm always here, at the end of a telephone. See?"

She said to the steady, smiling face, "You don't understand."

"Sure I do. You think because you said 'the soul' I think you're crazy. I don't. A lot of us go searching all our lives. That's fine. But, because you have an intellect as well as the —huh—equipment you mention, I want to appeal to it. One word of warning; know what it is?"

"I think so." She wished that he would take his hands off her shoulders.

"This impulse to quit—because you've 'come to the end'————— It's not new."

"No."

"It's just your old pattern, d'you realise?"

"Yes. I thought you'd say that."

"The same compulsion-neurosis operating again. Because you're tired; not surprising; you've worked damned hard. So you'll take your holiday—and you will, won't you—for my sake as well as your own—watch out?"

For the last time she asked him, "Why?"

"Well, I don't know what red-hot crusade you're figuring on, but I do know you haven't left yourself too many things to 'come to the end of'. And if this—whatever it may be—happened to fail you, you'd take a beating. You'd be back where you were last year, before you came to me. And that, sweetheart—wouldn't only feel worse—it would be worse. Believe me. And now—just move into the chair while I give you a treatment."

"No, thank you, Russ. Not tonight."

He was angry. His control held. "As you like of course. Good-bye, Linda. Take care of yourself."

There was the strong handshake, and the wide smile.

Only now that it was done did she know how much the prospect of doing it had frightened her.

She thought, 'If I could do that, I can do anything. I can pick up the telephone and ask for Long Distance and talk to David.'

DAVID

1956

THERE was no mistaking Ricky's farm. As Linda had said, you couldn't miss it. A corona of cut black metal topped the gate; some of it spelling RICHARD JAY POWERS and some of it shaped into a bull.

The drive wound on and up through fields; there was a lot of the drive before you came to the first farm-buildings. In the hot light of mid-afternoon, David saw the white barns, the white silo, the white cowsheds and the black cattle. They shimmered, as they did in the gravure section.

He came to the garden, that was astonishingly green, to the French house with the turrets; he saw the hydrangeas and the spreading trees. He remembered Devonshire, the obstinate earth and Ricky, in dirty flannels, riding the tractor. He brought Hunter's car, a five-year-old Chevrolet, up to the sweep of shallow white steps in front of the panelled door. A manservant in grey uniform came down the steps. He took David's suitcase, heavy with manuscript; he said that Mrs. Neilson was on the veranda.

"Air-conditioned to the hilt," David recalled, as he went through the high rooms. He was sweaty and rumpled after the three-hour drive. The cold air drenched him; the shadows made him blink. He took out a handkerchief and wiped his face; he smarmed his hair flat with both hands, as he used to when he was a small boy. Here were doors open on to the veranda; through the windows beyond he could see the green garden sloping down to the river. The veranda stretched away to each side of him like a long gallery. He stood halted in the doorway. He had said to Mary, "Pray for me." ("I always do, Mr. Neilson.") He found that his heart was beating quickly, up at the base of his throat.

He looked to his right; down the cool, luxurious gallery,

Linda came to meet him. As though he had made a magic in writing of her as she used to be, Linda echoed the girl from Dijon. He took her hands; they were quiet hands; they lay peacefully in his while he kissed the top of the fragile, boyish head. He looked into her face; she looked up at him steadily and charitably; she did not clown with her eyebrows. The Californian Linda was gone, like a changeling.

She said the words that were in his mind to say, "Ten years younger; that's what you are." She added, "You've turned bony again; bony and strong. Oh, David, I'm so glad to see you. I was beginning to be afraid you'd thought better of it. I waited lunch. Till half-past two."

"I'm so sorry. I'm using Hunter's car and he had to have it this morning."

"No car any more?" she asked wistfully.

"No anything any more," he said, grinning at her. "Don't worry. I like it." ('And I like to be with you again.') He watched her move to the bar; it was a full-scale bar, built in a curve at the top of the steps that went down to the pool. He thought that the back of Linda's neck still looked young and defenceless.

She turned, waving an arm towards the bar. "As you see, the choice is extensive. There's even some pink champagne; something of a political curiosity under this roof. What'll you have?"

"What'll I have?" he repeated stupidly.

"Drink, darling; you know. Alcohol; goes to the head; you must remember it."

"Sorry—I'm so much alone these days I'm hardly housebroken."

"Alone?" Why, he wondered, should that surprise her? "You mean—quite alone?"

He nodded. "And I don't drink any more."

"The wagon, eh?"

"Yes, the wagon, eh."

"Well, good for you, Mr. Neilson; but aren't you thirsty? The soft ones are numerous and nauseating. Want some of this thing? Alleged to have a passion-fruit base?"

David said, "What I'd really like is to plunge into that water."

The trunks were initialled R.J.P. When he came out of the

dressing-room, he saw Linda staring at him as though, stripped, he demanded her studious attention. He dived; the blue water was ice-cold; he came up, shaking his hair and blinking, to the sunshot, echoing coolness. He said, "There are some advantages in being Ricky."

"Well, let us say some advantages in being Ricky married to Primula."

He lay out along the water, holding the rail, looking down to the marble floor, looking up to Linda. "Is he bearable these days? Do you like them?"

She said, "I like them more than I approve of liking them, somehow. But I had to stop living with them; it was wearing holes in my integrity; even taking the holiday here does—a little. One remains invincibly Puritan inside."

"One does, eh?"

"Well," she said, "you know what I mean." She brought him a towel robe with the same initials on each lapel and he said, "I know exactly what you mean." They lay in long chairs by the pool, with the passion-fruit drinks; "only a preliminary for me, I warn you," said Linda. "Does it worry you when other people take a drink? No. Silly question, it never did; in Lent. Are you going to tell me about the book?"

He had dreaded this the most. He said, "All finished; tidy. And Mr. Vale swears he can read my 'beautiful handwriting'."

"Well, you have got beautiful handwriting," Linda said.

"Less legible than it was. But the firm will pay for the typing. And the price I pay for that is letting Vale read it first; not to mention this trip. Realise I haven't set foot in New York for a year?" He was chattering to stop the question; it came.

"What's the novel about, David?"

He hesitated. "Can't I hear your things first?"

"Not on passion-fruit, you can't, no."

"Oh yes. What was the work, Linda? You said you'd been working hard."

"Just a job. Over now. Let's skip that. The novel? You always *could* tell me," she reminded him.

"I know. It isn't that."

"Well, what? Would you rather I just read it? Or—or don't I have the right—any more?"

"Heaven, what a notion." Still, he found the words stuck. At last he said, "You may not like it; I'll understand entirely if you don't; but I had to do it. As Kipling said, one can only write 'what is laid on one'."

"Of course."

"This isn't a novel."

"No?"

"It's a book about Anne."

She looked paler, more stricken, than he had feared for. Her voice was a whisper:

"About—Anne."

"Do you mind? I was afraid you would. I suppose," he said, "you think it's unforgivable."

Her expression was wholly dazed. She repeated, "Unforgivable . . .? But why should it be?"

"Coming from me."

"But—who else? *Why* unforgivable?" It was still a thread of a voice; making his own seem harsh and loud.

"The thing I never forget is the thing you never forget, after all," he reminded her.

She went on looking beaten and baffled; after a time she asked, "And what is that?"

"That I was responsible for Anne's death."

She said, "You . . . Oh, but, David, that's the thing I never remember." She shut her eyes, she whispered, "Don't— please. It isn't true."

He should, he thought, be grateful. But he could only stare at her quiet hands and think, 'You have never known. You never saw me carrying that.'

Yet there were tears on her eyelashes.

"I'm glad you wrote it. May I read it, please?"

"It's a family portrait, Linda. It had to be."

She whispered, "Heartbreaking to do."

"Oh no. Not for a moment. It was like going home again. I've been travelling home, with both of you, for a year."

She turned away her head and gave him her hand, clutching his tightly. After a moment other thoughts came down on her and she drew her hand away.

"Early for a drink, a real drink," she said, "but I'd like one all the same."

After he was dressed he found her standing by the bar again. The manservant came to ask what time they would like dinner. Linda looked at her watch. "It's five now; half-past seven suit you, David?" The maid came to ask her if she would be changing for dinner. "No," Linda said, "I don't believe I'll change." Talking to the servants, she made him think of a child shut up for punishment in this palace, this hall of mirrors.

She mixed her drink and took a long swallow, still standing at the bar. She said, "You take the sofa; I'll sit here." There was room enough on the sofa, but she chose to face him across the low, glass-topped table. On the table there was a crystal cigarette-box and crystal ash-trays. Ricky's monogram was twined in the crystal; the book-matches had the same monogram. "All this identity—very tiring," Linda said. The sky outside was turning coppery above the garden that sloped to the river.

She took another swallow. "David, this isn't the prelude to an inquisition—but has Janet read the book?"

"Janet?" He was startled. "Good God, no, why should she?"

Linda's face was dedicated and solemn—the face of the girl at Dijon, studying the little stone figures that mourned on the sides of the tombs. She said, "But you love her, don't you? And that's all right with me. I can see why."

It was like listening to Chinese. When she had talked a moment longer, he said, "Oh, Linda, stop. This is pure imagination . . . I mean it. You're being very sweet and charitable but God knows where you got the idea. I don't love Janet—I never have and I never will." When she remained silent, gazing at him, he said, "You can cross *that* one off your list of worries."

He seemed to have stunned her. She turned pale, then flushed, then turned pale again. Then she laughed. It was a shaky laugh. She said, "The windmills . . . Dear God, the windmills."

"Windmills?"

"Quichote; tilting at windmills."

"I don't get it, Linda."

"Nor shall you." There was a glitter of anger. "All right. Leave me alone a minute—I'm adjusting." He saw that the quiet hands had begun to tremble. She laughed again. "Oh, anti-climax department. Oh, failure," she said. "Failure, failure. That's all there is . . ." She went on talking to herself. "*No*; not quite. If it hadn't been for that—never mind."

But much of her serenity had left her; she was twisting her fingers tightly around the glass and laughing again. "I really am very glad about that. I assure you. But this hotel—this roadhouse—Hunter's Tavern or whatever. Tell me—I've no picture."

He began to describe it. Suddenly it seemed very far away; it seemed longer ago than this morning since he had left. He saw the low-built pine house, with the trees and the hills behind; he saw Mary's small, defiant garden, watery with heat-haze; the yellow flash of a goldfinch darting down to the bird-table; the blisters in the new paint on the door of Hunter's tool-shed. He looked down the veranda, past the bar to the marble pool. He thought, absurdly, 'Either that is true or this is true. There cannot be the two places.' He looked at Linda, the slight and dangerous shape with the boy's head, the brilliant grey eyes watching him steadily.

"And that's enough—for you? Enough to have made you so utterly different? So happy? . . . That, and writing again." She finished her drink. "I do understand. I really do. And I won't disturb your peace—ever again."

He thought of his Bloomsbury room and the girl asking solemnly, "But don't you like to have your peace disturbed from time to time?"

Linda rose, went to the bar and mixed another drink. She said, "And God? How are you about God these days?" There was no mockery in her voice; she sounded solemn and interested.

He said, "Oh, much as I always was, I think. Why?"

She came back to the glass-table. He looked beyond her shoulder to the coppery sky and saw the leaves in the garden begin to shake; far thunder sounded in the valley.

Linda said, "I'll have to talk this through—the way you do when you tell me a novel—remember?" He saw her adopt his trick of looking away, as though at a screen where the story unfolded; it was shadowy here now; her head

226

glimmered, white-gold; her profile was as quiet as her voice.

"This isn't about last year; about my unspeakable behaviour. It explains that a little, but it begins before. Long before. Before Anne's death. I've told you for years that I'm more adult than you. It's a lie. You're the adult; I'm not only immature, I'm a case of arrested development. Now I look at it, I can see my bi-sexuality was just that; failure to grow up. I gave some other fine reasons for it. I was wrong.

"David, I've always been wrong. About everything. I've worked at it—given years of my life to being wrong. None of my solutions have worked out; they couldn't. I always wanted watertight facts; theories that added up, balanced, didn't leave a question-mark any place. Lord," she said, "how I worried at the question-marks. Like a bad-tempered dog. Remember me on religion—reading, probing, patronising, debunking, trying to get it out of the way? Of course you remember. Know why that was? Know what I was doing? I do, now. I was for ever trying to bolster up an insecure opinion; trying to prove I was an atheist. I couldn't."

"Agnostic——" David said. "You never claimed to be an atheist. No intelligent person ever does."

"Well, I couldn't make it; but I wanted to. I wanted a philosophy that gave a factual answer to everything. From Marxism to Rationalism and on to Freudian psychiatry . . . anything would do if only it would do that. And nothing did. I came to the end of them all. Then I found the apostle of the central nervous system—we can skip that, except I thought it was the answer. And it wasn't. Just another secular religion, like all the others I've practised since my freshman year. They've all failed me." She paused and turned from the invisible screen to look him in the eyes. "David, there's nothing left for me now but God."

She thrust the words at him and waited; they had the quality of a prepared phrase. Was there now, because he did not speak, a look of disappointment on her face? In this light he could not be sure. She began to talk again, speeding up her tempo.

"That's the only real thing—you're the realist after all and I'm the sentimentalist. Anything *more* sentimental than

227

my effort after Anne's death—anything more escapist—well, you saw it; you know. My runaway; my refusal to face the truth—my declaration of war on the past. And, dear God, the palliatives—skip them too, they make me blush. An adult doesn't need palliatives. You didn't. You accepted your grief and shouldered it. Because you knew there was a God, a designer and a design. Yes?"

"Yes."

"I think I know it now. It's come slowly and I wouldn't quite know how it came—from seeing my own failure——And from seeing all the people going up and down the steps of the church—does that sound silly? I took to going in, mostly late, when it was dark; it's right opposite where I worked . . ." she went on describing the street and the corner as though they mattered very much. "And something used to happen. I knew that there was somebody there."

Again she waited. "And that's as far as I've got." She spread out her fingers on the table; she said, without looking up, "Help me, David."

He said gently, "How can I help you?"

Linda put back her head and laughed. "Because I don't know what to do next. See? What *does* one do next?"

He smiled at her; he tried not to think, 'But this is kindergarten, still.' He said, "Only you can answer that."

"But I don't know. Talk to me about God, David, please." She repeated it, "Just sit here and talk about God."

It was like being told to say something funny.

She said, "It has to be you; we've talked the same language for so long. I wouldn't get any place talking to a priest. Oh, I could ask him to baptise me, I guess I ought to get that done right away." Now she looked at him sharply. "What's the matter? You can't think *that's* for comedy. . . ."

"No, no—of course I don't, God help me," he said, still fighting a giggle. "It was just that you made it sound clinical, like an inoculation or something. Sorry, Linda."

Her face flushed. "Well, there you are, you see . . . I don't even know how to talk about it properly. You must teach me."

He stared helplessly around the Powers' veranda. "I don't honestly believe," he said, "that I can be much use."

228

"Of course you can," she said violently. "You're the only person."

"Wait. Your mind's clear—you're at a practical beginning. Roughly, you've decided that God must be the right medicine for you because none of the others have done you any good."

Her flush deepened. "Who's being clinical now?"

"I don't mean it unkindly, darling. A lot of people have come to the truth that way; saying, 'We've tried everything else; now let's try God.' I'm not laughing at it or despising it." ('Are you quite sure you're not?' asked the voice inside his head, the voice that chose to make things difficult.) Linda was looking down at the table again.

"I swear I'm not," he said robustly, "I sympathise."

('Do you?')

Still she kept her head bent, not looking at him.

"Darling Linda . . . The trouble is I'm much too woolly and solitary and unorthodox to be able to take you on from here. I've been a sort of dumb yes-man to God all my life. My belief in him is automatic, like breathing. I couldn't teach anyone how to breathe."

She muttered, "Could give them sort of breathing-exercises, couldn't you? Couldn't you?"

He got up; she sat on, still looking down. He took a cigarette from the crystal box; he paced beside the table; looking at her linked hands, at the defenceless back of her neck.

"As an instructor, I'm out," said David to the bent head. "Truly. It wouldn't be possible. I'm the laziest Christian I know. I just potter into a church—any church—when I feel like it. And I pray, in my fubsy way. And I wish them all well . . . all the churches, because they're all trying to get to Him—even the ones whose views I can't take. At least a yes-man; not one of those Recherché No-Boys who thinks, because he's got his own private channel to God, he can afford to sneer at what he calls man-made religions. In my view, there's no such thing as a man-made religion. Man can't do that for himself. Even if he does it wrong, he does it because of God."

Linda raised her head. "Go on, David, that's what I want. Please go on talking."

Perversely, he found that this silenced him. He paced to the window; the storm was holding off; there was still the metallic sky, the leaves that shook, the faint bump of thunder a long way down the valley.

"Go on, David. Please." As he turned back he saw her sitting upright, tense and demanding. "*Give* me your God; I'll accept him; I want to."

She made him feel battered.

"But, darling—don't you see—I can't. To me he's a mystery. The mystery. One I can only know after I'm dead." Forgetting her for an instant, he added quietly and lovingly, "I can wait."

He had not meant it for her. He stood stupidly, seeing what happened because of it. She swept her glass from the table and it smashed on the stone floor; the soles of her shoes crunched the broken pieces as she ran at him. Her hands were raised; her face was the taut, furious mask that he had forgotten.

"*You* can wait—what sort of talk is that?" She was shivering; she clenched her fists and he thought she was going to hit him. "Damn you, yes, you can wait—— But I can't— why should I? *If I want it, I can have it, eh?*" There was the bitter mouth and the twist of the clowning eyebrows. "*Eh? Eh?*" she cackled at him. "Who said that? You did. And now you're so Goddamned smug you don't want me to have it. That's it, isn't it, David?" She slapped his face. "You'll take your God and your book and your smugness out of here. Now. Before you know what you've done to me." She began to cry hysterically, sobbing and shaking. "You don't know—you don't understand—— You must go. *Go*——" Somehow, astoundingly, she was able to turn off the hysteria; to ring the bell and say to the manservant in a quiet voice, "Mr. Neilson has to go into New York at once. Please repack his luggage and bring it down."

Her voice was still quiet when she spoke again, turning to him, shaking, with no colour in her face and cold eyes. "Wait here. Don't come after me, please. If you try to come after me, I shall ring again and you'll be shown the door. Good night, David." She went, walking slowly and steadfastly.

2

"You see," said Job Vale, solemn-eyed and fish-like, staring at David across the table, "where books are concerned, I'm equipped with a Geiger counter. I don't mean I know what'll sell. I don't know and I don't care. I do know what's good. That sounds conceited, but it isn't really. I doubt I've made a nickel for either of the two firms who've been good enough to give me gainful employment. My salary," he added, "is justly low. What I put on their lists is a circumstance called literature. You might say," he continued sombrely, "that I don't know what I like, but I do know about art. You, in my view, are an artist. In your popular days, you were a little too popular for anybody to realise how good you were. Anybody but me, I mean. Sure you won't have a liqueur with your coffee?"

"No, thank you kindly," David said. The unreality persisted. He could not believe that he was in New York again, eating lunch at the Algonquin, hearing a publisher talk about a book that was finished.

"Thank God, most people have forgotten your reputation," said Vale, shaking back his shaggy hair. "These six years in the wilderness have helped this book."

David said, "I can only hope so."

"And I promise you——" Vale now looked furious, "that I'll look after it. I won't let them play any of their embarrassing tricks on the production-side. I've gotten them fairly well-trained. They leave it to me to handle our limited supply of respectable stuff in a respectable manner."

"But you haven't *read* it yet," David said, not for the first time. Job glowered at the flat parcel lying on the end of the table. "I don't have to eat my egg to know it's bad—or good. Stay overnight and lunch with me tomorrow and I'll tell you how right I was."

If, David reflected, he told Vale that he couldn't afford to stay overnight, there would be the offer of the advance again.

"I assume you prefer to get out of this underwater hell at all speed," Vale said. David nodded.

"Then I'll call you in Putnam. On the condition that this time you *do* come to the telephone. Nine thirty a.m.?"

"You'll have to read all night."

"I generally do. Sure you won't have a cigar? What d'you want to happen to this book, Neilson? And don't say 'sales'; I won't believe you."

"They help, chum."

"Too true. But that isn't why you write, or why I publish."

"No, it isn't," said David. "Why isn't it?"

"You tell me. What's your wish for this one?"

"This one's important to me. I want it to live. I want it to live longer than I do. I never bothered about that before."

"Suits me," said Vale.

David said, "I'm not sure it will suit you."

Vale said, "Come again?"

"As you've discovered, I can't talk about work while I'm in the middle of it. That's not an act; it's an impediment in my speech; I've had it ever since I started writing. But you may be disappointed, as of tonight. This isn't a novel."

"You never said it was. You never said what it was," Vale reminded him. "Could be metaphysics, for all you've told me."

"It's a mixture of biography and autobiography."

"Well, all right. Swell," said Vale, blinking at him. "How did that happen?"

"I wanted to write about my daughter. She died when she was seventeen. I've written all I can remember. I think it comes out as if a painter were talking to his model while he worked; talking about himself, too; my own story comes in because it must. My life as it was, up till the time when she died; the person I was, in relation to her . . ." He stopped, finding Vale's concentrated stare too much for him.

"Well, that's wonderful," said Vale placidly.

"How d'you know it is?" David teased him.

Vale didn't answer. He seemed to be debating something in his mind. He called for the bill. Then he sat looking thoughtful and half-drowned.

Presently he said, "I don't know how much this matters to you. But I know your wife will be pleased."

3

"What time did she leave? This is her husband talking." The voice from the Powers' farm said that Mrs. Neilson had left early, about eight o'clock. The voice thought that she was going straight to New York.

"To her apartment?"

"She didn't tell me, Mr. Neilson. She said she wouldn't come back tonight."

"Have you her number there? . . . And the address?"

The voice thought so; it sounded puzzled, as if, being her husband, he should know. It came back and gave them to him.

He rang the number for a long time; there was no answer. He came out of the booth and walked to the parking-lot where he had left Hunter's car.

He had, he reminded himself, little reason to go in search of her. Yesterday was nearer than her meeting with Job Vale. That furious dismissal had ended everything. But now he could no longer see the face that had haunted him all night in the stuffy hotel room—the bitter mask of hatred.

It was foolish to be so deeply touched by what Vale had told him. It was idiotic to feel that all was still well between them because she had wanted him to write the book.

"Why couldn't she tell me? Why just look stricken and say nothing? And why has she come to New York? I must find her," he said, "I have to find her."

He picked up the car from the parking-lot and drove down-town. It was a dingy city now, with the heat like a dirty wet blanket lying over all.

He kept track of her in his mind. He kept track of her down the Avenue. He came to the corner that she had carefully described; he saw the church. "All those people going up and down the steps." They were there, a runnel of tired, shabby figures; women halting to cover their heads. He thought that he might find her in the church. It was a gambling chance, anyway. He had to drive two blocks west before he found a space to park. He walked back. He went up the steps. He walked through the candle-lit greyness, looking for Linda. She was not there.

When he reached the door on West Eleventh Street he was quite certain that she would be home by now. He looked for the name of Neilson under the mail-boxes and found the name Linda Platt. He went on ringing. Then she must, he

said, be on her way here. He refused to think otherwise.
He sat in the car and waited.

'Why? What will you say to her?'

'I haven't thought. I just want to see her.'

When he had been sitting there for twenty minutes, a
taxi came in from the Avenue and slowed down at the door.
He was out on the pavement beside it before he saw that
this wasn't Linda; this was a young, dark-haired girl, in
shirt and slacks; a terrier on a leash jumped down after her.
She went past him to the door, taking a key out of her
pocket.

"Excuse me," David said.

"I'm waiting for Mrs.—I mean Miss Platt. You haven't
seen her, have you?"

"Yeah, I saw her an hour ago. She was going out."

"You don't know where?"

"I don't know where." She looked at him levelly, sizing
him up.

"I'm her husband," David said, "and I do want to see
her." The girl holding the terrier frowned a little. She didn't,
he thought, believe the husband story. "Anything you can
tell me?" he asked.

"She was driving the big car. She'd come in from the
country, I guess."

"You didn't talk to her?"

"Well, yes; I asked her if she was feeling all right. She
looked rather badly." The girl paused again. He said,
"Well? Was she all right?"

"I couldn't hear what she said. Something about not
giving trouble . . . It *sounded* like that. She was just on her
way to the car. She drove off."

"But you wouldn't know where?"

"I wish I did; she worried me. You see, I don't know her
too well and I think I made her angry, asking . . ."

"Angry——" David repeated.

"Yes."

Though they still stared at each other, he thought that
only their eyes were interested. They were caught in separate
preoccupations; they had nothing more to say.

"She doesn't need anybody." Had the girl said it, or was
it the thought in his mind? He could not be sure. Suddenly

234

the search had gone flat. He was walking back to the car; he was driving away.

As he drove West towards the highway, the first heavy drops of rain spattered and starred his windshield. 'Here comes the storm,' David said to himself, 'and about time too.' He felt as though it were important, as though it would solve something that had been waiting since last night. Before he reached Tenth Avenue, the thunder cracked; the rain hissed. The rain was washing out today. He was back at their parting; back at his same defence-line. 'I didn't mean to hurt her; I didn't; I would have helped her if I'd known how. I was trying to help.'

('Were you? Are you sure?')

He was on the highway, driving past the docks; he saw the red funnels of a Cunarder anchored, the purple, pouring sky behind. The rain was a water-spout now; it was beating the windshield-wipers; he rubbed off the cloudy mist on the inside of the glass and still all was opaque, yellowish, a falling tent of water ahead.

'If this keeps up——' David thought, 'I'll never get home tonight.'

'Home. Where's home?'

'Once I'm back there, in my room, looking at the carved angel, going to the window to cool off and stare at the trees and the fireflies, all this will be gone.'

'Even Linda's face?'

'Yes. No. Back in the room I'll find her as she used to be: the person I wrote and remembered.'

'Are you sure?'

'It is all I want. To get back to there; to find her.'

'But she is here—in this city. Only you don't know where to look.'

'There is no need to look; not for that one; we have finished our conversation.'

'But she wanted you to write about Anne.'

'What difference does that make?'

'Every difference.'

On his left a sizzle of forked lightning went down into the river. The splitting burst of the thunder overhead made him think of bombs, of driving under bombs.

'No difference. The Linda who is somewhere in this city,

235

behind me, isn't the person I knew and loved; not any more.'

Another forked flash ripped through the sky above the Palisades; the bridge turned livid silver before it went. The thunder cannoned again. He could see the last lights beyond Riverside Drive; green, through the dun and watery glass. He put his foot down; there was only a strung-out line of cars ahead; he began to pass them methodically; these were old tyres of Hunter's; he dared not make too much speed.

'New York is over; and Linda is over. Oh, but she was over long before yesterday. You thought not, because you had lived with the other image. You tried to superimpose that one on this one; and it didn't work. Just for a little while you thought it worked. She looked like the other image, that was all. The Linda you knew wouldn't be in that place, kept by those people.'

'Be fair to her, can't you? She broke out of it and took the apartment and got away.'

'But she still uses the farm when she wants to, and the penthouse.'

The penthouse on Sutton Place . . . He had forgotten that. It hadn't occurred to him to look for her there. Too late now. He drove on, through the swish of the rain.

'She is changed for ever. And so, I suppose, am I. We aren't the people who first met, first loved each other. Why does that seem so sad—sadder than death?'

Suddenly, sharply in his ear, he heard Aunt Rachel's voice saying, 'Pooh to death. It's life that's the trouble.' He could see her face and her flower-pot hat. 'You're right,' he said to Aunt Rachel. 'The worst thing is that Linda and I are going on alone, in different lives. But it has happened. And I got over it a long time ago.'

A long time ago. The words stayed in his head, became a chant, with the noise of the windshield-wipers moaning across the glass, 'Long time ago—long time ago; long way to go—long way to go.'

For the first time in months, he wanted a drink.

'Oh pooh,' he said.

'What d'you mean, oh pooh? Nothing against taking a drink, is there?'

236

'You know there is. . . .'

'I do, eh?'

'Yes, you do, *eh*. You've a long drive ahead.'

'That's why I want a drink.'

'Well, cut it out. I wonder . . . *did* she go to Sutton Place? Maybe yes, maybe no. If they're in Europe, it's more than likely that the place is shut down, covered in dust-sheets, all the dust-sheets initialled R.J.P. Toll-gate coming up.' He fished for a dime.

The thunder was receding; there was a hollow light coming through the rain; a hopeless dazzle that strained his eyes. It stayed, becoming no more and no less, a mockery of daylight while the rain drummed down. He went on thinking about the penthouse. 'Of course,' he said to himself, 'she isn't there.'

'But I have to know if she is there.'

'Wait, only wait; in a few more miles, you'll stop worrying. You'll be away, really away.'

'It is no good. I have to know.'

He turned off where the first beckoning sign stood; below it there was the leaden figure of a huntsman in a scarlet coat; Cocktails, the sign said, in fluid red letters.

David parked the car; he saw a brown frame house, made elegant with window-boxes. He splashed through a miniature river on the gravel. He found himself in a long empty bar, with the barman seated in a chair at the further end, watching the television-screen.

"Quite a storm we've got here," said the barman.

"May I use your telephone?"

"Sure, help yourself. In the booth."

"Got a Manhattan directory?"

"In the booth."

He found the Sutton Place number. He was saying to himself, 'Once you've done it, once you have proved she isn't there, this thing in your head will stop and you won't want a drink.' He gave the number to the operator. He heard it begin to ring; it went on ringing, as he had known that it would. Nobody there.

Suddenly there was Linda's voice. "Hello. Who is that?" She sounded very faint and far away.

"David here," he said.

"David . . . Yes, I thought it was. Why did I think it was?" She said something else; he missed it.

"Could you speak up a little, Linda? I can't hear you."

Silence.

"Are you there, darling?"

"What . . . Oh, yes, I'm here." She sounded as though she were sleepy.

"Are you resting? Did I wake you up?"

"Sort of; not *quite*," said the drowsy voice; then there was silence again; then another muttered, broken phrase that he couldn't hear.

"Linda—what is it? Are you all right?"

He had to repeat it before the fading voice said, "Oh yes; surely. I think your God knows about this."

NEILSON

Neilson stood alone. The mist into which he had walked at the beginning was about him again. But the mist was thicker now. He saw it grey and cold, endlessly eddying, wherever he looked. There was no sound. While he listened for a footstep, he knew that none would come. Nothing would happen here. There was no past self to set free.

The self who once prayed that he might follow Linda through her loneliness had got his answer. 'But where is he? That different survivor who had, when I saw him, the look of a bright, untroubled spirit? He is gone,' Neilson thought. 'He will not come again. This time I defeated him. He was the remnant of good. I lost sight of him. I shut my eyes. And the blind-man's walk has brought me here.'

No past self to set free. The man who had listened to the faint, drowsy voice on the telephone was co-equal with himself, was indeed himself, now standing here awaiting other judgment, not his own; judgment for the worst thing of all. His memory was broad awake. He knew what the man had done after the drowsy voice ceased. He could remember every second, as far as the end.

'If I had known, if I had remembered before,' he said to himself, 'I could not have made this journey. They were merciful to hide it from me until now. And now I am stripped. I am nothing but my own guilt. I ask forgiveness, but I ask no further mercy. And I am ready,' he said to the grey nothingness about him, the lightless eternity, 'I await my punishment, even to damnation if that is your will.'

The grey mist was changing, thinning out. He could see dim shapes and lights beyond; at either side, on the hem of the mist there were flashes going by. He could not see what made them. There was still no sound, just the greyness where he stood, and the moving shapes that slipped past.

"Neilson."

He turned and the guide stepped through the mist and stood with him.

"I am ready," Neilson said.

"You are ready," the guide repeated; in the grey gloom his face looked ruined with weariness. Pityingly, the innocent eyes gazed at Neilson.

"No," said Neilson. "You must not pity me. I know what I did. How can they do anything but judge me?"

The guide said nothing.

"You will take me where I must go?"

The guide raised his head. He said, "Listen."

Neilson heard it, faintly at first, then growing louder; it was the sound of rain. After it there came other sounds, the hiss of tyres on a wet surface, the noise of engines.

"What is that?"

"Do you not remember?"

"What are those lights—those shapes moving past?"

"You have seen them before."

The mist grew thinner. Through it now he could see a wet road, and the shapes became the shapes of cars flashing through the rain.

Neilson shuddered.

"Why do you shiver? What does it remind you of?" the guide asked.

He said, "Of the highway; when I drove back to the city."

"It is the highway."

Neilson looked and saw it. It was only the ghost of the highway as yet; the two of them stood in the middle of it, on an island-refuge, with the ghosts of cars going past them on either side. If he shut his eyes, he thought, he could make it not be there. But the noise of the beating rain went on, and when he opened his eyes he could still see the ghost-road and the ghost-cars flashing.

He said in a whisper, "Why is it still there?"

"Because it is the road that you will take."

"No!" Neilson shouted.

"Yes."

"No!" He fell on his knees. "Not again. Not that again."

"Yes, Neilson."

"They cannot ask it of me."

"They do ask it of you," said the guide.

"Why? Why? I know it all. I went out of my life knowing

what I had done. All I ask is to be punished. Not to do it again. I can't do it again."

"Yes," the guide said, "you can."

"*No!*" He caught the guide's hand, clutching at it. It felt frail, remote, unkind. "In the name of God," he said, "I beseech you."

"I cannot change it. I can change nothing."

"Help me."

"I have no power."

"Oh please. I'll do anything . . . anything but that. I'll die again," he said. "But not the room. Don't send me in." He heard himself sobbing like a little boy. "Don't do it to me—please—please—please. Not the room."

The voice above his head was small and sorrowful. It asked, "Must you refuse now, having come so far?" Over it, inexorably, he heard the steel clanging and the deep chant of the builders. Monstrous up the sky, there climbed the skeleton towers; the city was closing in.

Now he was without hope. He was lost. He dropped the frail cold hand and covered his eyes. He cried, "Oh, hear me, God!"

The voice spoke differently. "He hears you," the guide said. "He has always heard you." Stooping, he raised Neilson to his feet and Neilson stepped forward into the rain.

DAVID NEILSON

THE rain was still falling when David came to Sutton Place; more softly now, thin silver needles flying down, hitting his cheek. Here, through a river mist, he saw lit windows hanging high. He stood looking up the side of a tower with lit windows. This was the end of the search. Linda was on the tower alone, behind the highest window. He rang the bell. The look on the doorman's face was familiar, a look that he remembered from older drinking days.

But there was no reason for it, surely. Surely he had taken only two quick drinks when he came out of the telephone-booth. Or was it three? His head was still clear and his thoughts lucid. There was no blurring of the immediate horizon. The drink had no effect on him, only on time; he seemed to have got here very quickly. In a few minutes, he thought, the wet ribbon of the highway pouring past, the cars that flashed, the toll-bridge, the lights at Ninety-Second Street and the smother of cross-town traffic had fled; giving place to this door and this man with the wary, questioning look.

"Mrs. Neilson, please. In Mr. Powers's apartment. She is expecting me," he said.

The doorman still looked dubious. "I didn't know there was anybody up there. I only just came on duty. They're abroad," he said.

"She is there. I just spoke to her on the telephone; I'm Mr. Neilson."

"Okay, sir. You know your way? Just press the top button."

The elevator had a looking-glass in one wall. He saw his own face reflected, a different face from the one that he had seen in recent months; the face made lively and larger-eyed with the first drinks. It wore a look of curiosity, as though having fun with the puzzle that it tried to solve; as though there were nothing in the mystery to make it afraid.

The elevator stopped and he walked out of it into the

lobby of Ricky Powers's apartment: he went ahead under an archway into the sort of room that he had expected, a grey and gold drawing-room. The furniture was sheeted. He went on and through. Now there was a grey-panelled dining-room, with glass and china in cabinets; a choice of doors. The first that he opened led into a study that shrieked with scarlet leather; he saw a Buhl desk, Chinese porcelain figures on the mantelpiece. The second choice took him into a long hall. He went down the hall, tapping at the doors, opening them one by one.

Then he stood still, on the threshold of a bedroom whose colours were blue and grey. There were net curtains over the windows; the satin curtains were half-drawn, so that the light in the room was dim. He was looking into a triple mirror that gave him the reflection of the bed before he saw the bed. It was wide, with a blue-grey coverlet. In the bed Linda lay asleep.

"Hullo," he said softly.

She did not wake. He tiptoed across the blue-grey carpet and stood beside her. Her breathing was quiet; the fair, fragile head lay easily, with her cheek pillowed on her hand.

He touched the cheek. Still she slept. Now he was more puzzled than afraid. He looked about him. The arm-chair had a dust-cover on it. There was nothing on the glass-topped dressing-table, no jars or combs or brushes. No sign of any personal possessions anywhere, not as much as a suitcase waiting to be unpacked. He opened the door of a built-in wardrobe and saw a dress hanging there; on the floor, below the dress, a pair of shoes. He shut the door.

The room, he thought, looked as bare as a room of its luxury could look. But on the painted writing-table under the window, the blotter was awry; the ash-tray was full of butts; and there was a bottle beside the ash-tray; a bottle of brandy and a used glass. He went to the table. A fountain-pen lay by the blotter. Inside the blotter there was one half-sheet of headed writing-paper. Looking down, he saw that the painted metal trash-basket was full, almost to the brim, with torn scraps. He could see Linda's handwriting on the scraps.

"Linda——" he said—"Linda . . . I'm here. Please wake up." He stepped back to the bed and shook her gently by the shoulder; she went on sleeping; she began to snore a little. It sounded like a purr, rather than a snore.

David saw his hand shaking, jumping at the wrist as he stretched it to the bedside lamp. He fumbled with the switch. Under the lamplight, on the bedside-table, there was a white telephone, a tumbler of water and a squat little plastic phial; any chemist's phial for pills. It was empty. He picked it up and read the label, a prescription-number, the name of the drugstore and the name of Dr. Russell Jones. He set it down again; his foot kicked something light that rolled, like a cotton-reel. He stooped. This was a second phial, of the same size, with the same label. This one too was empty.

Time went slow.

David set the second phial beside the first. He went to the writing-table, picked up the brandy and drank straight from the bottle. He repeated the swallow several times and then tilted more into the used glass. When he had drunk that, he found that his hands stopped shaking. He lifted the blotter; nothing there; he turned the torn half-sheet over; it was blank. He grabbed a handful of the scraps out of the trash-basket, sifting them through his fingers; they were torn very small; he could only find odd words: "Sorry"—"All of them——"—"Nothing left"—"Sorry"; he kept finding the same words again.

He went back to the bed and sat on the side of it. He took her hand.

"*I think your God knows about this.*"

Still he found it hard to believe. She looked so peaceful and lovely, lying there. He held the hand between his own, saying aloud, "Why, Linda? Tell me why?"

He answered for her. "Because of you."

"Yes. Because of me. I failed you. There was something I could have given you. Call it God or call it hope or call it life itself. I took it away."

He kissed the hand and laid it down. As he picked up the telephone, he felt that he was impertinent, that she would want him to guard this room, to let her be private here, to let it happen.

'I think you will have made certain that you cannot be saved. I think you have enough knowledge for that. But— forgive me, please, I must give them the chance to save

244

you. . . .' He found that he was listening to a dead telephone; she must have cut it off after she had spoken to him; the little switch with the extension figures confused him; he moved it one way and there was still no dialling-tone but the voice of an operator saying brightly, "Good afternoon. Can I help you?"

"Where are you?" he asked.

She sounded young, amused and flirtatious. "Why, this is the switchboard operator of the building you're in, sir. You flashed me. If you want to dial, you must turn the little gimmick to the figure Two. Or I can——"

"Wait. Is there a doctor in this building?"

"Sure. Dr. Mervyn Thomas. I'll get you his office; hold on."

The next voice said, "I expect him back in a few minutes. He's visiting a patient in the building."

"Ask him to come straight up to Mr. Powers's apartment . . . What? . . . Does it *matter* who's calling? All right—my name's Neilson—tell him it's very serious and very urgent." He thought that his voice sounded thick, blurred; was that because of the drinks?

Now he felt that he had betrayed Linda. He said, "I'm sorry, darling; I had to." He bent over her and kissed her. He tried to raise her head on the pillow; the gentle, purring snore went on; the head lolled heavily. He sat with his arm curved around the pillow, staring in a stupid way at the room. Looking at the writing-table, he thought suddenly, bemusedly, 'Those scraps of paper . . . Nobody must see them. She meant them for nobody, the discarded words. Nobody must try to piece them together.'

At the table, he drank again from the bottle of brandy. He picked up the trash-basket and butted his way around the table to the windows. They were long windows, opening on to the terrace that ran all round the penthouse; a terrace with a parapet and a striped awning. He buffeted the windows open and plunged through.

The rain had stopped. Water still dripped from the edge of the awning, sluiced down the slender struts that held it, trickled to the gutter below the parapet on this side. But the mist around him in the sky had begun to glow; the skeleton towers shone; all was turning to gold. He stood by the parapet. Now he knew how drunk he was. He was saying to Linda, "We are on the tower and it is the skies that are falling, not the rain." He swayed, and clung to the window-frame; he looked back into the room.

Above the pillow and the quiet, sleeping head, the light from the bedside lamp was spinning in circles, circles that haloed out and spread and blurred, circles of light spinning faster, wider. Just behind the circles, in the shadow, there seemed to be a figure standing, watching over Linda. The swaying lamplight and his own drunkenness had put it there; it looked like himself.

"That's right," he said thickly—"I'm there, beside you, all the time." Walking unsteadily, he ducked under the awning; he set the trash-basket down. No drips came through; the light metal would act as an incinerator; this was what must be done.

He pressed the scraps well down. He groped in his pocket and found the book-matches from yesterday, the monogram 'R.J.P.' He had forgotten it. He began to strike the matches. The scraps would burn away in a few minutes.

When he saw them smouldering, he said, "That's done, darling; nobody will see them, you're safe." He went back to the open windows; there were gold banners in the sky and the mist was shredding away; he could feel the wind on his face. Alone on the tower, he said, alone above the sunset, walking on the wind. Dizzily, he stepped into the room again; he went back to sit on the side of the bed.

Surely the doctor was taking a very long time. He picked up the telephone and the same bright voice said that he seemed to be in an awful hurry. "But I'll put you through to the number again." The voice in the doctor's office was exasperated; the voice of somebody who guessed that he was drunk. "I *told* you, Mr. Neilson, I'll give the message as soon as he comes in. No need to keep calling." She hung up.

He put his head in his hands and prayed, but the words meant nothing.

"You said 'Give me your God' and I refused. I laughed at you in my heart and I went away. Forgive me, Linda. Please forgive me." He bent over her again. Detachment came in spite of him, making him see the beauty of bone and shadow in the face.

246

It was impossible to think that this was the person with whom he had shared the long years. There was nothing here to remind him. There was no memory of any time at all. Nothing but this dying mask of beauty and his knowing why she died.

"But why do you wait?" he said, and the voice sounded like the voice of somebody else. He had left the windows open; a gust of wind pushed them wider; the net curtains bellied out. Between the windows, surely, there was somebody standing; somebody whose head looked dark and glowing, with the wet gold sky behind it. Who? This must be his drunkenness that made it be there, that made it move as he dipped his hand into the tumbler of water on the bedside, made it halt beside him and sweep its hand downward, the hand becoming his own hand that traced with the water the sign on Linda's forehead.

"I baptise you, Linda, in the Name of the Father, and of the Son and of the Holy Ghost," said the drunken voice of David Neilson.

Then he stood, looking down at the forehead; a little of the water ran down over her eyelid and he wiped it away. He thought that her breathing was quieter. The blowing, banging window made it hard to hear. As he went to shut the window, he remembered the burning paper. He could smell the smoke. Along the terrace the scraps came dancing to meet him, thin black flakes. Beyond the parapet he saw the rough gold sky, the towers that dipped. The wind was strong; this plunging sky would fall.

He stood at the edge of the awning, holding the strut. Smoke poured from the metal cylinder, the wind driving it down, scattering charred flakes and bright-edged burning scraps; he watched it; now there was a thin flame shooting up; now the wind scooped a blazing handful of paper and sent it up like a torch; it went nearly as high as the awning before it broke and fell.

'Get it out from under there,' David told himself. But the metal was too hot for his hands and he had to push at the basket with his foot, shoving it towards the gutter. It fell and rolled. The wind seized upon the burning stuff; some of it blew back at his eyes; the rest of it floated up on to the edge of the wet awning; blinking at it, he thought that it would blaze. He sprang on to the stone parapet to sweep the blaze away before it caught.

It was easy; balanced on the parapet above the gold rough sky and the towers; easy because he clung tightly to the awning's edge. But surely it should not be so slippery beneath his hands, surely it should be more solid than this, not bend like this, not push him out over the parapet into the wind. . . . There was the wind tearing him and his hands hurting; and then the wind was all that there was. He saw the side of the tower, rocketing past him, up and up and up, into the gold sky.

There was an end of pain. Dimly he could hear the murmuring of the voices above him; that one voice, a woman's voice, was still screaming over and over again, "So *silly*! So *silly*! Oh Christ, how *silly*!" but the screaming thinned into the noise of a siren and this faded. Although he could still see the mob of people, he could not hear them any more. He rose and walked away from them. He went on walking, lightly and easily. He looked to his right and to his left. He was back on the bridge.

THE GATE

NEILSON walked over the bridge. The coping on either side was too high to let him see the river. Ahead, he saw the backs of the slowly-moving crowd. It was a quiet crowd; there were no groups, each of them going on his way alone.

"This is well done," said the voice of the man who walked with him, the companion of the journey, who had been there since the beginning.

Neilson turned to him, silently, inquiringly.

"You thought you'd remembered it all," the guide said, "but you'd forgotten something. That was why there had to be the room again. You forgot the last thing you did for her."

They came to a bay in the bridge. Above the bay, the coping rose into a small, rounded turret, with the sun making a golden surface on the stone. At the foot of the turret, a flight of steps ran down. They went past the bay and the steps. They went on.

"And here, Neilson, we part," the guide said.

"Part?"

"At the gate, yes." He smiled, and as Neilson gazed at him he saw that the face with the innocent eyes was no longer tired, no longer the face of a man. For a moment, tall, perilous and shining above his head, there towered the wings.

Neilson said sadly, "But shall I never see you again?"

"You'll never need me again. Look up. This is the gate."

Neilson lifted his eyes.

For the last time, he was afraid. He said, "But I dare not go in. What shall I find?"

"What you lost," said the guide.

Still he was afraid. "It dazzles so. What shall I see?"

"You'll see them waiting for you. You haven't forgotten them, have you?" the guide said, laughing. "The three people. Your mother, your wife and your daughter. Look."

Neilson looked and saw them, standing at the beginning of the impossible city. He saw their faces; he saw their arms held out to him.

He ran in, through the gate.